I0761010

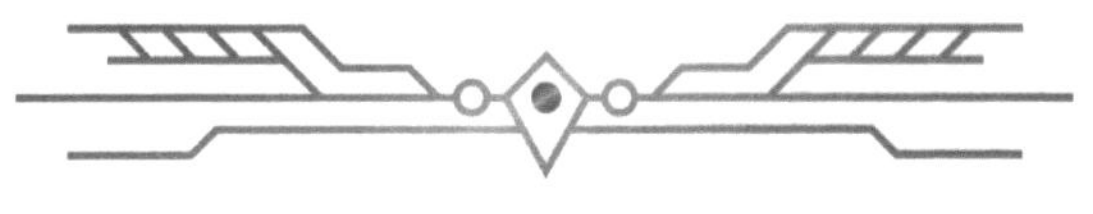

A KESTREL CIRCLES

THE CERVANTES FILES
BOOK I

G MICHAEL SMITH

Seattle, WA 98121
info@indieowlpress.com
IndieOwlPress.com

A KESTREL CIRCLES
THE CERVANTES FILES BOOK I

Illustrated by G Michael Smith

Cover art © Alter Dimension Design
Cover design & Interior layout/design by Vanessa Anderson
at NightOwlFreelance.com

Paperback ISBN-13: 978-1-949193-30-5
Hardcover ISBN-13: 978-1-949193-32-9

With eternal thanks to my two ineffable muses,
my wife Cheryl and my daughter Lindsay.

"I am a cage, in search of a bird."
– Franz Kafka

CONTENTS

CHAPTER 1 – THE PAST ...1

CHAPTER 2 – LOOKING BACK ...2

CHAPTER 3 – THE CHARGER ...3

CHAPTER 4 – BUSINESS IS GOOD ...6

CHAPTER 5 – THE PSYCHIATRIST ...8

CHAPTER 6 – THE POCKET WATCH ...12

CHAPTER 7 – THE MEETING ...16

CHAPTER 8 – THE SEARCH ...20

CHAPTER 9 – THE FLIGHT ...22

CHAPTER 10 – GOOD MORNING ...27

CHAPTER 11 – A KITKAT ...31

CHAPTER 12 – A MURDER ...35

CHAPTER 13 – POLICE AT MY DOOR ...39

CHAPTER 14 – SUBTERFUGE ...43

CHAPTER 15 – ESCAPE ...48

CHAPTER 16 – WAFFEN ZER HAND ... 52

CHAPTER 17 – REPLICA ...55

CHAPTER 18 – THE WATCH REPAIR SHOP ...58

CHAPTER 19 – POCKET WATCH SECRETS ...64

CHAPTER 20 – BACK HOME ...69

CHAPTER 21 – THE MICRODOT ...73

CHAPTER 22 – BAUBLES ...76

CHAPTER 23 – HIDE AND SEEK ...80

CHAPTER 24 – UNSATISFACTORY EXPLANATIONS ...83

CHAPTER 25 – ZEE PLOT, SHE T'ICKENS ...86

CHAPTER 26 – I'M A SUSPECT ...90

CHAPTER 27 – DECISIONS TO BE MADE ...95

CHAPTER 28 – A GIRLFRIEND? ...101

CHAPTER 29 – ALTERCATIONS ...106

CONTENTS

CHAPTER 30 – PROBING FOR INFORMATION ...111

CHAPTER 31 – TRUST ...116

CHAPTER 32 – WILL THE REAL HARRY KRUGER PLEASE STAND UP? ...122

CHAPTER 33 – A DIGRESSION: DRIVING LESSONS ...127

CHAPTER 34 – HOME INVASION ...129

CHAPTER 35 – WHAT TO DO? - WHAT TO DO? ...135

CHAPTER 36 – SELF-STORAGE ...139

CHAPTER 37 – PERFECT PAPER ...143

CHAPTER 38 – CLARIFICATION ...148

CHAPTER 39 – PRISONERS ...154

CHAPTER 40 – BOTOX ...160

CHAPTER 41 – ESCAPE ...164

CHAPTER 42 – BACK HOME ...167

CHAPTER 43 – BEAL DEBRIEF ...170

CHAPTER 44 – SOLVING THE MICRODOT ...175

CHAPTER 45 – FUN WITH MAGGIE ...179

CHAPTER 46 – DISCOVERIES ...183

CHAPTER 47 – OFF TO GERMANY ...191

CHAPTER 48 – TRAIN TO AMSTERDAM ...195

CHAPTER 49 – HOTEL "DIE PORT VAN CLEVE" ...199

CHAPTER 50 – COFFEE AT CAFÈ VAN ZUYLEN ...204

CHAPTER 51 – DINNER: BRASSERIE DE POORT ...208

CHAPTER 52 – BRUG 9 CELLAR ...214

CHAPTER 53 – OVERBOARD ...219

CHAPTER 54 – CANVAS DREAMS ...223

CHAPTER 55 – HACKED ...227

CHAPTER 56 – THE CEMETERY ...234

CHAPTER 57 – PLAN 'A' ...240

CHAPTER 58 – SURPRISE ENCOUNTER ...244

CHAPTER 59 – THE TRIP HOME ... 247
CHAPTER 60 – THE ULTIMATE DISCOVERY ... 255
CHAPTER 61 – TIDYING UP ... 261

WAYS TO CONNECT ... 264
ABOUT THE AUTHOR ... 265

A KESTREL CIRCLES

THE PAST

Thirteen years.
Old.
Different.
Not same. I was. Am. Is. Very.
Need to rush on.
Ahead.
Must tell.
Fast.   Quick. Speedy.   High velocity.
Accelerate. Jet. Mach. Sound. Light.
Words.
Too slow.
Words are shit.
Shit slow.
Can't keep up.
Slow.
Must tell with slow words.
Focus.
One after the other.
Prepositions.
Use.
Prepositions are brakes to flow.
The *the* **the.**
Riddling ideas.
THE Ideas. See! Obvious. Unnecessary word.
Meaningless.

LOOKING BACK

Fourteen.
Sky-high.
A bird searching.
Eyes closed.
Circling.
I have found a way.
Think first.
Pause. Edit. Think again.
Speedy fast.
Make whole.
Then translate.
Slow words.
For you.
Words for you.
Slow words for me to tell.
I will tell you the story.
My story.
Slowly.
The words will plod along and tell you the story.
They will slowly tell you my story.
I am smiling.
A proper sentence I have written.
Yes.

THE CHARGER

Older.
Now.
Past.
Young.   I am.
Reflection.
I reflect with words and proper sentences.

WHEN I was young, I was also blind to most things. I could see, using light, but what my eyes saw was always overlaid by a perforated screen of sorts: a canvas, like a fine mesh screen—a screen to keep flies out—filtered its way through from the real world. I have learned since, but I still see the canvas first. The canvas was/is fascinatingly filled with light and sound. It is not the kind of sound you can hear or light you can see with your eyes. It is a mixture of all sorts of radiation. I can see it in my mind's eye, but I must wait until the shifting hues reach a kind of focus. Not the best explanation, but as I said before, words are shit. There is never a truly perfect one. Maybe that is good. Life would be boring if all the words were perfect. I would not even need to tell this story. Perfect words would make it so obvious that you would not even listen.

I digress.

I am high above the canvas. I translate the shifting hues and tones. It was not something I learned. I must have been born with the skill. I have always just looked and then heard—mostly. Like music. I would hear a note and then pretty much know I had to follow the pattern. My parents often found me staring into space. That is how they would explain it to all those people they felt they had to explain it to.

There were a lot of them. That is how I learned to see the light coming through the perforated canvas. That is where they were. That is where they wanted me to be—to, at the very least, look. I feel I am a quick study. I like some phrases like 'quick study.' A phrase like that tells a lot with just a little. *'Quick Study.'* I realized I could get them to leave me alone if I occasionally attended to them on the other side of the canvas. I could even double-task. I find that funny because I have never just double-tasked. That would truly be a waste of resources. I just learned to set an alarm of sorts. When it went off, I would donate a part of myself to whatever set it off. It was my way of *'keeping the monsters at bay'* (love this phrase too) and limit interruptions to what the canvas was communicating to me sailing high above.

At first, attending to the radiation was just pleasant. Again, the words are limiting me—sounds, sights, thoughts, feelings—all of the above—filled my every waking moment. I did not have to look anywhere to experience the radiation. It was just there, and it was pleasant and calming. I mostly observed from high up. That way, I could see it all. At least I thought I could in the beginning.

It was calming at first and then my fixation on the canvas morphed it into a translation. In the beginning, it was only bits. A burst of color and sound followed by lines of organized static. The lines linked and soon became paths and the paths became pointers. They pointed everywhere. Where they were pointing from and what they were pointing at was the puzzle. There was never enough information to define more than that. Vectors. Vectors pointing everywhere from everywhere. Yes, the image I gave you is a mess. Just a bunch of lines crisscrossing the universe. And me circling high above, fascinated by it all.

You don't need to know any more about my early childhood than you already know, but you will learn more about my adolescence as we go along.

I started to feel that *'so what'* feeling as you may be feeling now. My fascination ebbed. The view from above was still filled with magic, but I started focusing more on what was happening in the physical world around me. I got older, and I had to. I was a grown man living on my own. Well, sort of on my own. My mother supported me, believing that I could never support myself. As long as I made weekly visits to the psychiatrist of her choice, there was always money in my account.

She was almost right about me not being able to make any sort of living. Any regular kind of employment would be difficult. I know I am not good at that sort of thing. Or at least that is what I thought. Don't get me wrong. I still felt, watched, and listened and, at some point, tried to taste the radiation, but it soon turned into a kind of static that I would attend to if I became stressed. It was one of those stressful moments when it happened for the first time.

I had misplaced the charger for my phone, and I searched the entire apartment, to no avail. I was in a bit of a panic and needed to calm down, so I stretched out on my sofa, closed my eyes, and let the radiation wash over me. I was trying not to think about the lost charger when I noticed something odd.

Something was odd about one of the vectors in the great wash of things the universe was displaying for me. I could see/hear the endpoint of this ripple of light-sound-idea-thing. My mind dove down to the detail. I sat up quickly. No vector had ever shown me its endpoint. Yet, there it was. It extended from somewhere out in the universe to its terminus. It was at that moment my lunch alarm sounded. It was time to eat. I shifted my focus to the world on the physical side of the mental canvas. That was the moment that changed my life. It made me what I am today.

I am the most sought-after detective in the world.

I can find anything. (Well, just about anything. More on that later.)

The terminus of that vector extended out into the physical world. At least it seemed to, but I suspect that was just my mind translating the concept of some sort of energy into a real-world image. No matter. It was pointing right at the recliner in front of the television. I walked over to it and, as I did, the vector shifted slightly to accommodate my new position. I looked down to where it was pointing between the folds of the leather recliner. I reached in and pulled out the lost charger.

BUSINESS IS GOOD

I was born Mathew Brown. I changed it. I had to change it. I never referred to myself until I was fourteen. I heard myself say my name for the first time in a psychiatrist's office. My mother was blackmailing me, as was her wont. "Mattie, tell the man your name," she said and pursed her mouth. That expression was well known to me. It said, "Do what you are told, young man." There was never a spoken 'or else', but it was there. It was kind of funny in retrospect in that I never thought to ask what every other normal child on the planet would have asked. And that was, "Or else what?"

I told the man my name, "Brown, Mathew J."

"Now, Mattie, there is no need to be formal with the doctor," said my mother.

The doctor must have responded, but this was before I understood the importance of not appearing like 'a retard.' I love that word. It is one of those words that communicates on multiple levels. That is why most people find it offensive. I do not. I simply do not offend. I understand the meaning of the word, but it carries no emotional content for me. Truthfully, there are no words that carry any sort of emotion for me. I think I understand their intent, but I simply have no need to feel their intent. This does not mean I lack empathy. I recognize the situations where empathy is required. I just don't feel it. I just feel what I choose to feel and not what others try to make me feel. (Maybe I do lack empathy.)

I decided to change my name when I became a detective. "The Brown Detective Agency" simply 'blew chunks.' That is another of my favorite phrases and yes, I am starting to appreciate words. They are much more versatile than I first thought. I wrote and spoke at least a thousand names in my effort to find a good one. Once I settled on something, I would hear something else that was 'cooler.' I have to say this once: COOL is my all-time favorite word.

I finally decided on Augustus De Marco Cervantes. I wear a hat. The whole package is cool. Did I tell you that I do not care what you think? Truly, I don't. Not caring is like a superpower. I have offices all over the US. Not really offices. They are actually just post-office boxes. I do have an actual office in Venice Beach. That's in California for those of you not from around here. I never know if I give too much information or too little. I probably give too much and usually not what is important or required. C'est la vie.

I live in the back of my office, just like a bunch of fictional detectives I have read. I think that is cool. I have a reputation. My card is simple. It just has my name, my post box address, and the words, "I am expensive, but I can find anything." The words are embossed in gold. The effect is very striking. My mobile number is private. If you want me to find something, you must ask the old-fashioned way and send me a letter. Typed letters are usually moved to the bottom of my pile. Handwriting holds personal flavor. I take out Ads in the cities where I have PO Boxes. All letters are forwarded to my office, and I pick out the ones I like. Business is good.

THE PSYCHIATRIST

I need to jump around a little. Don't worry. I will warn you so things in the past don't get mixed up with things in the present—unless I think they should.

I saw my first psychiatrist as heretofore (fantastic word) mentioned when I was fourteen. I remember him ordering my mother to leave the room. I don't think anyone had ever ordered my mother to do anything in her whole life. I doubt, after watching her reaction, that she has ever let anyone order her to do anything since. It was a first and a last, and I was there to witness it. More like, experience it. At the time it meant little, but now it is one of my favorite memories. I remember pretty much everything, like a 3D film clip.

Anyway, my mother reluctantly left the room. I watched her go. I did not have any need for her to stay or go. My mother was a fixture, so it did not matter to me, but it did matter to the doctor and her. She just looked at him with her 'don't fuck with me face.' He stared back with his 'I don't give a shit' face. It was a standoff. At the time, I didn't care and returned to explore the canvas. That is what I was doing when some sound filtered through. It was not my mother. I started to multitask. I heard the doctor ask me a question.

"Mattie, is it alright if I call you Mattie?" the doctor asked.

I answered simply, "No."

"Don't you like that name?" he asked in his HAL voice.

(For those to whom the reference to HAL means nothing—watch the movie "2001: A Space Odyssey." I apologize to those for whom I wasted their time with this note.)

I knew there was a correct answer. But I could not find it. I am not a cretin. (Maybe I am a cretin.) I said, "I have neither like nor dislike for that name."

"It is your name," he said.

I said nothing.

"Is it your name or not?" he questioned.

"It is not my name."

I then decided that I must socialize as my mother had told me a zillion times. In fact, it was the only reason she was sending me to the psychiatrist in the first place. I could hear her voice echoing in my head. My mother was the opposite of HAL in tone, but exactly the same in intent. She believed it was her job to make sure I survived and be damned if I or anyone else for that matter was going to get in the way. I still hear her screech, "You are not an imbecil and I am going to make sure the world recognizes that fact."

Before he could ask me my name again, I spoke in a pretend-normal voice, "My name is Mathew J. Brown. The J stands for Joel. My mother is a big fan of Billy Joel. She decided I would be called that, so when she heard any Billy Joel song, she would think of me. Perhaps she regrets it? I do not know?"

"So, is it all right if I call you Mathew?"

"Yes."

"Well, Mathew, I would like to have a conversation with you. Is that alright?"

"Yes."

"Good. You are here because your mother asked me to have a chat with you. She feels …" (He paused. I wasn't sure why at the time, but I think I have since figured it out.) "… that you are a little socially challenged. She tells me that you have problems concentrating when someone is talking to you, and she wants me to help you with that issue. How do you feel about that?"

I turned away from the canvas and looked at him. I figured this situation needed my full attention. I was right. I suddenly realized this man could actually get my mother off my back. (Great phrase—'off my back.')

At the time, I would not have understood it. When I was fourteen, all words were literal. Had someone said it to me then, I would have wanted to check myself out in the mirror to see if my mother had somehow slipped back into the room and climbed onto my back. As it was, I just said, "I am not a cretin." I was about to multitask again, for I realized this was not going to be a conversation, it was just him asking and me answering.

"What is a 'cretin'?"

"A cretin is someone of very low intellectual ability."

"Do you think you are smart?"

"Yes."

"Good. What do you like to do?"

I looked up at him. I thought he was trying to trick me. I did not know how to answer, so I just stared. I was about to go back to the canvas and see what had changed since I last looked two or three minutes ago, but I stopped myself. It was probably something entirely different, anyway. "You wouldn't understand," I said.

"Try me. I am a doctor, after all, and you have to understand a lot to become a doctor."

"I look at the canvas to see what kinds of noise it is making and what kinds of pictures it is drawing and other stuff."

"The canvas."

"Yeah."

"Where is this canvas?"

"Everywhere."

"Can I see it?"

"I have no idea."

"Where exactly do you look?"

I looked at the canvas and then I looked through the tiny holes in the canvas back at this man. The question was confusing. I did not like being confused when I was fourteen. I started to get flustered, and I did not want to answer this man's stupid questions, so I said, "I don't know. I must be a cretin." I stood up and walked to the door. I could hear him say something, but by then I was totally focused on the canvas and what was developing there. I swooped down. There were some very cool numbers bouncing around in a light-sound soup. In the waiting room, I saw my mother jump to her feet. "Time to go," I said and walked to the door. She did not know if she should talk to the doctor or follow me. She followed me. I guess she thought she could always talk to the doctor later. I hoped that I would not have to go back to see him again even after suggesting I was a cretin, but it did not turn out that way.

THE POCKET WATCH

I pay extra to have my mail pushed through a slot in my door. The letters fall into a locked catch-all box on the inside. The box is secure. It only opens when I stand in front of an almost invisible camera. I must be alive and sticking out my tongue. Tongues are as unique as fingerprints or irises. The tiny, almost invisible camera takes a picture of my tongue and compares it to the most recent picture of my tongue. That way, no one can enter or touch the letters or parcels once they have been delivered. I would not say I am paranoid. I just think that everyone out there is trying to expose me as a fraud. I am fairly famous among detectives. It is the mystery that keeps the fame alive. I must constantly update my security and thus maintain the mystery.

The entire building is located in the old section of Venice Beach. I own a small brick building that I have converted to meet my needs. The front office section is where I meet respective clients. It is decorated circa 1959-ish. My desk sits front and center. There is a line of gray-green filing cabinets along one wall. They are filled with yellowed files. I have an old rotary phone on my desk. It works sort of. I can make it ring if I want, but that only happens when I want to give a client a certain impression. Usually, I want them to think that they are not first in line. I do that mostly for entertainment value. What good is doing a job if it is not entertaining?

The walls remind you of a smoke-filled room. There is no actual smoke or even the smell of smoke. That would ruin it for me. It is all for me. It is an affectation that creates a specific effect—a 1950s down-and-out detective's office with a bathroom at the rear. Nothing in the room has any functional purpose, with perhaps the exception of the phone. Its purpose has nothing to do with its designated function. If I dial a certain number and then enter the bathroom, a panel opens that leads to my living quarters.

The rest of the building is where I live and where the real detective work happens. You might think I have walls of computers and hundreds of minions to help me find whatever needs finding. Well, you are wrong and right at the same time. I have just one computer that sits unobtrusively (cool word) in the corner of my lab. It connects me to a single company that hires a large number of other companies that get me the information I need to do my job. I pay them well.

I know you are wondering about the how. I won't keep it a secret. Here is how I can say with certainty that I can find anything you want me to find, as long as you know what you are looking for. That last bit is important. You cannot walk into my office and ask me to find you a pot of leprechaun gold. Don't misunderstand. I could find you that leprechaun gold if, in fact, you had actually seen it and were sure it existed. I cannot find imaginary things. Well, I could, but they would still be imaginary. I am not sure if that last part was funny or not. I find humor difficult, but I am getting better at it.

It is time to get on with it. I received this letter:

> *Dear Mr. Cervantes,*
>
> *I am contacting you as I am told that you can find anything. My mother is on her deathbed, and I would like to give her the one thing she desires most and that is something that was lost a long time ago—her father's gold pocket watch. My grandmother often spoke to her about it and how important it was to her husband. My grandmother is no longer with us. We think my grandfather died during WWII, but his remains were never found. I was told that his body might have been hit by a shell and torn apart. Perhaps they were unable to identify him, and his body is buried somewhere in Europe. I hope the watch was buried with him and finding it might lead to finding him and bringing him home.*

My grandmother searched for him after the war, but his body was never found. My mother wishes she could hold the watch for a little while. She thinks she would die peacefully holding something her father cherished.

I would like you to find my grandfather's pocket watch. He always kept it next to his heart. My grandmother's picture was inside the lid.

I have some pictures of the watch that were taken for insurance purposes. I also have a picture of him wearing it before he went off to war, if that would help. Do you think you can find it?

Sincerely yours,
Sandra Beal

P.S. I am unable to travel due to my mother's illness. If you take this case, I request that you come to San Francisco to see me. I will gladly pay for your time and travel costs.

I was intrigued, so I decided to fly to San Francisco. I love to go to new places. I didn't when I was younger, but once I traveled to Dallas with my mother (she forced me) things changed. It was like the altitude made the canvas clearer—more vivid. I spent the entire flight immersed in a myriad of patterns that I later defined as vectors. Now I think of an object that I have seen in pictures and practice finding its location. The better my sense of the object, the better the chances of finding it in the great flood of data that paints the four-dimensional canvas. Sometimes I can only find where the object was at some time in the past. I figured out this indicated that the object had somehow been destroyed. It no longer exists in the present. Lately, I have been trying to locate possible future objects, but I have not been successful. Perhaps it is because my concept of what they actually are is wrong. I have decided that it is a little arrogant of me to think I can find the location of some object in the future.

However, I do have a plan. I experiment with the location of future objects by having an employee hide something very common so that finding it in the present would be an impossible task as there would be billions of them. We will decide on a particular coin. They tell me that in six months they will take a felt pen and mark the object with a shape. They show me the object and the kind of mark they will make. I will search for it as if it has the shape in the present. My task will be to find it before my employee actually marks it. Who knows? I might add God-like powers to my repertory of skills.

Just so you know, I am smiling at the prospect.

THE MEETING

I flew to my meeting with Ms. Sandra Beal. She was a woman in her fifties. She invited me to her residence. It was on the ground floor and had a small yard at the back. She said she lived alone, but I suspected that was a lie. Several items in her condominium seemed odd for a woman who lived alone. When I used her bathroom, it became obvious that a man was living with her. I did not press the issue, but I did wonder why she chose to lie.

At the meeting, I nodded and listened. I asked a few questions.

"So, you want me to find this gold pocket watch that belonged to your grandfather—a Samuel A. Adare?"

"Yes."

"And you are sure it was on his person when he died?"

"Yes. I was told that he always carried it. He wanted my grandmother's picture close to his heart."

"That sounds a little…," I searched for a word that would not offend. "… romantic."

"Maybe it is, but that is what I choose to believe. If you find my grandfather, you will find the watch."

"So, it is your grandfather's remains that you actually want to find. That might be harder. It has been a long time. There might be nothing left to find."

"No. I want the watch."

"Don't you mean your grandmother wants the watch?"

There was an irritation creeping into her voice. "We both want it."

"But for different reasons?"

"Yes."

"I apologize, but I need to understand as much as I can about this situation. Finding the watch will depend on it. The more information I have, the easier it will be to find."

"I am sorry; my mother's illness has made me a little tense. She is very frail."

I smiled at her. I changed my tact. "So, what did your grandfather do in the war? This will help with my research. I can narrow down the possibilities if I know where he was stationed and when he went missing." I expected an answer along the lines of—*He was killed when the Americans entered Berlin* or some such explanation.

"He was a photographer turned spy. At least, that is what my mother told me. He was in Amsterdam on May 10, 1940. That is when…"

"When the Nazis attacked. It started with paratroopers dressed as Dutch soldiers."

"Yes." She looked at me and arched her eyes. "Not many people know that."

I shrugged. "You said he died in the war, but his body was never found. How do you know he died? Did he die in Amsterdam?"

"My grandmother told my mother he died. I don't know where."

"How do you know he was in Amsterdam in 1940?"

"I have his effects. He left some letters."

"I don't mean to be exasperating, but how did she know he died? Did she get a notice from the war department?"

"I don't know. She just said that he never came back from the war. He was assumed to have died. She did say that the CIA had informed my grandmother that he was presumed dead."

"That is odd. The CIA was not formed until 1947. Are you sure it was not the OSS—Office of Strategic Services?"

"No—I remember—she told me that it was the CIA. My grandmother tried for three years after the war was over to find out what happened to him. They finally told her that all records of my grandfather's activities during the war were destroyed and he was assumed to be deceased. At that point, they stopped looking."

"Did they send her his personal effects?"

"Yes."

"What was in them?"

"Just his military dress uniform and his kit."

"And the letters?" I arched my eyebrows. "Can I see them?"

"No. They ended up in his footlocker. They were destroyed when the basement of my mother's house flooded." She paused as if she were considering my next question. "I remember looking through the footlocker before that happened."

"Did you read them?"

"I glanced at a couple. I don't remember much. They just chatted about common stuff. Mostly about house repairs."

"So, everything was destroyed, even the letters?" She paused. I observed her pupils dilate. I expected that she was about to lie. This often happens with clients. They want to employ you to do something, but they do not want to give you all the information. They want to keep certain things hidden. She was definitely hiding something.

"Everything was ruined. The letters were unreadable. I'm not sure what happened to the uniform. The only things that might have survived were some photos inside the lid. There were pictures of my grandmother holding my mother when she was a baby. There was one of my grandfather in a graveyard. He was standing with one foot on a small fence that surrounded the grave. His hobby was taking pictures of graveyard headstones. One of his buddies must have taken the picture."

"Do you know what he did in the war?"

"No one seems to know. As I said, all his records were destroyed. I assume he was doing some sort of spy stuff." She pointed at a picture on a side table. It was a man in a suit with a camera around his neck. He was standing in a graveyard. He had one foot on the small fence surrounding the grave. "That was sent before the war. It is similar to the one in his footlocker."

I glanced at the picture. "One last question—I understand your dying mother wants it to provide comfort, but why do you want the watch?"

Her demeanor changed. She spoke sharply. "I have told you everything I know. Why does it matter why we want the watch? Can you find it or not?"

I stood. "Yes. What would you like me to do when I know where it is?"

"Pardon?"

"What would you like me to do with the knowledge of its whereabouts?"

"I assumed you would get it and bring it to me."

"I don't usually do that. Knowing where something is and actually retrieving it requires two very different skill sets."

She frowned.

"Let me explain. Say you wanted to know the location of a diamond-studded broach your gangster ex-husband took when he left. I could tell you exactly where it is, but I am not going to mess with gangster ex-husbands to get it back to you. That would be your job." I paused. "Do you see what I mean?"

"In that case, what would it require for you to bring it to me once you find it?"

"I don't know." At that point, I made a decision. I knew I would search for the watch and considered what retrieving it might require. I did know people I could call on if I needed something distasteful done, and I was getting bored with my present cases so I said, "Yes, I will take the case. As far as retrieving it, if and when I find it, well, I cannot guarantee success. I will not charge you anything beyond my usual fee, plus travel expenses if I cannot retrieve it." I took out one of my cards. I handed it to her. "Just so you know, I travel first class, and that can be expensive."

She took the card. She looked up at me. "Fine. When will I hear from you?"

"I don't know, but I have your email. That is how I will contact you when I have found the watch, that is, if it still exists." I shook her hand and stood to leave. She stood in the doorway as I walked down the sidewalk. I had already shifted my focus to the canvas. I had a couple of photographs in my pocket and would spend the return flight studying them. I was troubled but not sure why. I pushed away a sense of foreboding.

THE SEARCH

IT never took very long to find a thing if I had a good concept of what it was. In this case, I had an old photograph. Once I was back in my residence, I stared at the canvas space and blotted out everything else. The silence was perfect in my soundproof rooms. The canvas energy would hiss and buzz. The light would assemble into vectors of different colors and intensities. The incredible volume of vectors caused them to blur into a sort of white noise. Unless I had a hook. It was, in many ways, like fishing. I would cast my knowledge of the object into the morass of energy and inevitably hook it—hook the vector that was beckoning to me. Once hooked, I could lift it out and follow the line to the location of the object. I became much better at finding whatever I needed after the first time: finding my charger.

The end results are seldom what I or my client expect. This was definitely true in "The Case of the Spy's Pocket Watch" as I like to call it. I spent the flight home searching the canvas. At the start, I just pictured the watch in my mind. At first, there were simply millions of vectors pointing every which way. I rolled the 3D image over in my mind. After some time, I noticed a thinning of the vectors as the mist parted and the light brightened. There were still too many to search each one, but experience told me that following one to its terminus would help me thin the herd. I chose the one that extended vertically down and fell with it. It ended with a burst of light as if it were an exploding firework. The points of light faded, and I could see a map of Europe spread out below me.

I felt a bump, and the canvas vanished. The plane had landed. I was irritated that I was unable to pinpoint the watch's location. I chastised myself for my arrogance. This was not going to be as easy as finding a charger that had slipped between some cushions. I had narrowed it down to the entire continent of Europe. The likelihood that it was anywhere else was slim to none.

I spent the remainder of the day in my residence looking for some clue as to where the watch was specifically located. I started with what I knew. The Spy had been in Amsterdam in 1940. I decided to follow him, assuming he had the watch on his person. I had limited success in this endeavor. The vectors flashed into existence and crisscrossed Europe with rapid transitions. It was extremely difficult to follow. They were often blocked by a yellowed image of a paper filled with letters. I knew that following things far in the past was often problematic and confusing. The Spy had been very active during the war. I would try to stop time from passing quickly to get a clear picture of exactly where Adare was at any given moment. The vectors split and pointed in two separate places at the same time. The lettered paper caused some of the vectors to reflect while others simply passed through. It was confusing, to say the least, until I realized that the confusion had a cause. The Spy did not carry the watch with him on all his missions as I had assumed. The Canvas was attempting to show me the watch and The Spy at the same time, but the two were in different places. I changed my tactic. I had to assume that Adare was deceased, so I focused on the watch at the present date. That is when I found it. The lettered paper disappeared. Doing this had some drawbacks, in that I would have no idea how the watch got to its final resting place.

The final location of the gold pocket watch was a small Irish village just outside the city of Limerick and not on some forgotten battlefield. My first thought was this soldier's remains were transported and buried there for the vector stopped over an old church in the center of the village of Killaloe Ireland.

Getting the watch was an entirely different proposition. In this case, I was intrigued and decided to take a little holiday. Ireland would do nicely. I sent a brief electronic message to my client: "Know where it is. Gone to try to fetch it."

THE FLIGHT

HOW could a pocket watch belonging to a photographer who was a spy in WWII find its way to a small church in Ireland? This part of my job needed some good old-fashioned detective work. I was looking forward to it. On my way over the Atlantic Ocean, something important happened.

As I told Ms. Sandra Beal, I fly first class. First-class allows me to do what I love to do: explore the canvas. It is never the same. Ever. The best changes are not slight shifts in tone, hue, or style. They can do that, but that is not what makes them cool. What makes them cool is the way they can become new and filled with new possibilities. All I have to do is glance away for as little as a second and Zowie-Pow the entire canvas has transformed into something new. Major changes don't occur when I am looking. They might shift as if the perspective had changed, but that is all. This often created problems for me when I was young. I would be in the middle of a safari of sorts and was just about to part the lush green fronds and expose some light-sound-magic thing when my mother would demand that I give her my attention.

Multi-tasking is often defined as doing two or more things at the same time. I don't think anyone can do that. Multi-tasking is simply being able to shift from one thing to another quickly and appear to maintain constant attention on it all. (Well, nearly constant.) The problem is, the canvas doesn't play that game, or maybe it plays it but doesn't care, or maybe it plays and is trying to fuck with me. I don't know, but if I have to glance away, even for a second, the whole thing will change and I will never know what was hiding in the grass. When I was young, that would piss me off and I would blame whoever was the source of the demand that I attend to them. If it was my mother, I soon learned that I could ignore her by becoming zombified (Mother's word). She would simply leave me be to do whatever I was doing. It would be better for both of us if she did. When I was very young, the school counselor would say to me, *This is a special school because you are special.* That is what they tell all the kids that went there. UGG. That used to make me puke. The counselor always wanted to *"break open my shell"* because he knew I was "*beautiful inside.*" (You had to read that last part with dripping sarcasm. Later I will tell you how I came to understand sarcasm. I didn't get it for the longest time, but now it is one of the most beautiful aspects of communication—at least from my point of view.) Anyway, he was the most useless twat on the planet.

Oh my God—get to the point. Sorry. One thought is always grabbing onto the tail of the preceding one. The point is, I don't like being interrupted when I am exploring. One interruption can ruin an entire session. Hence my soundproof apartment. Flying first class allows me to tell the flight attendant that I do not wish to be interrupted even if the plane is falling out of the sky or should I say, "Especially if the plane is falling out of the sky." I want to spend the remaining few minutes of my life exploring a new aspect of the canvas rather than engaging in a scream fest with all the normal people. I keep my seatbelt on to avoid the most common interruptions.

LAX was in its usual chaotic state. I don't like airports mostly because I don't like being touched—more specifically, I don't like anyone brushing up against me. Deliberate touching is okay. It is not my favorite, but I usually know when it is about to happen. I prepare for the where and the how and can mitigate the duration and location. Brushing up against me leads to some crazy notions running through my brain such as *Who touched me? What part of them touched me? What or who did they touch before they touched me? Did they touch me on purpose? If so, what was their purpose?* And on and on until my brain explodes.

I arrived at LAX and headed to the Oneworld Alliance Lounge. I was flying British Airways direct to Heathrow and then taking a short hop over to Shannon Airport on Aer Lingus. I hired a car and driver to pick me up. The lounge was not crowded. I sat alone with my dark glasses on and explored the canvas. I did notice, through the net of the canvas, a woman watching me. She was being a little furtive. That is to say, she was looking at me sideways when she looked up from the book she was not reading. I don't think she turned the page once, which, needless to say, was odd for someone who was actually reading. I did, however, dismiss it when she was joined by a tall blond man. The woman was also blonde. They reminded me of middle-aged Barbie and Ken. They moved away and sat at the bar on the far side of the lounge. I soon boarded the flight. Both the man and woman were also on my flight, but I did not notice that until much later.

Don't think I have forgotten. I have not forgotten about 'the something' that happened. I am going to get to that now. I was soon settled in my seat. I chatted with the attendant about my needs. He seemed to understand what I wanted. I hydrated, snapped on my seatbelt, set the privacy panels, and slipped a sleeping mask over my face. The sleeping mask is to conceal the fact that my eyes roll back into my head while I am exploring the canvas. I think a smile must come over my face when I become immersed. The image is rather odd: a smiling face with eyes that drift back into their sockets. When I think about it, I imagine seeing someone else's face doing that and the picture is not an attractive one. One might say it would look rather macabre.

A couple of hours passed on the uneventful flight. I was immersed in the canvas. I was trying to narrow down the location of the gold pocket watch. A church built in the 13th century would have many possible hiding places. I needed to go as directly to the location as possible. There is an oddity in my ability to find things. The closer I am to the object, the more accurate my location vector will be. Maybe that is not so odd—after all, the universe is an ordered place when it wants to be. Five hours had passed and, as per my instructions to the steward, he touched my shoulder. "Mr. Cervantes? Five hours have passed." I set this alarm so I could use the facilities. If I put this aspect of the human body off too long, I would be very uncomfortable later.

"Thank you," I said quickly. The interruption was a serious case of bad timing. I was much closer to the exact location, but the interruption blurred that knowledge. All I knew was that the gold pocket watch was not in the church proper. It was just outside. I reached up and pulled down the mask. I headed to the facilities and relieved myself. I exited the washroom and, on impulse, I reached up and parted the curtains between first and second class. The tube that made up the plane extended away from me. I was staring at the far end. I slowly ran my eyes up the rows of seats and finally rested on the passengers right in front of me. Sitting in the seats directly behind the first-class curtains were the man and the woman from the airport lounge. The three of us made eye contact. They both stood and stepped toward me. The man reached up and put his hand under my left arm as if he were helping a disabled person. He pulled me to the side, and the woman slipped past him, heading toward one of the first-class washrooms. As she did, my sports jacket caught on her handbag. As it fell closed, the man released my arm.

"Sorry, my wife was trying to get past you. She has a bit of an emergency. You know, female stuff." I nodded and turned back through the curtain just as the washroom door closed. I hurried back to my seat. The steward brought me a sandwich and a bottle of water as per our agreement. The sandwich was supplied by a small Deli in Venice Beach. I had ordered it specifically. I started to eat as my brain began to race. The man and the woman had both brushed against me. What was their intent? The timing was very odd, almost deliberate. I put down the sandwich and felt under my arm where he had grabbed me and pulled me to the side. There was nothing. I remembered my jacket flapping open as the woman passed. I felt in my pockets. There was nothing. I usually do not use pockets. I always feel better when they are empty. I had not put anything in any of my pockets. I was sure of that. As I patted, I started to relax. Perhaps it was all just an accidental encounter. There was nothing in my pockets. I did not leave anything to chance and opened my jacket to look at the lining. This particular jacket had a small pocket low down. What it could possibly hold was beyond me, but I patted it, anyway. There was nothing. I stuck a finger inside and felt around. That is when I found it. It was stuck to the jacket side of the pocket. It was a disk about one centimeter in diameter with the thickness of a dime. It was soft and pliable and barely detectable. I could not feel it by simply patting the outside of the pocket. They had planted something on me. My mind raced as to the what and the why and, most importantly, the who.

GOOD MORNING

MY first impulse was to remove my jacket and get rid of it. I could ask the steward to throw it in the trash or just stuff it in one of the overhead compartments and leave it on the plane. I searched for a good and proper word here, but the closest I could come to how I felt was 'infected.' I had been *infected.* Perhaps 'compromised' would be better, but that word did not carry any sense of impending doom while 'infected' did, at least for me. I felt infected as long as I kept the jacket.

I sat back in my seat. My pulse was racing. I went to the canvas and it calmly, slowly enveloped me. I began to think a little more rationally. I need you to understand something here. I want to stop you from assuming that thinking irrationally is a bad thing and that the opposite is a good thing. That is not so. I have done some of my best work while in a totally irrational state. However, I must admit, this was not one of those times. As I became rational again, I saw the silliness of throwing away a perfectly good jacket given that the persons causing the infection would know that I was no longer carrying the device they had planted in my pocket. I did not want them to know that. I assumed it was some sort of tracking device. Knowing of its existence and knowing they did not know I knew put me in a powerful position.

They must want something from me. I started to review all my most recent cases. None seemed to involve anything of great value that might cause some person to follow me to Ireland. The only thing that might be valuable enough was the gold pocket watch. But its value would not even cover the price of a plane ticket, let alone two of them. It was of sentimental value only. At least that is what I was led to believe by my client. Maybe that was not true. I smiled and rubbed the section of the jacket that held the device the man and woman sitting in the first row on the other side of the curtain had so surreptitiously placed there. At that instant, I heard the washroom door open behind me. The steward's voice could be heard. I turned and saw him quietly speaking to the woman leaving the washroom. His hand gestures told me he was telling her that she was not to use the washrooms in first class, as they were reserved for first-class passengers. She was trying to explain that it was an emergency and as a result, I got a very good view of her. I studied her face. She was a woman in her late thirties—early forties. Her hair was blonde, but not naturally so. There was a dark streak down the roots. It was straight and flipped up and in at the end. When she tilted her head down as she did when nodding affirmatively to the steward, her hair fell forward, exposing her ear. I caught a glimpse of a small device embedded there. The steward held open the curtain, and the woman passed through, out of sight.

I concluded that I was under surveillance. They were listening to me and tracking me. I wasn't concerned about the listening, as I seldom said anything of import. The tracking was another matter. Since there was little I could do at the moment, I settled down in my seat and was about to pull the sleeping mask down over my face. I glanced to my left and caught the eye of a gentleman staring at me as if I were a rare and precious object. He took the opportunity of our temporary connection to speak. "Hello," he said. I simply nodded and started to prepare myself to explore the canvas. He continued unabated. "I think we have met." He paused, waiting for me to respond. Since he had not asked anything, I did not feel a need to agree or disagree with his statement. I do realize this is a shortcoming. Most people would have translated his statement into a question and answered it as such. I have rationalized my shortcoming as simply a measure of respect for the other person, for they might not want me to assume to answer the non-question. He continued, "Maybe I just saw you in the newspaper or some magazine. I am an avid reader and I like to keep up. Are you from LA?" Before I could even nod, he rushed on, "Of course you are. At least that is your likely home, as that is where the plane departed."

I smiled one of my practiced smiles and said, "Yes."

"Are you famous? I assume you are or else you live in my neighborhood, and I saw you at the Deli or some such place and I don't remember. What do you do?"

I leaned forward. "I am a detective. I find things."

The man snapped his fingers. "Got it. You are that detective from Venice Beach and yes, you find stuff. You find stuff that has been lost for a long time. I read that you once found an old wedding ring with an inscription that was dropped down a drain some thirty years ago. The building where it was lost had already been torn down and a new building was erected over the spot. You found the ring in the city sewer system. A bit of cracked concrete had caused an eddy when the sewer water rushed past. The ring had been trapped in the eddy."

A surge of pride welled up, and I quickly pushed it aside. "Yes, that was me."

"I often wondered how you found it. I am a writer, and I would love you to explain your process and any other interesting cases you may wish to tell me about." I smiled as dismissively as I was able. I was obviously not very good at dismissive smiles, for he continued. "What do you say? We can share any profits if the book sells. I am pretty sure it will sell. It could make you even more famous than you already are."

"I don't want to be any more famous. I am always busy." Suddenly it occurred to me that this encounter on the plane to Ireland might not be serendipitous at all. What if he was in cahoots (very cool word) with the man and the woman who planted that thing in my pocket? The 'WHY' question was asserting itself. It did, as you probably already suspect, occur to me that the encounters had something to do with the gold pocket watch. I needed to give the recent events some thought. I turned to the man. "I am not interested in your proposal. I need to rest. Good morning," I said dismissively. I sat back in my seat and settled in to scan the canvas. For some reason that I have yet to discover, I could not focus on anything other than a crazy quote that popped into my head.

"Do you wish me a good morning, or mean that it is a good morning whether I want it or not; or that you feel good this morning; or that it is a morning to be good on?"

The magic of these words from Tolkien's "The Hobbit" simply overwhelmed me.

A KITKAT

SOMETIMES, I find it elucidating to go back and watch the memories of past events. I increase my understanding when I do this. I often return to the second visit to the psychiatrist my mother decided would be good for me. I remember waiting in the anteroom just outside his office. It was a large room, as it served several medical personnel. I was at least 30 minutes early because my mother needed to meet someone, so she just dropped me off and told me to wait if she was late picking me up. This was her usual modus operandi. It was only recently that I figured out what she was doing when she left me somewhere. She had a lover. I don't think she still has one.

I seldom talk about my father, mainly because I barely know the man. He lived in the same house as I did, but that was all. We did not interact at all. We still don't. I have a few vague memories of him picking me up when I was very young. I remember crying and him putting me down and walking away. Anyway, the point is, he was there, but not. I think that is still the case. They live in the same house. When I visit, which is rare, I do not, as a rule, see him. He lives in a separate apartment in the house. I do not have any negative feelings about either of them. When I was fifteen, my mother having a lover was a good thing in that she spent less time trying to fix the unfixable in me.

The anteroom at the doctor's office was filled with people. This was my second appointment, but the first time I was left to wait. There were all types of patients. They were waiting to see various medical specialists. I was about to conjure up the canvas and lose myself when this one patient caught my attention. He was sitting opposite me. He was wearing a cardigan sweater with at least thirty buttons down the front. I can see it clearly as it was covered in patches of various animals on one side and various cars on the other. It was an odd combination. His hair was clumped together in tufts. When he leaned forward, I could see he had multiple hair whorls. I have learned since that they are called trichoglyphs. There were at least four of them and seemed to be fighting with each other as to which would be in command of the direction of the hair. None of them were winning, but the fight was forcing the hair to stand up on end like little armies forever on alert. The only thing that changed their position was when he ran his fingers over his head and disrupted their orders, forcing a different whorl to be dominant.

It was not his hair that interested me, although, at the time, I found it captivating. It was just an oddity of nature that once explored, became accepted. What really caught my attention were the buttons. There were a lot of them close together. They were multi-colored. He was focused on them and kept unbuttoning them and rebuttoning them. That is how I got such a good view of the top of his head. He kept looking down at the buttons of his sweater. At first, I just felt like I was normal when juxtaposed with this person. He was really weird and had no problem displaying his weirdness to the world. Back to the buttons—as I said, they were multi-colored and he would unbutton them all with deliberate care and then rebutton them in what I initially thought was a random order. He started at the bottom. I remember the bottom button was yellow. He would then find the next yellow button—fourth from the bottom—and button it in the second hole. The fifth button was red, so he buttoned the three red buttons in a row, letting the unbuttoned ones bunch up the sweater. Then the next five blue ones. The image I want you to see is that his sweater was being buttoned up all wrong. Some buttons were simply left out because they were the wrong color. When he got the five blue ones buttoned, he turned to green and buttoned seven green in a row. When he finished the green ones, he started on black, and I suddenly knew that he would not be successful, for he would need eleven black ones to continue the pattern. There were not eleven black ones. It was a pattern he was after. He was buttoning the prime numbers. When he realized this, he unbuttoned all of them and started again only from the top. The first button was red. I know you might have found this whole button business dreary, but I wanted to show you that it helped me come to terms with who I was and how I was viewed by the outside world. People thought I was weird in the same way I thought the button-prime-number-multiple-trichoglyphs guy was weird. That didn't mean I felt a need to change who I was, but it did give—and continues to give—me some insight into the need to present myself to the world in a somewhat "normal" way.

By the time I got into the psychiatrist's office, I was changed. I was determined not to present as a weirdo. As you will see, I needed more than determination:

"Hello, Mathew. How are you today? Would you like to sit down and have a chat?"

"Good." I gave a brief pause. "No." I answered both of his questions.

"I will rephrase. Please sit down in that chair so we can talk." I sat down in the chair. "Tell me a little about what you have been doing."

"I have been sitting in your office. I was watching some of the people sitting out there. I rode here with my mother in her car. I had eggs and toast for breakfast. They were hard in the middle. I …" The doctor raised his hand, indicating that I should stop. I did.

"Let me be a little more specific. What have you been thinking about? Anything interesting? Last time you were here, you talked about the 'canvas.'"

"Yes."

"I think I need more detail, Mathew. Can you tell me more about the canvas?"

"Yes," I answered.

The doctor was beginning to see what was happening. He rephrased his statement to a request. "Please tell me more about the canvas."

"I'd rather not."

"Why not?"

Here I blurted. I don't usually blurt. I am measured. But I blurted, "Because I don't want to appear like I am a weirdo."

"I won't judge. I can help you overcome those kinds of feelings."

"You don't understand. It is not the feelings I need to overcome. I know I am weird. I like being weird. I never want to change that. I just do not want to appear to the world as a weird cretin."

"Why is hiding the appearance of your true self so important to you?"

"Are you kidding me? It is so obvious." I rolled up my sleeves and displayed my gravel-burned elbows. "I got pushed down in the school parking lot last week. I was just standing, waiting for my mother to pick me up. I was looking at the canvas when a couple of kids from one of the behavior classes decided to shove me around for their entertainment. I didn't notice them until it was too late."

"I'm sorry."

"Why?"

"I mean, I understand your feelings." He paused and opened his drawer. He took out a couple of candy bars and tossed me one. I caught it. He opened his and took a bite. "Eat," he said.

I opened the candy bar. It was a KitKat. My favorite. I like it because it is a perfectly organized candy bar without bumps and odd shapes. I carefully broke a finger off of the bar and nibbled. "Thanks."

He watched me for a while as I ate the candy bar. He smiled and said, "I have a confession to make." I looked up. "I did some investigation and found out that your favorite candy bar was KitKat. Is that ok?"

"Is what OK?"

"That I investigated you?"

I shrugged.

"Good. Let's chat about your 'canvas' next time." We continued to eat our candy bars in silence.

A MURDER

I arrived at Heathrow and traveled as quickly as I could to the designated gate for my flight to Shannon Airport. I did not see any of the three people who had contact with me on the plane. I took a taxi the 50-or-so kilometers to the Lakeside Hotel in Killaloe. I considered leasing a car and driving myself but soon dismissed the idea as not compatible with my skill-set or my tastes. I hate driving. One has to give the task one's full attention. There would be no looking at the canvas while driving. The village was just a short walk across the River Shannon over the Killaloe Bridge. I checked in and walked a few hundred meters down Lakeside Drive to the pub on the corner. It was open late. My previous trips to Ireland were before the country-wide smoking bans and, as a result, I had never been to a pub on the Green Isle. I had checked out the area on Google maps and was expecting a pub called Molly's, but instead, I found it had changed to Bóruma Gastro Bar. The food was not memorable. That is not to say it was not good, I just don't remember it. I left the pub late, walked to the middle of the Killaloe Bridge, and stared down at the river swirling in eddies around the bridge pier below. In the morning, I would begin my search in earnest. It was a cool May evening. The wind off the river was chilling me. I did up the buttons on my jacket and turned to walk back to the hotel. My hand skipped to the hem of the jacket and felt the small soft disk embedded there. Once back at the hotel, I would explore it further. I turned to head back when I heard someone yelling.

A man was standing on a raised platform overlooking a small boat moorage. He was alternating staring down into the water and calling out to someone at the restaurant.

"Sean. Sean," he called over and over. No one by that name answered. Several people turned to look in his direction. Finally, he seemed to recognize one of the people congregating in front of the restaurant on the other side of the road. He called out, "Mary. Mary, go get Sean." The woman turned and ran into the restaurant. A few seconds later, a man came out. At the same time, the people in front of the restaurant and those on the bridge started to move toward the man. I stared at where he had pointed. I could see what looked like something light-colored floating in the water between a couple of small boats. I suspected it was a body. By then, the man called Sean was jogging across the road. He looked over the rail at whatever was floating in the water. He took out his phone and called someone, then both he and the other man proceeded to keep any onlookers away from whatever was floating in the water. I left the bridge, turned left, and stepped over a meter-high metal railing surrounding a few benches and tables used by the restaurant when the weather was warmer. I strode toward the raised platform, staying as close to the stone wall and hedge that separated the area from the edge of the river.

The two men now stood at the fence opening at the end of the crosswalk. I walked quickly behind them and was about to step up on the raised platform that probably held pumping equipment when a man named Sean noticed me and turned.

"Sir, please step away from there. The police have been called," he said and took steps toward me.

This is where I pulled my superior card. It took me a long time to develop this skill but, once I had it mastered, it never failed to put me in a top position. Once there, a little bravado kept me there. I could ask questions and look at whatever needed looking at. I always carried my private investigator badge and license. I flipped it open just long enough for someone to see what it was without allowing them to see any detail. "My name is Cervantes. I am an investigator. Please step back. I would like you to continue with your efforts to keep the curious public away." I glanced down at the river between two moored boats and determined that it was a body floating in the water. "Is there anyone here that can help me get the body out of the river?"

He hesitated and then, like a switch went off in his head, he was all in with me being his superior in this situation. He turned and called to a man on the other side of the road. "Ken, go and get Ian and get over here." Ken jumped to it and the two men were soon attempting to pull the body from the water. One was lying on the deck of the nearest boat and the other was on the narrow sidewalk that ran past the moored boats. They slowly pulled the body from the water and deposited it on the concrete walkway. I turned it over and found myself staring into the face of the man from the flight to London who offered to write my memoirs. There was a red spot the size of my thumbnail right in the middle of his forehead. It was obvious to all that he had been murdered.

I turned toward an approaching siren sound that was soon accompanied by flashing police lights. The two men were staring at the body and then at me. I knew I needed a few minutes alone with the body. "Go and tell the officers that the body is down here." One of the men turned to go while the other younger man just stared at the body. "Both of you. Go." My voice carried authority. I watched them disappear, and I was soon alone with the body. I felt his pockets for some kind of ID. I needed to know who he was. Something was going on and I needed to know if I was the focus or if this situation was merely a coincidence. I highly doubted it was the latter.

I pulled out a wallet from the inside of his jacket. I glanced at his ID. His name was Harold W Kruger. I felt in all his other pockets. The only other thing was a very wet folded piece of card stock in his front pant pocket. I did not try to unfold it, but I did slip it into my jacket pocket beside the tracker. I had a strange thought that the tracker might be able to read what was on the folded paper. I shook my head and chastised myself for being silly. Men were approaching, so I quickly returned the wallet and stood back away from the body. I quickly walked down the concrete walk past the raised platform. I slipped off the small pier and onto the sidewalk, going in the direction of my hotel. No one noticed my disappearance, for they were all staring at the police as they went to inspect the body staring blankly at the sky with very dead eyes.

Once back at my hotel, I went to my room. I could see the flashing lights of the police vehicles on the walls of my room. I closed the curtains and sat at the small desk. I carefully opened the folded card secreted in my pocket. It was one of my business cards. I wondered where he had gotten it. I definitely did not give it to him. The last person I gave a card to was Ms. Sandra Beal. Perhaps she didn't trust me to get her watch. Or maybe she wanted the dead man to steal it from me so she did not have to pay my fee. Someone else also wanted it so badly they would kill for it. The pocket watch was much more valuable than a memento for an old dying lady. I threw the wet card into the trash and lay down on my bed. It was time to do some high-flying over the canvas. I needed to sort out the rather bizarre sequence of events of the last, very long, day.

POLICE AT MY DOOR

WHEN I was fourteen, my psychiatrist asked me a question about the canvas that I could not answer. "Where exactly do you look?" he had asked. I still did not have an answer that was, in any way, definitive. Everyone I have talked to about this since had assumed that the canvas was in my head and that somehow, I was exploring a thing in my mind. I assure you that it is not in my mind. I do know where it is *not,* but I cannot tell you precisely where it *is*, in the same way, I cannot tell you *what* it is. I have been looking for something analogous that I could use to explain it, but nothing seems to fit with any degree of precision. All the comparisons are like gloves that are too large or small or have the wrong number of fingers. When I try to slip them over the canvas, they just do not fit. I once thought that the clouds in the sky on a blustery day might work. With some measure of imagination, a person could see anything in the cloud formations, just like I can see things on/in the canvas. But it was just too simplistic. I have concluded that I no longer care. I see the canvas. The canvas is intriguing, and that is enough for me.

Somehow, I can see into this opening while others can't. My mind can perceive things that are on constant display. It is a bit of a mess, and it has taken me a long time to sort it out. Imagine a thousand movies being projected on a screen at the same time, with Dolby sound turned up high. One has to tune some things out while others are tuned in. I separate the streams. That is how I find things. A separate stream carries its own vectors, and I am able, to a limited degree, to follow them. I still have a lot to learn.

I stretched out on the bed in my hotel room in the village of Killaloe, Ireland, and circled the canvas from a height like a hawk searching a field for just the right kind of motion. I would know when I saw it. I was sure of that. I needed an exact position of the pocket watch that was of interest to more than myself or my client.

The thought of my client blurred the canvas. There was something odd. I made a mental note to myself to find out more about her. That information might just lead to some clarity of why someone else was also after the pocket watch. Someone wanted it badly enough to kill for it.

I returned to circling the canvas. I pushed everything else aside. Do not think that I am circling a map or picture. It is not like that. It is more like energies that rise and fall, flow and ebb, shift in hue and intensity of color combined with sounds from sharp isolated tones to dull hums. To find something, I ask myself—what kind of energies would a pocket watch lost in WWII produce? The pocket watch might have a picture of a woman inside. It was owned by a specific person who looked like the photograph I was given. I pictured the watch in my mind and turned it about on all axes so I could see all the details. Details are important because they differentiate this watch from all the other watches that look like it. As I went through this process, a vector started to form. It started near me and pointed to the object's location. Then information about the location coalesced and showed me details. Usually, if I am close, I can see the precise location. This is what happened. I saw a church graveyard. St Flannan's Cathedral. It was just on the other side of the river. But a graveyard in an active church was not somewhere I could search. I especially could not dig. I needed more precision. I concentrated on the vector and forced it to refine itself. I could see a brass ball in front of a large gravestone. The detail gradually filled in and I had a clear picture of a two-meter-high grave marker surrounded by a short grave rail with posts capped with brass knobs. One of them held the watch. I was sure of that. I could not get exactly which one, but that did not matter. I was sure I could make that determination once I was on site. I smiled and opened my eyes just as there was a knock on the hotel room door.

I stood and looked through the peephole. I suspected it was a hotel employee come to turn down my bed or some such silliness. It was not.

There were two uniformed persons at my door that I assumed were police officers. I wondered if my little inspection of the body had been noticed. I opened the door. I smiled at the policeman and policewoman at my door. I said nothing.

"Sir, may we speak to you?" said the woman. She held a small notepad in her hand. The man held a camera. It was obvious he wanted me to see it. I simply nodded my assent to her request. I did not invite them in. "Would you please tell me your name?"

"Cervantes," I said calmly. The trick was not to give any more information than was absolutely required and still give the impression that you were being totally cooperative. I added, not really needing an answer, but, as it turned out, was valuable. "What are your names?"

The man spoke, "This is officer Roth, and my name is Fallon." He cleared his throat. "Mr. Cervantes, have you been out this evening?"

In another situation, I would have answered this question with a terse 'yes,' but that would have, as I have learned, appeared combative. So, I attempted to answer the question in such a way that the officers would not find me odd. I tried to give lots of information in an attempt to avoid further questions. As it turned out I was not successful in that endeavor. "Yes. I went out to dinner at that delightful restaurant on the corner. A bistro? Or. A pub? Anyway, it was a very filling and tasty meal. I had the lamb. Have you ever eaten the lamb at Molly's? Oh, yes, it is not called Molly's anymore. What is it called now? No matter. I did enjoy it." The woman started to write in her notepad.

"What time did you return to your room?" asked the man.

Answering this question was tricky. I could not lie, but I could be obtuse. "Oh, I am not sure. A little while ago. I was just about to go to bed."

"You have an accent. Where are you from?" said the woman. "California, I bet. You sound like that is where you are from."

"Yes. Venice Beach."

"What is your business here, Mr. Cervantes?"

"No business. I am just a tourist. Lovely town. I am interested in old churches, and you have some really old ones here. I plan on visiting them tomorrow. What do you recommend I do so that I get to see all that there is to see?"

"Wouldn't know, sir," said the man.

"I saw some flashing lights through my window. Is there anything happening that I should be concerned about? Was there an accident? Anyone hurt?"

The two officers looked at each other and the woman spoke. "There has been a death. That is all I can tell you. The forensic team will be here soon, so I recommend you close your curtains. The lights will be flashing for most of the night. We wouldn't want to discourage tourists."

"Are you staying at the hotel for a few days? We may wish to speak with you again."

"Yes. I think I am. I have not booked a flight home yet. I thought I would play it by ear. You have so many beautiful old churches to explore."

"Yes, well, thank you for your time," said the woman. They both turned to leave.

"You are most welcome. Glad I could help." I was about to close the door when I thought of something. "Officers?" I called to their retreating backs. They turned.

"Yes, Mr. …," she looked down at her notepad. "… Cervantes."

"I was wondering if you have noticed any other tourists as you go about your interviews. I was supposed to meet a couple from home, but they have not shown up and I have not had time to search for them."

"Sorry. We haven't seen any Americans," said the man.

"If we encounter a couple with an American accent, we will let them know you are looking for them," said the woman amiably. "Don't let it be said that we do not treat our tourists well." She smiled.

"Please. No. I want to surprise them. I would appreciate it if you would leave a message for me at the desk if you encounter them. That would be much appreciated." They both nodded, and I closed the door. I realized I had very nearly exposed myself more than I intended.

SUBTERFUGE

THE next morning was filled with self-created problems brought on by my inability to decide what to do next. There was no need to look at the canvas. I knew it would not provide me with any solutions. I had to figure it out on my own. The primary question was what to do with the tracking device in the pocket of my jacket. I was going to explore the graveyard at the church to see if I needed the cover of darkness to retrieve the pocket watch. If tools were needed, that might be the deciding factor. I couldn't very well take a hacksaw to the grave fence knob in the middle of the day. If I went there to do recon, whoever was tracking me would now know where to look. If I left the tracker in the hotel room and left, I would most certainly be followed and they would know I had found the tracker. I needed to keep them thinking that they could depend on the tracker. They needed to think that they knew my whereabouts without physically following me. I was sure they were watching the hotel and would see me exit. I needed to take the device so they would relax their surveillance and just depend on the tracker.

Once the germ of an idea came to me, I set about making it work. I needed an accomplice. I needed someone to do a series of little tasks for me. The tasks needed involved travel to several locations in and about Killaloe and the nearby city of Limerick in order to deliver a specific item all the while carrying the tracker while I visited the graveyard.

Finding someone to act as my accomplice might not be so easy to achieve. I had only spoken to one person other than the hotel clerk and the police officers. That person was Sean from the restaurant. He was my height and was impressionable. If I suggested that I was working with the police to try to find the perpetrator of the previous night's murder, he might be willing to help me. I needed to dupe my trackers into thinking they were following me. Some subterfuge was in order. I would offer Sean some remuneration for his time. I called the front desk and requested the number of the bistro formerly known as Molly's. I called this number.

The voice of a young woman answered, "Good morning, Bóruma Gastro Bar. How may I help you?"

"Hello. My name is Cervantes. I would like to speak to Sean. Is he available?"

"Won't be for an hour or so. Want me to have him call you?"

"No thanks. I will come in and have breakfast and wait for him. Can you reserve me a table by the window? I will be there shortly."

"No problem, Mr. Cervantes. I will see you soon."

"Thank you," I said and hung up. I went to the closet and took out my raincoat and hat. I removed the tracking device from the pocket of my jacket and concealed it in the pocket of my raincoat. I looked out the window. The weather gods were smiling at me. It was drizzling outside and looked like it was not about to stop. I put on a windbreaker. I concealed the small collapsible umbrella in the pocket of the raincoat and slipped it on along with my hat. I grabbed a stack of my business cards and left the hotel room. I walked down the street to the restaurant, all the while keeping an eye out for the couple from the plane. I did not see anyone and was soon seated at a small table near the window. The early breakfast crowd was finished, leaving just a few latecomers. I ordered coffee and an omelet. The young woman assured me that she would ask Sean to drop by my table when he got in.

The breakfast was adequate. I sipped my coffee and stared out the window. There was still police barrier tape across the entrance to the moorage on the river. I wondered if they had found anything. I doubted it. The water would have washed away any trace of evidence. The only thing they would have was the bullet, and it was probably still in the poor dead *'I will write your memoirs'* head.

In a little over an hour, the young woman led the man from the previous evening over to my table. I stood and asked him to join me.

"You are the detective from last night. Have you found the murderer yet?"

"No sorry. We are still following up on the identification of the victim. I spoke to officer Fallon and Roth last night." I threw out the names so he would assume I was working closely with the police. "They wanted my help." I left out the part where they just wanted to know if I had seen anything. "To give them my time, I need to hire someone to do a few things for me. I thought of you. Are you available today?"

Sean was a little hesitant. "What kind of things? I must prepare the menu for tonight, so I won't have a lot of time."

"It won't take more than a couple of hours and it pays well." I slipped three 100-euro notes onto the table.

His eyes widened. "It is not illegal, is it?"

"No, I assure you, it is completely legal." I took a stack of my business cards and placed them on top of the money. I took one card and handed it to him. I need these delivered to all the lawyers' offices in the area." He looked at me with a puzzled expression. "I guess you call them Barristers and Solicitors. I am expanding my client base."

Sean read the card out loud. "*I am expensive, but I can find anything*. That is quite a statement." He looked up from the card. "Anything?"

I kept my expression flat. I was used to those who did not believe my claim. "Yes. I can find anything as long as it exists. I am not stating I can retrieve it, but I can tell you where it is if it is on the planet. For example, if you ask me to find a long-lost, stolen painting, I can pinpoint its location to, at the very least, 10 meters, usually much closer, but I cannot break into the place that has it and get it for you."

"Are you trying to find the murderer?"

"I am sorry, but I cannot divulge any information regarding the case. I do need someone reliable to make these deliveries, as this crime will require my full attention. I only have a few days before I am due back in LA." I paused and looked at him. "You will need to find the addresses of all the Barristers and Solicitors in this area and Limerick, deliver one of my cards to the front desk in every office, pick up the cards of the lawyers, and return them to me so I have a record of the deliveries. I expect you to do a minimum of 10. Do you think you can do that?" I asked as I slipped another hundred euro note onto the pile.

He glanced down at the money again. "Yes. I can do that. When do you want me to start?"

"Now," I said and pushed the banknotes and business cards across the table. He picked them up and slipped them into his shirt pocket. "There is one other thing." He looked up. "You need to wear my raincoat and hat. You need to look a little like me while you do it. Do you think you can do that?" He did not answer. "I am not at liberty to tell you why I need this, be it sufficient that I want it done this way." With that, I took out three more bills and held them in my hand. "At five this afternoon you will return here, give me the cards you collected, and I will give you this little bonus." I looked down at the money in my hand. "Come in the front door as if you were me. Go into the washroom. I will meet you there. We will go there now so you can dress like me and leave to do your tasks."

He nodded and stood up. "I will be three minutes. I must get Margie to prep the menu." He stood, and I waited a moment. I scanned the room and looked out the window. I did not expect to see anything suspicious, and I didn't. A few minutes later, Sean left the restaurant, and I slipped out the back door with my umbrella concealing my face.

I walked quickly over the bridge and headed to St Flannan's Cathedral. I scouted out an entrance to the graveyard of a small car park. I walked up to the largest stone gravestone and looked to see if I was being observed. I knelt as if I was praying and tapped the two brass balls topping the grave fence. They made different noises. I reached out to turn each of the balls. The one on my left would not budge. The one on the right seemed somewhat loose. I rocked it back and forth and it came off in my hand. I bowed down as if I was giving penance for some past discretion and peered into the ball. There was an object wrapped in a piece of oilcloth inside. I pulled it out and slipped it into the pocket of my windbreaker. I quickly replace the ball and walked out of the graveyard. I concealed myself by keeping my umbrella tilted in front of my face. I returned to my hotel, entering through the underground car park and back into my room. I opened the oilcloth and stared at the pocket watch. I not only found it; I had retrieved it. I felt a rush wash over me. I had not gone and retrieved an object I was asked to find before this one. It was a first. It felt wonderful, and I knew it would not be the last.

ESCAPE

I turned the watch over in my hand. The outside was greasy from the oilcloth. I wiped it down with a cloth from the bathroom. It shone like a brand-new watch. I think it was gold, but not being an expert in metallurgy, I was not sure. I pressed the catch and the front cover flipped open. I expected to see a photograph under the cover. There was nothing. The watch had not been wound in a very long time. I wondered if it still worked. I wound it and watched the second-hand sweep around the face. I glanced at my watch to see the time to set the watch. I pulled out the stem and turned the watch to the correct time. It seemed to be working fine. I inspected the inside cover a little more closely. Besides some stamped numbers and letters on the inside, there was nothing. They were part of the manufacturer's codes. At least I assumed that they were. The rest of the watch held nothing I thought might give it any more value beyond being a memento of a lost grandfather. I would need to take it to an expert if I was to find out more. Perhaps I would spend a day or two in London and seek out a watch repair shop.

I set the timepiece down on the desk and closed my eyes. The canvas filled my visual cortex. It was swirling. It had been a few days since I had immersed myself. I relaxed into it and let myself sink into a giant eddy of light and sound. When I reached the swirling vortex, I let it suck me in until I was no longer conscious of anything outside. The new reality opened, and I was now circling a brand-new but blurry landscape. I was a bird of prey, scanning and dropping through the mist and clouds that distorted my view. The vectors were everywhere. They all pointed in the same general direction. I spiraled down in an ever-narrowing circle as the vectors coalesced into a single snake. I followed it. I suspected it was taking me to the location of the pocket watch owner. He must be dead and lying in a grave somewhere. It would be a bonus for my clients to be able to tell them where their great-grandfather was buried. My eyesight was as sharp as the bird the canvas had transformed me into.

I was over a city. I did not know where. I figured it must be somewhere in Europe. As I neared the tops of some of the buildings, I realized this was not a modern city. It was somewhere in the past. I looked for something that would identify where this was. A sign was close but not yet clear enough to read. I swooped lower. It was nearly clear when something rattled the whole canvas. This had happened to me before. Something from the outside world was demanding my attention. I was just too close to leave. I might never get this kind of clarity again. I pushed the outside noise aside. Words on a large sign were starting to come into focus. I could read fragments from one. '*ama ar*' I pushed harder and caught another fragment: '*mster*'. Then everything swirled upwards. I opened my eyes. Someone was knocking on my door. I slipped off the bed. My visitor started to pound harder on the door. Suddenly, I was hesitant to open it. My mind jumped to the Americans I had met on the plane. My mind was racing. Perhaps they would go away if I just pretended I was not here. Then I heard a voice call, "Mr. Cervantes, it's me, Sean. I need to talk to you. The hotel desk said you were in. My friend works at this hotel, and she assured me you were here. Please open up." This was followed by more knocking. "Mr. Cervantes, please." I opened the door. "Thank God you are here."

Sean stepped into the room. He was now carrying my hat and raincoat. "I thought we were going to meet back at the restaurant?" I said. He stepped into the room and nearly collapsed. I reached out and led him to a chair. He flopped down. I could see blood on his face. He had a cut above his left eye and a split lip. "What happened?" I asked. I was seriously concerned.

"I was attacked."

"By whom? Why?"

"I was assuming you could answer that," he said and wiped the corner of his mouth.

I went to the bathroom and brought back a wet cloth. I gave it to him, and he pressed it against his cuts. I closed the hotel room door and stood before him. "Tell me what happened."

"I was doing what you asked. I was just coming out of the fourth solicitor's office. The office was a little hole in the wall off a small lane. I had just stepped down the stairs that lead up to it when three men stepped up to me. Two of the men grabbed me by the arms and dragged me further down the lane. I struggled. The third man punched me in the gut. When I straightened up, I could see a knife flashing beside my ear, so I stopped. I figured they wanted my wallet. I didn't bring the money you gave me, and I only had a couple of quid on me, so I figured that the joke was on them. Struggling was not worth getting stabbed, so I stopped."

"What did they want?"

"Not my wallet, that was for sure. The man with the knife who had punched me asked who I was and what I was doing?"

"Just like that. '*Who are you and what are you doing?*'"

"No, more like, '*Who the fuck are you, and what the fuck are you doing?*' Then he spoke to the blokes holding me. '*Search this motherfucker,*' he said. He had an American accent. The guys holding me found nothing. They looked in my wallet. The American looked inside and started calling me Sean." He coughed. "Hey, could I have a drink of water?"

"Sure." I gave him a drink of water. "What happened next? Can you describe the American?"

"He was tall and slim. He had blond hair. I don't think it was natural. The other two were local thugs. The guy with the knife took my raincoat—your raincoat—and searched it. They found the business cards. Most were yours, but a few were from the solicitors I had already visited. He looked at yours and cursed. He found something in one of the pockets. I could not see what he found, but he was not happy that he had found it. He cursed a lot after that. Then he nodded at the assholes holding me. They started to work me over." He touched the cut on his forehead. "They tossed my wallet at me and left. I came straight back here."

"I'm glad you did. I am really sorry. I had no idea that someone would do that to you."

"Look, Cervantes, I don't want to know what you are into. I know I did not complete the job you hired me for, but getting beat up was not part of the deal." He stood. "I want the rest of the cash. I think I deserve it, considering." He held out his hand.

"I do too." I walked over to the drawer, took out the promised banknotes, and gave them to him. "I am really sorry."

"Thanks." He turned to go but turned back as he reached for the door. "Mr. Cervantes, stay away from my restaurant. Find somewhere else to eat." He left.

I knew now that I must be on my way. I called the front desk, checked out, and requested a car to take me to the airport. I packed quickly. Once at the airport, I would find a flight to London. Whoever was following me wanted the watch. That I was sure of. They had made it clear that they would do pretty much anything to get it. The murder at the river and the attack on Sean were strong indicators that these people were dangerous. The phone rang. It was the front desk informing me that the car had arrived. It was waiting for me in the rear parking lot. I slipped the pocket watch into my jacket pocket and walked to the elevator. It opened to a near-empty lobby. The woman from the airplane was chatting with the receptionist. She did not see me slip out the back door. I hurried to the parking lot and waved at the waiting driver. He swung the car around and was about to get out and help me with my bag when I signaled him to stop and opened the back door of the car and swung my bag inside. "To the airport. Please go quickly," I ordered him and closed the car door. He sped away. I relaxed. I did not want a confrontation with anyone, especially the American who had accosted Sean. I was not afraid of a confrontation. I was quite capable—no—I was extremely capable of defending myself, but I did not want to cause anyone to pay any more attention to me than was absolutely necessary.

WAFFEN ZER HAND

I was fourteen when I first entered high school. I was not what you would call a social butterfly. I simply minded my own business. My typical day was going to class, completing assignments, and indulging in the exploration of the canvas. It was not like the canvas I see today. It was much less expansive, but it was, for a teenager like me, very enticing. I was addicted and spent all my free time wandering around that wonderful place. Today the canvas is just a tool—a fantastically cool tool, but still just a means to an end. Back then, its exploration was all I wanted. That resulted in problems—social problems. I was beaten up three times in my first week. I had this habit that came about through my experiences with my mother. Whenever she wanted my attention and I did not want to give it, I would dismissively wave my hands and tell her to *'piss off.'* I did that to the students at school and it did not go over well.

One day I was absorbed, and I did it to a girl who wanted me to move from in front of her locker. Her boyfriend was nearby, and he took offense. He asked me what I had just said, so I repeated it, assuming he was hard of hearing. I can't remember what was so important on/in the canvas, but it must have been at the time. I gesticulated at him and told him to *'piss off'*. He punched me in the stomach. I doubled over and he kneed me in the head and proceeded to slam my head into the locker behind me. He then grabbed me by the scruff of my neck and the back of my belt. He walked me to the nearest door and shoved me out. I soon became the joke of the school, or should I say 'dummy'. That is what they all called me. It got to the point that I could not walk down the hall without someone taking a shot at me. In class, I sat alone and was pretty much left alone, but once

I reached the hallway, I was the preferential target for anyone wanting to take out their aggression. I never reported it, but it was noticed by one of my teachers and I assumed they called my mother on the same day I came home with a cut beside my eye. That was when all hell broke loose. She threatened to sue the school for all they were worth if they did not do something to protect me. The problem was that I did not want anyone's protection.

My mother then decided that she would take matters into her own hands. My father became involved. It was one of the few times he paid attention to me. I was enrolled in a series of self-defense courses. They did not achieve what my parents wanted. The other students pretty much used me as a punching and kicking bag. I did not want anything to do with self-defense until my father hired a special teacher to tutor me individually. He was a funny little German man named Fritz, who spent the first two lessons talking to me. I told him about the canvas, and he just listened. I remember this interaction like it was yesterday.

"Mathew," he said, "stand in front of me and close your eyes. Do not conjure up the canvas in the usual way. Paint the canvas with what you hear, feel, and remember. Inspect all the details and react to what you sense."

"Yes," I said. The mention of the canvas held my attention. No one ever suggested that I use the canvas. They always wanted me to stop my obsession. I did what he said—or more accurately—I tried to do what he said.

"I want you to see me. I want you to hear me. I want you to sense what I am doing without using your eyes. Would you try that for me?"

"Yes," I said and tried to see him using only the canvas. At first, it was weird. I kept devolving into strange and interesting canvas stories, but each time I did, he would tap me somewhere on my body. These were not love taps. They hurt but did not do any real damage. After a while, I became ultra-aware of him.

"Block me with your arm each time I am about to strike you."

"How do I block you?"

"Don't use any real force. Just stick your arm in front of the location of the strike. That will tell me that you know where I intend to strike you. I will simply stop and look for a new location. Understand?"

"Yes," I said. I quickly raised my arm to block a hit on my forehead. No blow landed. I then blocked my stomach and my groin in quick succession. I did not feel any hits. Suddenly, he punched my arm. I yelled out.

"Mathew, that was excellent."

"But you hit me, and it hurt."

"I know. I used my other hand. You blocked everything coming from my right hand. You did not see the left."

This is how the training went. Week after week. I liked the sessions. I became more and more efficient at protecting myself. He was my teacher for two years. He taught me a form of fighting called "Arnis" or as it is sometimes called, "Kali" but he did not call it that. Arnis is the national martial art of the Philippines. He modified it. He gave it a German name—"Waffen zur Hand" which translates to "Weapons at Hand." I am now rather efficient at using whatever is available to protect myself.

My problems at school stopped partly because I learned to see past the canvas and stopped waving my hands and telling people to piss off and the fact that they were not able to lay a finger on me anymore. I graduated with honors, but I did not have a single friend at school. The closest I had to a friend was Fritz. After two years, the classes stopped. I don't know if they stopped because I graduated or because my father stopped paying for the classes. I prefer to believe the former. I have not seen him since he left.

REPLICA

A few hours later, I was heading to London in a taxi. I asked the driver to take me to a hotel downtown—something boutique. I wanted something small so that anyone able to follow me would be easy to detect. I did not want a crowded lobby. He took me to a little mid-range hotel. I checked in and asked for directions to the nearest watch repair shop. I stressed that I did not want anything fancy. I wanted someone knowledgeable about pocket watches circa 1930. The receptionist laughed. I then set a 50-pound note on the desk and told her another would be forthcoming. She smiled and said that she would investigate and get back to me. I flopped down on the bed in my rather tiny room, especially by American standards. The canvas beckoned me.

I noticed that the canvas had become more of a landscape extending to the horizon in all directions and I became a bird that would fly high above like an eagle or a hawk only smaller. I was a falcon. No—less romantic—I was a kestrel; a small and brown. I was an unobtrusive observer until the canvas decided otherwise. I was searching for the city and the sign. The word fragments "*mster*" and "*ama ar*" floated like dandelion seeds sailing on the updrafts. I was willing them to set down, take root, and grow into whole words. I had a feeling they were the key to where this pocket watch mystery was leading me. I was now sure that the watch was the tip of some very secret and hidden metaphor for a story.

My canvas eyes caught movement. A rodent scurrying over and under an energy pattern. It was dragging a gold watch that clung to the canvas pattern like a Dali painting of a melting pocket watch. The face was distorted. The rodent stopped and looked up at me as if daring me to swoop down and crush his skull with my talons. Sorry for the cobble of images. Sometimes I get carried away. Anyway, I swooped and landed in his path. The watch he was dragging lay still and became the pocket watch. I reached out to open the cover to see if the canvas was trying to tell me something—to direct me to a solution of why it was so sought after—to reveal the secrets I was sure it held when something strange happened.

As I neared, the watch's face darkened and began to shrink. The closer I got, the darker and smaller it became until it was just a small black dot on the undulating surface of the canvas. Just then the rodent that, up until that moment, was nondescript, transformed into a rather nasty-looking rat with big yellow teeth. It exuded evil. It dashed out of a dark and dirty hole in the ground and grabbed the tiny black dot the watch had turned into. It turned to run back and disappear into the dirty hole when I grabbed its tail with my talon and held it as it scrabbled the ground to escape.

My phone rang. The canvas faded, and I sat up and picked up the receiver. "Yes."

"Mr. Cervantes, this is the front desk. I have the address you requested. The shop is closed until tomorrow."

"Thank you. Leave it there. I will pick it up a little later and leave you the promised gratuity."

"You are welcome. I will leave it here for you." I hung up and fell back into bed. I was tired. It had been a very long day. I planned to order room service and crash. I ordered a rare steak with crisp asparagus and a glass of merlot. I am not a big drinker, but steak without red wine was almost a sin. I waited and started to reflect on what the canvas was trying to tell me. It did not usually speak to me in such a cryptic way. I thought about the rat trying to steal the watch or the black dot the watch had become. I had to stop that theft from happening. That was obvious, but the significance of the black dot was not. I needed to take some precautions. I had the watch. Whoever was following me did not. I had to keep them from getting it, and I needed something more than a kestrel claw holding a rat's tail to the ground to be successful.

My dinner arrived. I ate, lost in thought. The last sip of wine finished my plan. To have it work successfully, I needed a replica. I flipped open my laptop and searched 'pocket watches for sale in London.' I opened a site called Selling Antiques. It listed dozens of pocket watches and I found what I was looking for almost immediately and the price was within budget. It was listed as a "1930s Waltham Full Hunter Pocket Watch." It was also American-made. It looked much like the one I had, except it was rather plain. It was listed at £135. I called the number. I did not expect an answer, as it was after hours. I left a message on the machine outlining my need to purchase this watch as soon as possible. I left my particulars along with my hotel and room number. I stated that I would be willing to pay an additional £50 if I could have it delivered to my hotel by ten the following morning. I hung up with the feeling that my plan would be successful. I deposited my dishes in the hallway and fell asleep.

I dreamed. I do not often dream.

THE WATCH REPAIR SHOP

I must have needed the sleep, for I did not wake until 9:00 a.m. the next day. I was surprised for I seldom slept longer than five hours. I ordered room service. A note arrived from the front desk along with my breakfast. The watch I had ordered the night before would be delivered before noon. I spoke to them and requested they cover the cost of the delivery I was to receive and just charge my card. I sat back and chewed on a delightful piece of crisp bacon. I thought about indulging in a few minutes of the canvas, but I knew a few minutes could easily turn into the entire morning and I had other things I needed to do. I was not sure when I would get back to the office, so I needed to call my assistant. I sat down at my laptop and sent an email to her. My instructions outlined the tasks I needed her to do for me. My mail was primary. She needed to go through it and send me brief outlines of each request. I would then tell her to ignore, politely refuse, request additional information, set up a face-to-face, or accept the contract. Accepting a contract without additional information did not happen very often anymore. In fact, it had only happened once when I was a bit of a neophyte in the detective business. That had been an error. I won't go into the details, but it was definitely a learning experience. I learned the most valuable lesson for a detective and that is: everybody lies. Some lies are bigger than others and those are the ones you must be careful of, for really big lies often look like the truth.

Once I finished my tasks, I started to write a note to my client. I was well into telling her that I had found the pocket watch in Ireland and I would return it to her soon when I realized that giving her this information was premature. All the events, including the murder outside the restaurant in Killaloe, were still troubling me. There was something else going on. There was more to this situation than a lost watch. There was a missing spy. A spy that did not have a history beyond 1940 and yet he lived to at least 1945. There was no record of his death, so he might have lived a lot longer. The last musing was doubtful, for I had found the watch. It was unlikely he would have hidden it and not retrieved it after the war. But why hide it in the first place? I picked up the pocket watch and held it in my hand. I smiled, for a silly image of the watch giving away its secrets while it was in my hand wiggled its way into my mind. The watch held secrets, and I needed to find them.

The front desk called and informed me that the package I ordered had arrived and I could pick it up. I got myself ready. My windbreaker as well as my coats and jackets were designed especially for me. They were constructed with pockets in peculiar places. I know I said I didn't like to put things in my pockets, but these were purposeful pockets. This jacket had two pockets at the very top of the inside of the sleeves. A small object placed in one would fit neatly in my armpit when my arms were at my side. When I raised my arm, the pocket and anything it contained would slide up my arm to just below the elbow. A search could easily miss it. I slipped the pocket watch into the left one and put on the jacket. I had never had the opportunity to rely on it working, so I tested it to see if it functioned as designed. It made a small zipping noise if I raised my arm quickly. I practiced raising my arm more slowly. It worked perfectly. I would put the replica in a more obvious location. I was kind of hoping those mystery people who wanted the watch would try to steal it. That would do two things. First, it would give me some idea of who they were and what they were after, and second, it might keep them from following me to wherever I was headed next. The only thing that worried me was the fact that they had already killed for it. I was sure they were responsible for the murder in Killaloe. I did not have a weapon, but I was sure that if the situation called for it, I could protect myself. With that mental reassurance, I headed down to the lobby.

I stepped out of the lift. I liked that word better than elevator, for it was one syllable as opposed to four. I started to walk to the front desk when

I noticed a woman sitting in a large lobby chair just to the left of it. She would be privy to anything said to the receptionist. As I had to discuss the watch I had purchased and did not want anyone, especially a spy to know about it, I turned and acted as if I had forgotten something and returned to the lift. I had to wait, for the lift had been called by someone else. I used the opportunity to surreptitiously glance at the woman. I was trying to decide if she was the woman from the plane and the hotel lobby in Killaloe who had put the tracker in my jacket. I remembered that woman was a bleached blonde, but that is all I could remember. This woman looked like a natural blonde. She was staring at me and quickly looked away when our eyes met. I continued to stare with obvious curiosity. I was trying to decide if this was the woman who had bumped into me on the plane. She was the right height. She glanced up and again our eyes met. This time, she smiled at me. At least that is what I thought until I realized that the lift had opened behind me, and a man had exited. He went straight toward her. She had been smiling at him, not at me. I watched them walk out of the lobby onto the street. They were obviously tourists. There was no need to do anything other than return to the desk and retrieve the watch that was waiting for me, along with the address of the watch repair shop.

Thirty minutes later, I found myself outside a small shop on a nondescript lane. A simple sign hung over the door: WATCH REPAIR. I entered through a marred wooden door. The room was very small. So small that one had to step to the side to close the door. Opposite was a door that I assumed led to the back of the shop. In front of me was a counter with a glass top. Under it were a series of watches in various states of disassembly. The inner workings of many different kinds of watches were on display. I could see that there was a drawer that held them. Perhaps the owner used them to explain the repairs required. On the wall behind the counter were several charts that surrounded a curtained-off area. They showed exploded diagrams of clocks and watches. They were yellow and curled in the corners. There was no one at the counter. I gently tapped the bell meant to call the proprietor and waited.

I was about to ring the bell a second time with more force when a woman stepped through the curtain. She did not look like someone who repaired watches. To start with, her hands were not right. She had fingernails that were so long that I was sure they would be a serious detriment when it came to manipulating very tiny watch mechanisms. She was dressed in what could only be described as a business suit. Her makeup was minimal, but effective. She appeared to be forty-ish. I am not good with the ages of women, so I could be off by decades. I started to wonder if she was the woman from the plane, but her hair was auburn. I chastised myself for seeing boogie women everywhere.

"May I help you?" she asked.

"Yes. I would like someone to look at a pocket watch."

She reached down to a shelf below and came up with a small envelope and a pen. She set it down on the counter and looked up at me. "Give it to me and I will have my husband look at it when he gets back. Write your particulars on the envelope," she said and held the pen out to me.

I took the pen. "I would rather not leave it. When will he return? I will come back then." It was then that I heard a thump from behind the curtain. The woman glanced behind her. The curtain was closed. "Is he back?" I asked and pointed the pen towards the curtain. "It sounded like someone is back there."

"I assure you, sir, there is no one there. My husband won't be back until after the shop is closed. If you want him to service your watch, you will have to leave it here." She seemed to be getting somewhat agitated. That is when I became super sensitive. Something was wrong. It was her accent. It was American, not British. I was surprised I had not noticed it immediately.

At that point, I turned to leave. "I will find someone else to look at it," I said. I reached out to open the door, but from my present position, I would be behind it with no space between it and the counter. I had to move to the other side of the room before opening the door. I stepped forward and turned my back on the woman.

I heard a bang and turned to see the woman hit the counter with her hand. "Fuck," she said, "He is going to leave. Get out here."

The door to the back room opened and two men stepped into the small space. One was short and one was much taller. They stepped to either side of me and hauled me through the door into the back area. The first thing I noticed was a man in a chair. He was tied up and gagged. He attempted to speak, but the sound came out like a moan. He wiggled back and forth in the chair. The tall man stepped forward and held up his hand as if to strike the man tied to the chair. He paused at the apex of his swing. "Shut the fuck up," he said. The man tied in the chair stopped, winced, and turned his head to the side. He was trying to avoid the impending strike. The hand wavered above him and a churlish smile formed on the attacker's face. He waited for the prisoner to turn back and when he inevitably did, the hand swept down with force and struck him. Blood spewed. The attack did not stop. The man tied to the chair was struck two more times. He whimpered and closed his eyes.

The woman was standing in the open curtained doorway. She moved into the room and let the curtain close behind her. "Stop. We need him. Just get the watch."

At that moment, I decided to play dumb. "What is going on here? What do you want? Leave that poor man alone," I shouted. I took a step back. I was pushed forward and held in front of the woman by the man behind me. "What do you want?" I spoke. "I have a few pounds in my wallet. Take it. Just don't hurt me." The last part came out as a whimper. I was deciding what path to take. I could easily subdue these assailants. I scanned the room for objects that could be used as weapons. There was a kettle on the side counter and a series of screwdrivers attached to a magnetic bar. I had already planned the sequence of events. I would stomp on the foot of the man behind me, and when he lowered his head, my elbow would smash into his nose. I would step to my right and pick up the kettle with my left hand, turn, and snatch a screwdriver with my right. I would continue the pirouette and smash the kettle into the head of the man nearest the bound watchmaker. I would continue the spin, bringing the kettle to bear on the side of the first man's head. I would drop the kettle, step in front of the woman, and put the business end of the screwdriver under her chin as my left hand held her head from retreating. My objective was an interrogation.

Or I could play along and get as much information as possible before any violence was required. I decided on the latter.

The man behind me hit me in the center of the back. "Shut the fuck up and give us the watch."

"Watch?" I retorted, expecting another bit of encouragement from the man behind me.

"Search him. He must have it on him," said the woman, who was obviously in charge. The man stood behind me and started to pad my pockets. I decided then that I needed to put up more of a fight. I leaned away from the man when he bent to reach into my pocket. I raised my left arm and smashed my elbow into his face.

He staggered back. "Ahhhgg," he screamed and grabbed his nose.

When I looked up, there was a pistol pointing at my face. "Mr. Cervantes, I advise you to stop." She looked up at her accomplice. "Search him, you idiot."

He wiped his nose on his sleeve. He was bleeding. He continued to pad my pockets until he found the replica I had received that morning. He took it out and handed it to the woman. She inspected it and then nodded at the tall man beside her. It was then I realized I had made an error in not dealing with these people. I felt a blow to the back of my head and then blackness.

POCKET WATCH SECRETS

THE pounding in my head pulled my consciousness up and out. It demanded I feel the pain. I opened my eyes and tried to move. My hands were above my head. They were chained to a pipe that entered the top of a steam radiator. I heard a rattle as I tried to pull them free. I scanned the room. My feet were extended out in front of me. I could see the watchmaker still tied to the chair. He was gagged. He saw me wake and I could see the panic in his eyes. He shook his head and moaned a warning. I looked around the room. We were alone. The watchmaker kept tilting his head toward the doorway that led to the front of the shop. I turned to the doorway just as the curtains parted and one of the men entered. He had a swollen nose. He was the man I had elbowed. He limped toward me. "So, you are awake. Good. I want you to feel what I am about to do to you."

"Haven't you done enough already? What do you want?" I demanded.

"Shut the fuck up," he yelled and stepped toward me and raised his hand. As he did so, I pulled my legs up and leaned back as far as I could. He moved closer, and I watched his hand form a fist and his lips pull back from his teeth in a snarl. He was going to punch me in the face. I turned my head to the side and flicked my foot up. I caught him in the groin with a hard kick just as his fist clipped a glancing blow to the top of my skull. I reacted instinctively. As his body twisted to one side. I lifted my legs and spread them open to receive him. His body continued turning. I squeezed my thighs together with a snapping motion and caught him around his neck. I continued to squeeze. His weight did the rest. I felt him go limp. I held him as I considered what to do next. He must have the keys to the cuffs, but there was no way for me to get them. I looked at the watchmaker.

They had tied the rope around his chest and the back of the chair. His legs were tied just below his knees to the legs of the chair. His hands were free from the elbows down, but his arms were securely pinned to the chair. It struck me as funny. All I could think of was a pantomime of Dirk Doogood tied up by the evil landowner.

I was sure my hands could free the rope if only he could scooch his chair over to me. "Can you try to get close to me?" He nodded his assent and began to wiggle back and forth. He slowly moved toward me. The body that was still cradled in my lap was definitely in the way. I twisted it to one side and kicked it away from the path the watchmaker was taking. "You will need to turn around. Do you think you can do that?" I asked. He did not respond. He tried to pirouette on one leg of the chair by pushing to one side and leaning forward. He nearly fell over. "Careful," I knew that falling over would end all our hopes of freeing ourselves. He tried again and slowly twisted so his back was facing me. He shuffled again until the ropes holding him to the chair were within reach of my handcuffed hands. The knot was high up and I picked at it until it came loose. The man on the floor moaned, and I realized that speed was of the essence. I pushed one finger into the loosened knot and worked the rope free. The watchmaker wiggled until his shoulders loosened the rope even further. His hands were free. He reached down and undid the rope around his legs, and stood. "Quickly. Search him for the key," I said.

He looked at me. "This ain't a movie. I don't want this crap to wake up and jump me while I'm searching his pockets." He walked to a corner of the shop where there was a bin holding umbrellas. He reached down and lifted out a cricket bat. He spun it in his hands as a rather macabre grin crept over his face. "Better safe than sorry," he said, and he hit the semiconscious man on the head. "You deserve more than one, you fucking bastard." He proceeded to search him and produced a key. He walked over and unlocked the handcuffs. "Drag that bastard over here and put the cuffs on him." I rubbed my wrists to help with the return of circulation. The watchmaker still had the cricket bat over his shoulder, so I decided to do what he said. In the end, it took both of us to get him over, sitting up against the radiator with his hands cuffed to the pipe.

"How long was I out?" I asked.

"Ten minutes at most. The tall one and the woman left with the watch they took from you. I heard her say something about someone they called Botox."

"What did she say, exactly?"

He looked at the ceiling as if trying to remember. "Something like, 'Botox's guy will find it' and she dangled the watch. That watch was nothing special. I don't know what they were expecting to find."

"They are not going to find anything, and they will soon realize that. Did they say what they were looking for?"

"Nae. But it couldn't have been very big if it fits inside a pocket watch. They intend on returning," he said and cocked his head toward the unconscious man attached to the radiator. "I am phoning the police before they get back. A couple of coppers hiding behind the door will take care of them."

"Not yet," I said. "I would like you to do something for me first." I slipped off my jacket and retrieved the actual pocket watch. I held it out to the watchmaker. "This is why I came here in the first place. I would like you to search this and tell me if you find anything that should not be there. I will pay you twice the going rate. I will require you to never reveal what you find."

The watchmaker reached for the pocket watch. He turned it over in his hand. "This is a Waltham full Hunter circa 1935-ish. It looks practically new. Usually, the gold layer will wear thin, exposing the brass. This one is pristine, like it had never seen the inside of a pocket." He turned it over and stared at the back. He picked up the loupe and stared at the bottom edge. "Some letters here. SAA. It looks like someone's initials." He snapped it open and walked over to his workbench. I followed. He sat, popped a loupe into his eye, and turned on a small, highly focused lamp. He pressed the top and the front cover popped open. He inspected it. "Nothing unexpected here," he said. He picked up a tool, pried the back of the watch off, and looked carefully. He turned to me. "Nothing unexpected so far." He tapped a section of the open watch. "This is the dust cover. The works are inside here." He used the same tool and the dust cover popped off. "Looks good. No dirt." He pulled the watch closer to his eye. He picked up a tiny screwdriver and poked a section of the watch.

"What do you see?"

"There is a black spot on one of the screw heads. Looks like dirt. This watch is too clean for dirt to have gathered in this one spot." He stood and opened a cupboard. He took out what looked like a small video screen. He placed it on the bench and plugged it in. He opened a small drawer below the screen and set the open watch inside. He twisted some knobs, and the pocket watch workings filled the screen. He zoomed in on the suspect screw head. The screen was filled with a black dot. He zoomed even further and exposed what appeared to be white lines on the black dot. "Well, lookie here. I have never seen one of these up close before. Only pictures."

"What is it?"

"Well, I could be wrong, but it looks to me to be a microdot. You know. Old-fashioned spy stuff. You will have to find someone with some very specific equipment to read it."

I immediately realized this was why the watch was hidden and if these people wanted it, it must have some interesting secrets. "Close it up. Give it to me." I was now concerned about possible visitors. I took the watch and put it back in the secret pocket of my jacket. I took out my charge card and waved it in front of his face. "Where is your machine?"

"In here," he said and walked through the curtain into the front of the shop. "I'm a little old school. Still using these." He picked up a manual credit card printer and swiped the card. "How much did you say you were going to pay me to keep my mouth shut?"

I reached up and took the card from him and signed the slip. "Put down whatever you feel is fair. I trust you. You better call the police now. I advise you to tell them the truth about what happened here. Just leave out the part about this." I patted the secret pocket. "Just say that I left, and you never even got my name. Make sure that you don't let the other two get away." I left him fanning himself with the credit slip. I assumed he was trying to decide how much to put down. I was not concerned. The card I gave him had a bogus name and a limit. I called a cab and headed to the airport. I now realized the Barbie and Ken couple I saw in LAX, the couple on the plane, the woman at my hotel in Killaloe, and the two that left with the replica watch were all the same. Their hair color changed, but they were definitely the same couple. They were probably responsible for the death of the supposed writer found floating in the Shannon River with a bullet in his skull. I shook my head and felt for the watch in my jacket. I touched the reassuring lump. The watch and its secrets would give me some insight into this mystery.

BACK HOME

I settled in my first-class seat on a flight to LAX. I knew I needed to be home to recuperate. For the first time in my life, I did not heed the call to the canvas. The opportunity was perfect, but the desire was muted. I reviewed my encounters in obtaining the watch. First, there was the man that wanted to write about my life. He ended up in the Shannon River with a bullet in his head. Then there was the couple on the flight from LAX that planted a tracker and showed up in Killaloe. There was the American that beat up Sean, the man I enlisted to help me. I was pretty sure it was the same man I met on the plane. I reflected on Sean and what happened to him. I had to be more careful next time. It was not fair to him. I exposed him to danger. Then came the woman in the watchmaker shop who took the replica watch. I hoped that the watchmaker had phoned the police and was not hurt. I decided to check in with him once I was back in LA. And finally, who the hell was Botox and how did he know that the watch held a clue? A clue to what? These people obviously knew more than me. I definitely had some research to do and questions to answer. I hoped the microdot would answer all my questions.

I closed my eyes. I realized I was exhausted. I let sleep take me.

I woke halfway through the flight. It was the movement in the first-class section that brought me back. The steward was preparing an in-flight meal. He leaned over my inclined seat. "Sir?" I looked up at him. "Sir, would you like something to drink before the meal is served?"

I nodded. "Could you please bring me some water and a can of Ginger ale?"

"Certainly." He stepped away, presumably to fetch what I had requested. I looked around the section to see who my fellow passengers were. There were only three other people in first class. None of them were paying me any attention at all. I unbuckled my seatbelt and walked to the washroom. Before entering, I peeked through the curtain that separated my section from the rest of the passengers. I was looking for anyone who might be there to keep tabs on me. In the seat right in front of me was a child, a girl, I think, given that it had long curly hair, but I could be wrong. It smiled at me. I smiled back and quickly closed the curtain. Children scare me. I can never discern their motives. That is silly, I know, but the knowledge does not change how I react to them. I used the facilities and returned to my seat. I was fairly sure that none of my pursuers had followed me onto the flight.

I ate a typical in-flight meal. I did not have time to preorder anything and had to make do. Four hours were remaining on the flight. I decided to use the time with the canvas. Perhaps it would provide some answers. I slipped on a pair of very dark glasses I always carried with me as the canvas opened like a gigantic iris. What was laid out before me was not what I expected. I was not floating above in the shape of my chosen bird. I was down on the surface. I was sitting on a pile of trash in a small clearing. All around me were mountains of trash. As was usual, the images constantly changed, as if time were speeding by. Some of the mountains slowly shrank and others grew. I could also see the pointers extending out from where I was sitting. Most of the endpoints were not discernible, for they simply entered the mountains of trash and disappeared. It was all too much. I stood and looked down at the pile on which I was sitting. I gave it a nudge with my virtual foot. That proved to be a scary moment, for hiding under the small pile of trash were at least a dozen rodents of various sizes and colors. I jumped back at the unexpected flurry of multicolored motion. All the rodents were gripping in their jaws, what I can only describe as words made of metal, like metal typesets. Each rodent scurried away in an attempt to conceal themselves and their word from my view. I was able to read a few of them before they disappeared under or in cereal boxes and tin cans. I saw the words "hard" and a part word "...arkle" as well as "...nger." That was all. There was nothing to give the words any context. Was it a warning? The last word could have been anything. I only saw the end of it. Maybe it was "anger" or "danger" or "scavenger" or "stranger." There were a lot of possibilities. As I considered these possibilities, I began to rise up and transform into the kestrel that was the usual form I took when exploring the canvas. I swooped down to try to uncover more of the word-carrying rodents. I desperately wanted to decipher the message that the universe wanted to tell me. I overturned cans and newspapers and anything else that might conceal one of the rats to no avail. They were gone. Frustrated, I flew higher until the landscape was far below. I continued to rise. That action gave me new insight into the nature of the canvas. It was now all around me, as if I was in the center of a gargantuan sphere. Vectors were pointing in a million different directions. There were so many it was pointless to track any of them. One quickly got lost trying to follow any line. You were never sure if the line you were following was the one you started to follow or if you had accidentally crossed over to some other line. It was impossible.

I shook my head and removed the dark glasses. Nothing I had seen made any sense. It was not like having an object you wanted to find. I could always discover the right vector and follow it to its endpoint. The canvas was showing me clues to the confusing events I had experienced. If that was the case, it was much too cryptic for me to make any sense of it. I slipped the dark glasses into my breast pocket and took out the pocket watch. I pressed the latch and stared at my distorted reflection on the shiny golden inside cover. I hoped the microdot if, in fact, that is what it was, would clear up the mystery of why so many people wanted the watch.

I sipped my ginger ale and just thought like a normal person might. Sometimes using the canvas made even simple things appear overly complex. This was usually not a problem when the thing or question I asked was highly specific but, in this case, nothing was specific. I remembered my psychiatrist telling me that I needed to develop non-canvas ways of solving my problems. His exact words shocked me at the time, but I guess that was what he wanted—to shock me and make me reconsider how I went about dealing with my world. He said, "It seems to me—and I am not trying to insult you—that you are seriously slow when it comes to seeing your way to extremely simple solutions to your problems." He went on to give me an example of how I might solve the problem of getting continually mocked and harassed by other students. I would spend my free time exploring the canvas. That would often be in the middle of the hallway or standing beside my locker or in class after I had completed an assignment. He asked me how I might stop this from happening. I shrugged my shoulders. The 'slow' remark was still stinging. He asked me why I thought it was happening. Again, I shrugged my shoulders. I clearly remember his words, "When you do that thing you do, your eyes roll back into your head. You give the impression that you are about to pass out. It is very odd-looking and attracts attention. You just need to conceal what happens to your eyes. Look down. Wear dark glasses. Whatever works at the time?" Those were his exact words. I remember them like it was yesterday. Near the end of the session, he told me why he used the word 'slow.' He said it was to get my attention, not to insult me. He often felt I was somewhere else when he was talking to me, and he needed me to be in the moment.

I considered this and decided to explore my problem like a proper detective without the advantages, or in this case, disadvantages, of the canvas. I would start with an examination of the microdot that was still in the watch. I did not have any experience with microdots, but I thought the microscope I have in my workroom would allow me to see what is on the microdot. Once I have removed it from the watch and read its contents, I will take the watch back to my client. She said she wanted the watch, and that is exactly what I would supply. I was looking forward to that meeting. I had some questions to ask, but I was unsure if I would get any real answers. I would wait until I had any new information that the microdot might provide.

THE MICRODOT

I took the microdot from the watch and placed it on a microscope slide. I projected the image onto the pull-down screen in my lab. I could not see all of it at once. I had to move the slide back and forth and up and down with the microscope controls. It appeared to be a spider web. I fiddled with the image until I was able to get a series of four captured pictures on my computer. I put them together as one image. I used some software to sharpen the image lines. This helped considerably. Now when I zoomed in, the image did not become fuzzy and I could make out the details.

The lines were in the shape of a series of nested half-circles crossed by radiating black lines. It actually looked like half of a spider's web. I spent some time zooming in to see if there was more detail or something other than lines. Perhaps there was a clue as to why someone would have created the microdot and concealed it in the watch in the first place. There were still some artifacts that were the result of my manipulation of the image. I inspected and rejected a number of these but I wanted to be sure I had not missed anything that might be a clue, so I continued. I zoomed in on a section left of the middle. I noticed what, at first, appeared to be an artifact. It was a smudge, but when I zoomed in, it looked like a series of dots and lines. I zoomed in further.

I thought it was a seven-legged spider-like creature that was waiting on a web of its making for something to wander out and become prey.

I stared at the screen image but nothing seemed to tell me anything about what it was or why someone would put these things on a microdot and conceal it in a pocket watch and then hide the watch in a graveyard. I had a ton of questions and absolutely no answers. My eyes were burning, so I shut down the projector, placed the slide with the microdot in a case, and put it in my safe, along with the pocket watch. I sat down on my lounge chair. I closed my eyes and conjured up the canvas.

I was a kestrel, once again soaring the updrafts of a mental canvas. I had often wondered if it was something that I had created. I could never come to terms with that hypothesis. If it was something that I created, then everything I had ever found or encountered was just part of me. I knew that was not true. I had found things on the canvas that I could never have had any contact with. The canvas had to be external to me. I must be able to tap into something. Exactly what was a problem for another day. I dismissed the thought and stared with my hawk eyes at the sweep of the canvas below. I circled and waited for something to happen that might give me insight into the puzzle of the microdot.

I seldom thought of anything else but the canvas in front of me, but today was different. I seemed to have become a victim of my own abilities for the extent of the canvas had vastly increased and, as a result, my ability to find something had decreased in equal proportion. Or maybe I was flying too high. It did not make a lot of difference. If I came closer, the amount of area in view decreased. I imagined a microscope with multiple lenses. A lower power showed the entire field of view without much detail, while the higher power allowed you to see with much greater acuity but a smaller area.

I knew I needed some time to let the microdot business settle. A few days away from the problem might help with clarity. Clarity often dictates action. I was not clear about anything regarding the microdot. I was stuck. I still had to return the watch sans microdot. I felt a little twinge of guilt for deciding not to return the microdot with the watch, but I quickly justified my actions. My logic was twofold. Firstly, it was not what I was paid to recover, and second, several threats to my life needed to be addressed. I set about notifying Ms. Sandra Beal. I decided I would not be a delivery boy. If she wanted the watch, she would have to travel to me to get it or run the risk of shipping. Her choice might indicate how much she valued the watch. I sat down and sent an email to such an effect. I discovered that my messages had piled up. I needed to deal with them and settled down to read what my assistant had culled from the hundreds of messages I received every month. I dismissed a series of really boring ones. I stopped at a request to find an emerald ring that was stolen from a safe deposit box in the early '70s. The emerald was 6.23 carats and certified as flawless. The thieves entered the bank in broad daylight to steal cash. The ring's owner was placing some papers in his safe deposit box when the thieves broke in and discovered the ring. They were never caught and the ring was never recovered. The ring was valued at $7000 in 1969. Its present value was estimated at $300,000. Attached to the message were images of the certification papers, along with some rather grainy images of the ring itself.

I like shiny baubles. The more unique they were, the easier they were to find. I found this intriguing and decided to take the case. I sent my assistant my decision and requested that she prepare the contract and gather any pertinent information I would need. I closed the laptop and closed my eyes. I was tired. I needed a good night's sleep. I would start this new case in the morning.

BAUBLES

THE next morning, I was refreshed. With my morning coffee in hand and the papers regarding the lost emerald ring my assistant had delivered, I sat in my favorite recliner. I studied the papers and sipped coffee until I was able to picture the ring in my mind. I closed my eyes and opened the canvas.

I started high. The kestrel circled on an updraft. A single vector formed and stabbed down. Experience told me that a single vector was incredibly rare. I usually had to hunt through hundreds to find the dominant one. I followed it. My eye caught some motion, and I swooped down and landed in a large oak tree. The vector vanished. This was how it worked. Once I was close to my goal, the vector was no longer needed. The scene below was not like anything I had ever seen before. I was looking down at an open field with a small outdoor stage at one end. In front of the stage were people sitting on blankets watching actors perform. I could not discern the words being spoken, but the costumes were from a period piece. Perhaps something from Shakespeare. The audience was laughing, so I assumed it was a comedy. There was nothing here that gave me any idea about the ring. I scanned the audience to see if the ring was there. I could discern nothing. There were a lot of women wearing rings, but nothing fit the description of the ring in question. I lifted off of the branch and rose up. The vector appeared again, and this time I followed it precisely. It was pointing at the stage. I circled directly above it. The vector was pointing backstage. Suddenly, it began to shift. A woman dressed in a long gold-colored tunic walked on from stage left. All the actors turned to her and knelt in supplication, like you would do before royalty. Then it occurred to me this woman must be wearing the ring. I focused on her hand. I could see three rings on her right hand and two on her left. I identified it as one of the two on her left hand. I could see it catch the light. It was a huge bauble just like the one I was looking for.

I returned to the oak tree and waited for the play to end. I did not have to wait long. I watched the audience laughing and clapping and the actors bowing. It occurred to me that I was no further ahead than when I started. I still did not know who or where this woman was. I could not report that I had found the ring and some unknown female actor was wearing it somewhere.

I watched the audience pick up their belongings and head out to the parking lot. I waited for the actors to come out. I would follow the woman and find out who she was. After a short time, I saw her start to walk to the car park. I flew up from my perch and I followed. As I gained altitude, everything became fuzzy. The entire canvas was enveloped in mist except for the field, the stage, and the edge of the car park. I quickly swooped down to see if I could spot the ring on the woman's hand. There was nothing but a simple gold band.

I realized that the ring was being used as a prop, along with other costume jewelry. It was probably locked up somewhere backstage with the rest of the props and would be taken out for the next show. All I needed to do now was to find out where this little stage in the park was located. By now, the only thing not covered in the fog was the stage. The canvas had shown me where the ring was on the micro level, but that was no help at all if I could not find the stage, or the park, or city, or the country, for that matter.

I was about to begin looking for some detail that would provide a clue, but the fog rolled over the entire scene and I was left with nothing. I circled for a few more minutes, but nothing changed. The vector was gone. It seemed that it had decided that it was no longer needed, as it had done its job.

I opened my eyes and looked at my watch. A lot of time passed in the real world. At least six hours. It was late afternoon. My stomach growled. I wanted some food. A small Deli with a half dozen tables was just a few blocks from my residence. It was my go-to eatery. With a sense of depression for not succeeding at finding what I was searching for, I headed out. Venice Beach in the late spring was a delightful place to walk. I slipped on my dark glasses and headed to the Deli.

There were few people for the first few blocks, but as I approached El Secundo Blvd, the number of pedestrians increased. I was a half block from my destination when the hackles on the back of my neck stood up and sent a chill down my spine. I glanced around. Someone was following and watching me. I could see no one. I hurried to the Deli and slipped into a seat that looked out on the street. I scanned the area. The Deli was just opposite the Old Town Music Hall that was advertising a jazz concert. The late afternoon sun was shining through the Deli window. I knew the reflection would conceal the fact that I was staring out the window searching the faces. A group of people were looking at posters of the coming events at the Music Hall. Further down the street was a large parking lot. It was there that I noticed a man leaning against the front of a truck. He kept raising his hand to his face as if he were using an invisible spyglass. I suddenly realized that he was doing exactly that. He was staring directly at the window of the Deli. I had no idea if I was as concealed as I had first thought. He dropped his hand that was holding some small high-tech spyglass and raised the other to his ear. He was talking to someone. I scanned the area again just as two men previously studying the upcoming shows at the Music Hall turned and strode across the street. They disappeared as they passed a parked car. I had to assume they were now coming up the sidewalk and would soon enter the Deli.

I started to panic. I was not used to this kind of intrigue. My mind jumped to what happened in the London watch repair shop. Part of me said, "RUN" while my more daring part said let them come. *You need to know who these people are and what they want.* I thought of the microdot. I was sure these people tracking me also wanted the microdot.

I got to my feet and walked toward the back of the Deli. The owner approached me. He was carrying a brown paper bag. "Mr. Cervantes? Here is your order," he said and handed me the bag. I always ordered the same thing, and the Deli owner automatically prepared it when he saw me enter.

Everything I ordered went on account.

"Thanks, Eddy," I said and took the bag from his hand. "Eddy, I have a favor to ask."

"Anything for you, Mr. Cervantes."

"Some men are going to enter the Deli in a few seconds, and I need somewhere to conceal myself and watch them. Can you help me?"

"No problem. Follow me."

I glanced toward the door. They had not reached the entrance. I followed Eddy. He took me to a small room with four monitors that showed the exterior and interior of the Deli. I could see the men approaching. They entered and surveyed the room. One of them walked to the rear door of the Deli while the other stood at the front. A waiter approached him and asked what he wanted. The waiter gestured to an open seat, but the man dismissed him with a wave of his hand. The camera facing the rear parking area of the Deli showed the second man exiting, looking around, and re-entering.

"What do they want?" asked Eddy.

"I have no idea," I said and stared at the monitors. I watched the man that re-entered go into the restrooms. As he exited each, he shook his head. The man waiting in the front touched his ear and spoke. They both turned and left out the front door. "Hey, Eddy, could I have a copy of this footage?"

"Sure, Mr. Cervantes." He reached into a drawer and removed a flash drive. He inserted it into the recording device. A few minutes later, he handed it to me.

"Thanks, Eddy. I owe you one."

"No problem, Mr. Cervantes. Glad to be of service. Enjoy your sandwich."

"Thanks. Mind if I leave out the back?" Eddy nodded toward the rear entrance, and I slipped out.

HIDE AND SEEK

I took a circuitous route back to my residence. The entrance is off the back alley. Entering involves standing in a meter square alcove. I look straight ahead and stick out my tongue. Like my mail safe, a camera reads an image of my tongue and compares it to the one on file. An invisible door on my right slides open and I sidestep through. The door closes quickly behind me.

Once inside, I sit at my desk. Above me are monitors attached to my security system. I glance at the cameras that have a view of the back alley where I entered. I was curious if anyone followed me. There was no one, but there was someone in my front office. They had obviously picked the simple lock, for there was no other damage. Two men were going through the file cabinets. They were careful to conceal any action that might alert me to their trespass. I could hear them talk to each other.

"These cabinets are filled with a bunch of old files." He holds one up. "Fuck. This is at least 50 years old." He looks around the office. "This whole office looks ancient. Are you sure this is the right place?"

"I'm sure," said the other man. "Keep looking."

"Why do you think he would hide a pocket watch in here? If it is valuable, this is a really dumb place to hide it."

"You're right. Put everything back as you found it. We're outta here."

The two men replaced all the files and closed the drawers of the desk. They quickly slipped out the front door of the office. I saw this as a perfect opportunity to get some information on the people who were after the pocket watch. I slipped on my coat and hat. It was time to be a real detective.

I opened the passage door to the office washroom, entered the office proper, and crept up to the window. I could see the men standing a few feet from the office entrance. They were waiting for the after-work traffic to ebb so they could cross. I watched them run to a car parked on the far side. Once I identified the car, I would exit the office in an attempt to get a plate number. I did not own a vehicle, so following them was out of the question, but a license plate would give me a place to start. 4 GXH 619. I memorized it and turned my back to the leaving vehicle. These were the same two men I had avoided in the Deli.

I returned to my residence and ate the Deli sandwich. I wasn't really hungry, but I knew it would fortify me. I needed to sit and explore whatever the canvas had to offer. This exploration was just that, an exploration. It was like I was a kid of fifteen again who used the canvas for entertainment. I would conjure it up and let the colors, smells, and sounds wash over me. I sat in my recliner and relaxed.

I was not the kestrel this time, mainly because I was not looking for anything. I was sitting in a rather spooky wood with trees all around me. The green moss beneath me was warm, dry, and soft. I leaned back against a large moss-covered boulder. I was startled when a spider dropped right in front of my face. It was suspended from a glistening thread of web. The spider was odd-looking. I had seen it somewhere before but could not place it. Then it came to me. It looked just like the drawing on the microdot. Almost immediately, many more of the odd-looking spiders dropped on top of the first one. They clambered over one another. Their legs joined and formed a series of tetrahedrons that also joined together until the result looked like a grid of spiders—only they did not look like spiders anymore. They just dangled in the breeze. Nothing else happened. This was an odd event.

The canvas did not just show something and then stop. But here it had done just that. The grid of spiders that were not spiders dangled in front of me as if I was to cull some sort of meaning from it all. I did not cull anything. The puzzle was enigmatic. I knew it had something to do with the pocket watch and the clue secreted inside. The canvas faded.

I got up and went to my desk. I emailed my assistant and requested she use her contacts to determine who owned the vehicle with the license number I had recorded. Ms. Beal replied to my email. She would be in Venice Beach the following day and wanted to meet me so she could get the watch and make the final payment for my services. I replied and set the time for 4:00 p.m. at my office.

I felt a little out of sorts. I was not used to the canvas giving me this many cryptic clues. It was historically straightforward. I would gather information about a thing and the canvas would point me in the proper direction. The microdot had not supplied me with anything useful. I suddenly realized something and jumped to my feet. The image on the microdot looked like a spider web with a tiny spider on one of the radiant lines. The canvas also showed me spiders. A lot of spiders joined together. I could not figure out what it was trying to tell me.

I reflected on the canvas. It had changed somehow. It was trying to give me information that I had not asked for. Information about what? That was the question.

UNSATISFACTORY EXPLANATIONS

MY next appointment with my psychiatrist was memorable. He wanted information from me. At the time, I did not understand why. Only years later, when he asked me to be part of a publication on odd psychological conditions, did I understand. He did not use my name, but as I read the article, I knew it was me he wrote about.

As usual, my 15-year-old self-entered his office and sat waiting to be called in. There was no one there besides me and the receptionist. That in itself was odd. There were always other strangely behaving patients sitting near me. To be truthful, I was disappointed. The receptionist actually spoke to me. That was not something I was used to. People never spoke to me. At least they never spoke to me more than once. It may have been due to my penchant to whisper 'piss off' repeatedly when someone was bothering me. By bothering me, I mean any sort of interaction. Back then, I did not want anyone to interject themselves and demand my attention. Except for the psychiatrist.

The receptionist spoke. "The doctor said to go right in. You must be special. He cleared all his afternoon appointments."

I got up and entered the office. I went directly to the chair opposite his desk and plunked down. I flipped one of my legs up and over the arm of the chair and said, "Got any KitKat bars?" The doctor opened a drawer in his desk, retrieved the requested chocolate bar, and tossed it at me. "Thanks."

"Mattie," he said and noticed me staring up at the ceiling with a KitKat finger in my mouth. He spoke again, "Mathew, I would like you to lie down on the couch. Would you mind doing that for me?"

I got up. "Cool, just like in the cartoons." I lay down on the couch or settee or davenport or chesterfield or whatever psychiatrists call it. I still had the KitKat in my mouth. I chewed and swallowed.

"I would like to know more about this thing you call *'the canvas.'* Would you mind answering a few questions about it?" I shrugged. He continued, "I'm intrigued and would like you to explain it in more detail. Are you willing to answer a few questions?"

I shrugged again. "Don't know what else to tell you."

"The last time we spoke, you gave me the impression that you would help me understand. The time before you got upset when I questioned you about the canvas. You said …" He flipped through his notebook. He stopped. "This was our conversation." He read:

Me: "Where is this canvas?"

You: "Everywhere."

Me: "Can I see it?"

You: "I have no idea."

Me: "Where exactly do you look?"

You: "I don't know. I must be very slow."

"Do you still feel like you are slow when you talk about the canvas?"

"No."

"How come?"

I grinned at him and put another finger of the KitKat bar in my mouth. I did not say anything.

"Is it because I gave you a chocolate bar?"

"Maybe."

"Do you trust me a little more now?

"Maybe. I don't know. Why do you want to know about the canvas, anyway?"

"Well, it is rather unique, and unique things interest me."

"Ok. I will tell you whatever I can. Lots of stuff that happens while I am with the canvas is…" I paused, "…confusing." I looked up at him. I remember thinking that he might be someone I could take advantage of. Like my mother. "Got any more chocolate bars?"

He opened his desk drawer and took out an O'Henry. "I just have these." He tossed it at me.

"Not my favorite, but it will do," I said and put it in my pocket. I knew I could not eat an O'Henry bar in public. I always felt an urge to smooth out the bumps before I put a piece of it in my mouth. That was a messy procedure. "Ask away."

"Great. Before I do, I would like you to lie back and relax."

"Are you going to hypnotize me?"

"Actually, that is exactly what I would like to do. Do I have your permission?"

I remember nodding my head and listening to his voice. I do not remember much else about that session. I have often wondered what transpired. Several other sessions left a lot of blank spots in my memory. I now suspect that he placed a hypnotic suggestion that enabled him to put me under quickly. I never really knew if he understood what the canvas was. I doubt it, in that it was my canvas, and I didn't know much about it. You do not have to know how many things work to use them effectively.

ZEE PLOT, SHE T'ICKENS

I spent the next day trying to remember all the details of my time watching the play, the outdoor venue, and the surrounding area. I could think of nothing that might identify where this took place. Then I remembered that the audience and the actors all left in vehicles. Seeing a license plate would have narrowed my search. I could not remember even looking for a plate at the time. I decided to use the canvas and have another look—that is if the canvas was willing to show me.

I sat in my recliner and relaxed into it. I was once again the kestrel circling above a wooded area. Everything beyond was shrouded in mist. There were no people anywhere. There was just the empty stage and grass field. It was raining. I was surprised. I expected something more cryptic. The canvas was always cryptic. What it had shown and was now showing me seemed straightforward. A female actor was wearing the ring as part of a stage costume. She was not wearing it when she left—ergo, it was still in the theater. But where was the theater? My alter ego swooped down and landed on the lip of the stage. There was a small music pit just off to the side. I glanced at it and noticed a rain-soaked paper on the floor of the pit.

I flew down and looked. It was a play program. I flipped it over. In doing so, I exposed a small hole that was filled with tiny spiders. Instead of scattering, they clung to one another and formed a lattice of spiders that slowly covered the hole. The misty rain clung to the lattice. It sparkled as a ray of sunlight pierced the clouds. I could not see into the hole. The lattice of spiders was concealing whatever was inside. I looked at the paper program to see what it might tell me. In that instant, the spiders disappeared along with the hole. The writing on the program was almost illegible. All I could make out before the program simply disintegrated was *The Persephone Players*. All that was left was a glob of white mush.

The canvas faded, and I stood up. The name of the theater group was a very good place to start. I sent an email to my assistant requesting she search for *The Persephone Players*. Once found, I was sure I could locate the ring. Getting it might prove to be more difficult.

I got out of the chair. My thoughts returned to the very odd image of spiders linking together over a hole. Images of spiders were asserting themselves again. The canvas had never jumbled up the information before, but it seemed as if there was some crossover. Perhaps because I thought there was a spider on the microdot, the canvas was using that information to tell me something.

I shook my head as if it might help me reach some sort of answer. It did not. I started to prepare for my meeting with Sandra Beal. I went to my safe and removed the pocket watch. I asked myself again if I should return the microdot to the watch or not. I decided that if the microdot was more important than the watch itself, then Ms. Beal had misrepresented herself. I would not return the microdot to the watch. It was a mystery I could not abandon. I hoped that the future would bring me some insight and allow me to solve it. I was about to have a look around the canvas to see if it would give me a new clue when there was a beep from my surveillance system. I glanced up and saw Ms. Beal standing at my office door. I slipped the watch into an envelope and took the passage from my residence to the office lavatory and from there to the office proper. I answered the door.

"Hello, Ms. Beal. I'm glad you could make it. Did you have any trouble locating me?"

"No. Your instructions and my GPS brought me straight here."

"Come in," I said and gestured to one of the chairs near the desk. "Have a seat."

"I don't have a lot of time. I assume the watch is here."

"Yes." I removed the envelope from my pocket and put it down on the desk. She reached for it, and I placed my hand on top of the envelope. "Payment?"

"Oh yes," she said and reached into her purse. She removed a fat envelope and placed it beside the watch. "I brought cash." I lifted my hand from the watch and picked up the fat envelope. "Your assistant informed me of the amount. You're right in saying you aren't cheap." I opened it and fanned the $100 bills. "You can count it if you wish. It is all there."

I set the money down. "I am sure it is," I said and leaned back in the chair. She picked up the envelope containing the watch, took it out, and pressed the catch that opened the front cover. She looked up at me. "Did you remove anything from the watch?"

"Such as?" I asked. I was curious as to what she thought I might have removed. Did she know about the microdot?

"The picture that my mother said would be right there," she said, and she pointed at the open cover.

"I am sorry, Ms. Beal, but there was no picture under the watch cover. Please accept that. It is the watch you asked me to find. Your grandfather's initials are scribed on the back." She turned the watch over and stared. "Here is a magnifier. Look right there. You will see his initials. SAA for Samuel A Adare."

"Yes, I see them." She lowered the magnifier. "Thank you. Where did you find it?"

"It was in a graveyard of a small church in Killaloe, Ireland, concealed in a brass ball of a grave marker fence."

She perked up. "Was my grandfather buried there?"

"No, he wasn't. I wonder if you know why the watch was hidden there. Do you have any relatives near that town?"

"None that I know of. He was a spy, after all. He was probably very good at keeping secrets."

"Yes, I suppose so." I stood. I held up my part of this bargain. At least, that is what I told myself. She stood and walked to the door. We both smiled weak smiles. She exited my office, and I closed the door behind her. I watched her. She took out her phone and made a call. She crossed the street and waited. She was glancing around. I assumed she had called a Taxi or Uber. A car pulled up beside her and she got in and closed the car door. I was about to look away when the car door opened again. Ms. Beal was getting out of the car. Suddenly, I saw a hand reach out of the car and grab the back of her coat collar. She was pulled violently back into the car. The driver got out, glanced around, circled the car to the open door, and slammed it closed. He returned to the driver's door, got in, and drove away. I stood up and ran out to see if I could get a plate number or something that might identify the vehicle. I got the first group of letters before the traffic blocked my view.

I knew that I needed to report the incident. I did not, however, want to talk to the police. I checked my pockets for some coins. I did not have any. I opened the desk drawer. There was a roll of quarters placed there just for this kind of situation. I took out three and walked over to the Old Town Music Hall. There was a payphone just to the right of the entrance. I dialed 911, covered the mouthpiece with a tissue I was carrying and reported what looked to me like an abduction. I answered their questions but refused to reveal who I was. I wiped the phone receiver with the tissue, returned and dropped the unused quarters back into the desk drawer. Whoever had grabbed Ms. Beal was most likely the same group that was following me. They knew about Beal and waited for the perfect opportunity to grab her and take the pocket watch. I felt vindicated for not including the microdot with the watch. I wondered if the couple had tracked me back home and waited for Beal to show up so they could steal the watch. They were ruthless. I also felt concerned that I would be their next target.

I knew I had to study the microdot in more detail. These people knew about the existence of the microdot. It must hold clues to something that would make these people commit crimes to get it. That something must be very valuable.

I'M A SUSPECT

THE next morning, I was waiting for my assistant to give me some information about the license plate I got from the two men who broke into my office as well as the partial plate number from the vehicle that took Beal. Once I knew, I would share the info with the police. Anonymously, of course. I was also waiting for the location of *The Persephone Players*. Since I had to wait, I decided to spend some time exploring. Maybe the canvas would show me something that might connect at least a few of the dots. I settled in.

The last few times I had chosen to be the bird. I figured it gave me a better perspective, but I was getting nothing but confusing information. I decided to take a different tack. I sat on the ground and waited to see what the canvas was offering. I found myself in a grassy meadow surrounded by deciduous woods. The sun was directly overhead. There were no vectors, as I was not looking for anything specific. It reminded me of canvas exploration in my youth. I would just watch and enjoy whatever the canvas was offering. Today it was offering little. I lay back in the tall grass. I was about to close my eyes when the light caught a spider spinning a web between two tall stalks of grass. It was fascinating to see the web take shape. I tried to memorize the web. I was concentrating when a small flying insect collided with the web and stuck. The vibration alerted the spider. It ran to the struggling insect and spun its web around it, binding it in place. It must not have been hungry, as it quickly retreated to the top of the web and hid behind a seed kernel. The web quivered in the breeze. I continued to study the shape of the web. I wanted to compare it to the web on the microdot, so I proceeded to memorize it.

A bell chimed. The surveillance system had detected someone banging on my office door. I abandoned the canvas and stared at the monitor. Two men were calling out my name as they banged on the door. I headed to the passageway through the washroom to my office. I called out, "Who are you and what do you want?" My first thought was that these were the people that grabbed Beal and I was next, given that they had not found the microdot in the watch. I cursed myself for not taking a gun with me. I had a license to carry one, but I never did. Guns, as far as I was concerned, inspired violence and killed too quickly. They never gave the shooter any time to consider other possibilities. Things were always black and white. There were no shades of gray. It was a situation of—*I'm afraid—bang—you're dead.*

"We wish to speak with you," he said and pressed his ID badge to the glass.

I opened the door. "Yes, officer?"

"Are you Mr. Cervantes?"

"Yes."

"May we come in?"

"What is this about?"

"We will tell you in a moment. Please?" he said and gestured to the office behind me. I nodded, and they entered. We sat. "Mr. Cervantes, may we see some ID."

"I left my ID in my residence at the back of my office." I removed one of my cards from the desk drawer in front of me. "Will this do?"

He took the card and stared at it. A grin crept onto his face. "So, Mr. Cervantes, you are a detective and …," he raised my card and read it. He said, "… you claim you can find anything."

"Yes, that is true. Now, how can I help you?"

"Find anything, eh."

I answered matter-of-factly, "I have not failed yet. Now, how can I help, gentlemen?"

The other officer spoke accusingly. "Do you know a woman called Sandra Beal?" I nodded my head in the affirmative. "Please speak your answer."

"No." I was getting irritated at these officers' attitudes.

"Why not?"

"The only reason I would have to speak out loud is so you could tape me. Are you recording this?"

The other officer jumped in. "What he means is a verbal answer is clearer. We cannot misinterpret a verbal answer where a gesture can be."

"You didn't answer my question. Are you recording this interview?"

"We were, but if you don't want it recorded, we will stop."

"Yes, stop." I waited until the first police officer reached into his shirt pocket, remove, and shut off a recording device. "Now, how can I be of service?"

"Do you know a woman named Sandra Beal? We found one of your cards on her person."

"I do. She is a client of mine. I was engaged to locate and return a lost pocket watch."

"Did you?"

"Did I what?"

"Find and return the pocket watch."

"I did."

"When and where did you return the watch?"

"What is this all about?"

"Answer the question."

"If you are not going to inform me why you are interrogating me, I would like legal representation."

"Ms. Sandra Beal was assaulted yesterday. She is in the hospital."

"Is she alright?"

"She was in a coma. Her assailants …," he paused and stared at me, "… or assailant left her for dead. She regained consciousness a few hours ago. We questioned her to determine the reason for the attack. She was not very forthcoming. She claimed she could not remember anything past going to meet you. That's what this is all about," the police officer practically spat out the information.

I stood up. "Do you suspect me?"

"Hey, Gord, this guy is quicker than I thought, but I am not sure he could find his own face if he looked in a mirror."

"If you think insulting me is going to entice me to cooperate with you, you are sadly mistaken. Now arrest me or get out." I pointed at the door.

"Look, Mr. Cervantes, I am sorry about Sammy here. He gets a little too aggressive. We just want to know where you were yesterday evening."

"Was that when she was assaulted?" Gord nodded. "I was here, and I live alone so no one can corroborate my statement. I have no reason to hurt Ms. Beal. She hired me to find her grandfather's pocket watch. I found it and yesterday she paid my fee, and I gave it to her. She left in an Uber, as I recall."

"A pocket watch? Was it valuable?"

I shrugged. "Worth a couple of hundred or thereabouts. I think it had more sentimental value."

"So, it was unlikely the pocket watch was the motive." I shrugged again. "How much was your fee?"

I looked at him and shook my head. "Seriously?"

"Did she pay you in cash?" I nodded. "Look, Mr. Cervantes, if she was carrying a large sum of money, that would constitute a robbery motive. Perhaps the perps thought she still had the money."

"Without being exact—it was in the low five-digit range."

Sammy whistled. "You don't come cheap. We are definitely in the wrong business."

"You gave her this pocket watch yesterday?" I nodded. The officer looked at his notes. "Well, she never mentioned a missing pocket watch."

My curiosity peaked. "Where was she found?" The two police officers looked at each other. "I'm a detective. Perhaps I can help you find the perpetrators. After all…"

"… You can find anything. Look, Mr. Cervantes leave attempted murder and robbery cases to the professionals," said Sammy.

"If you continue to insult me, I will be forced to end this little tête-à-tête."

"Mr. Cervantes, she was bludgeoned and dumped."

My interest was growing. "Where was she dumped? Exactly. That information would provide me with a starting point."

Gord blurted, "She was found in the skate park this morning." Sammy elbowed him.

"Thanks for the info. Do you have any more questions for me? I will let you know where I am if I need to go out of town."

"Not at this time. And a word of advice—don't go snooping into things better left to the police." The two men stood. "Good afternoon," they said and left my office. I remained. I stared out the window at the two officers walking to the parking lot of the Old Town Music Hall. They got into their car and drove away. My mind started to race. Once again, dozens of unanswered questions pelted my head like hailstones begging for an answer.

DECISIONS TO BE MADE

I needed to talk to Beal. I sent an email to my assistant and asked her to find out which hospital Ms. Beal was presently in the care of. I sat back and waited for a response. I had a lot of questions and I hoped I could convince Beal to answer some of them. She did not want to talk to the police. Perhaps she would talk to me. After all, I had found the watch for her. If someone took it from her, and I suspect they did, she might want me to find it again. That would lead me to whoever kidnapped her, and they would not want to be found.

I also realized that they would probably come looking for me once they did not find whatever they were looking for in the pocket watch. I suspected they knew about the microdot. That means they got the information from the same place that Beal got the information—Adare's footlocker or from Beal herself. I thought of my meeting at her apartment in San Francisco. A male was living there or visiting often. Perhaps there was more intrigue around the contents of the footlocker than she was admitting. I would visit her in the hospital tomorrow morning. Right now, I wanted to find the town where the Persephone Players hailed from.

There was a note in my email from my assistant, Billie, regarding the Persephone Players. She was brief. It was one of her personality traits that I loved. Our professional relationship started a few years earlier. I needed someone to look after those parts of the business I was unwilling to spend time on. She was my accountant, paralegal, assistant, security chief, and technology guru, all in one package. I had advertised for a company manager through an agency. They set up a series of interviews. She was my third interviewee. The first two people seemed to think that they needed to interview me. One asked me a series of personal questions I was unwilling to answer, so he walked out of the interview. Billie was different. Her first words were, "If I take the job, what are my actual responsibilities? The description of the job is rather vague." I remember smiling at her. She had a penchant for large and bizarre earrings. I pointed at her earrings and asked her what they were made of, for they looked like brown lumps. She said they were coprolites. I must have looked puzzled. I was puzzled. She explained that coprolites were dinosaur poop. I laughed. At that moment, I figured that anyone who could wear fossilized poop as jewelry was someone I could work with. I told her what I needed and that she could hire whomever she wanted to aid her. I would provide her with an office that she could set up as she saw fit.

She wanted the job, and I wanted to work with her. We seldom met face to face, but we communicated regularly. She looked after all the company's needs so I could focus on finding things. She even helped me with many of my cases. I read her note:

Cervantes
The info you asked for:
Persephone Players - They do shows in Gorman Park, Freeport Maine
Beal is in Cedars Sinai Marina Del Rey Hospital
Billie

The location of the ring was definitely not optimal. Maine was just about as far away from Venice Beach as you could get and still be on the continental USA. I had a few options. I could go there, spend two days traveling, and get the ring myself. Or I could send someone in my stead. Or I could simply tell the owner of the emerald ring where it was, and they could retrieve it themselves. The last one was the most desirous, as it would not require me chatting up the actress from the players and convincing her to give me the ring. Or simply stealing it from backstage of the theater. That would require some level of stealth and planning. As much as I wanted to be able to put the ring in the rightful owner's hand and collect an exorbitant fee, I decided to simply tell them where the ring was and be done with it. After all, that was what I was contracted to do.

I contacted Billie. Thanked her for the information and asked her to inform the clients that I had found the ring and where it was located. I gave her the details she needed to impart so they could retrieve the ring in a way that best suited their skills and sense of propriety.

Ms. Sandra Beal was next on my list. I hoped she would be healthy enough to answer a few questions. I needed to know if she still had the watch. Perhaps she was able to hide it from her attackers. If they had it and discovered that it was just a pocket watch with no special information inside, they would be coming after me. They must have some information about it from an alternate source. Perhaps Beal would be able to enlighten me. I decided to be blunt with her. I called an Uber to take me to Cedars Sinai Marina Del Rey Hospital.

I seldom looked around when traveling in a car. I always saw it as an opportunity to spend time with the canvas. Normally, I would slip on my dark sunglasses and drift away. Today was different. I found myself constantly glancing around at the traffic. One time, I fixated on a car behind me in the left lane. I was trying not to be obvious, but I failed. My driver spoke. "No one is following you, if that is why you are concerned. I used to have a different job that required me to notice stuff like that. Old habits die hard," the driver said calmly.

I looked at him in his rear-view mirror. He glanced back and smiled. I decided not to question his stated expertise. "Thanks," I said and relaxed. He pulled up to the hospital visitors' entrance. I paid with a generous tip and headed into the hospital. I suddenly felt more exposed and glanced at every person in the hospital atrium. I was looking for a middle-aged woman with a tall man. I recognized no one who fit the description I had recorded in my head.

I requested the room number and headed to a bank of lifts. I was soon standing outside Sandra Beal's room. I walked past and glanced into the room. It was a private room. I knocked softly on the door jamb and stepped inside so she could see me. Her eyes brightened, and I took that as a good sign. I entered the room and stood at the end of her bed. There were several scratches and contusions on her face and arms, and she had a black eye.

I suspected her nightgown was concealing many more injuries.

"Mr. Cervantes, it is nice to see you. I am going crazy. They won't let me go home until they are sure I can do so safely. Since I live in San Fran, they strongly advise me to wait a few more days."

"The police interviewed me and told me you were in the hospital. Are you alright?" I asked, not wanting to get straight to the reason I was visiting.

"Just a few scrapes and bruises. They say I have a slight concussion. They must have dumped me out of the car. I don't remember very much."

"What did they want?"

"Money, I guess. I was going to the bank to get the money to pay you, and that is the last thing I remember. I am sorry I did not make our meeting. I assume you still have the watch. Be assured, I will pay you for your services."

I stared at her. I was trying to discern if she was being honest with me. I saw no signs of deceit. She seemed to have no memory of anything past her arrival.

My reaction to her made her suspicious. "Is something wrong? You do still have the watch." I was stunned and did not know what to say. I said nothing. I simply turned to leave. "Where are you going?" she demanded.

"Ms. Beal, I will be right back," I said quickly. I left the room in search of her doctor. I approached the desk and queried the nurse. She pointed to a doctor who was approaching. I stepped up to him and spoke. "Doctor, my name is Cervantes and I would like to talk to you about one of your patients. Ms. Beal." He nodded, and I continued. "Do you know that she has no memory of the last 24 hours?"

He looked at me blankly and turned to the nurse at the desk. "Could I have Ms. Beal's chart?" The nurse picked up a tablet, selected something, and handed it to him. He scanned it and then looked up at me. "You say she has no memory of the last 24 hours? How do you know this?"

I glanced around the room. "Is there somewhere we could talk that is a little more private?" He indicated a small room to the side. We entered it.

"Now Mr. …"

"Cervantes." I fished out a card and handed it to him.

He stared at it. "Find anything? That's quite a claim, even for a detective."

I shrugged. "This isn't about me. Did you know she has lost a whole day?"

"I did not," he said flatly.

"I just spoke to her, and it seems she has no memory of a meeting we had yesterday."

"What was this meeting about?"

"She hired me to find something. I found it. She gave me a sum of money and I gave her the item she hired me to find. She does not remember any of that, and that puts me in an awkward position."

"How did you know she was here?"

"The police visited me this morning. They were able to piece together her travels. She was taken after leaving my office. She was robbed and beaten and dropped at the skate park. She was unconscious when someone reported finding her."

The doctor glanced at his tablet. "She is scheduled for a CT scan. That will tell us more."

"I have an idea that might help her understand what has happened. Will you come and talk with her?"

"Sure."

We entered her room. Ms. Beal was trying to get dressed, but her balance was off. She tried to lift her leg into her slacks but fell back onto the bed. The doctor called out, "Nurse!" He went to her and supported her shoulder. The nurse entered.

"What is going on, Cervantes?" Beal demanded.

"Ms. Beal, I am going to ask you some questions, and your answers should bring clarity." She nodded at him. "When did you leave your home in San Francisco?"

"Let me see—it was a Tuesday. May 12. I am sure because it was garbage day, and I put out the can."

"Great. Now, what is today's date?"

She looked at him as if the question was absurd. “Today is Wednesday, May 13.”

I looked at the doctor and nodded. The doctor spoke. “Ms. Beal, today is May 15—Friday, May 15. I suspect your concussion is much worse than we thought. You have lost at least a day and a half. I think Mr. Cervantes knows what happened during that missing time.”

She turned to me with an expectant look. I explained what had happened between us and what had probably happened to her after she was taken. I could see the color drain from her face. She started to slip down from her sitting position on the bed toward the floor. The nurse stepped in. “This is over. Please leave Mr. Cervantes. You can come back tomorrow.” She tucked Ms. Beal into the bed.

As I left the room, the doctor spoke to me, “We will know more tomorrow. Come back then.”

I was feeling a little helpless as I rode down in the lift. The doors opened in the lobby, and I was about to stride quickly out when I heard a woman call my name—the name I was born with.

“Mattie Brown—is that you?”

I considered just ignoring this person and running away, but then I looked up. She was right in front of me. It was Maggie Browling. In high school, her name was always called just before mine. We even had a thing—if you can call what happened between us a thing.

A GIRLFRIEND?

The last year of high school was generally not memorable. Not much happened. I had finally gotten an adequate understanding of the social thing. Everyone left me alone for the most part. At the end of the previous year, I was put in a situation where I had to defend myself. A gang of grade-10 children decided they would make a name for themselves. They were not students from my school, or they would have known better. An after-school basketball game had just ended. I had spent the last hour sitting quietly in the cafeteria exploring the canvas. I was on my way out when this group of thugs decided I was the perfect target to take out their frustrations of losing the ball game. I was walking down the steps at the front of the school when they surrounded me. At first, I was just pushed like a pinball from person to person. I did not react. I simply thought they would get bored and leave me be. That was not to be the case. My lack of reaction seemed to anger them. They pushed me harder and started to punch me in my torso and arms. I decided that it must end, so I tried to break out of the circle. That seemed to enrage them. They began to call me names and chant, "Hit the dummy. He is trying to get away. Punch him in his stupid face. Let's fuck him up." There were other epithets, but you get the idea.

The first kid who swung his fist at my face paid the price. I think I broke his elbow. My training kicked in. I grabbed his arm at the elbow, pushed it past me, and slammed his forearm in the opposite direction. I heard a crack. He screamed. I stomped on the foot of the kid behind me. I raised both my arms, so my hands were in front of my chest and my elbows were level with my shoulders. I slammed my elbows into the noses of the kids on either side of me. That opened a hole in the circle, and I stepped backward. The kid right in front of me screamed, "You fucker!" He ran right at me in an effort to tackle me. I stepped aside, stuck out my foot, and pushed him in the center of his back. He stumbled forward and fell on his face. I attempted to extricate myself from the situation and leave them to wallow in their anger and their pain. As I walked away, I heard one of them running up behind me. I quickly turned and calmly stared at him. He suddenly stopped. I assumed this was a case of "discretion being a better part of valor." I heard him mutter, "Shit," as he walked back to his buddies.

I walked down the sidewalk. I was heading home. As is my wont, I pushed the altercation aside and considered my next meeting with the canvas. That is when it happened. Maggie Browling ran up to me. She was in most of my classes. We were lab partners in chemistry class. She stopped right in front of me and smiled and said, "That was fantastic." She did something that I still think about. She threw her arms around my neck and kissed me full on the mouth. It started as a friendly peck but soon became a wet tongue-filled face suck. I started out as a passive observer until she bit my lip. At that point, something else happened in a different part of my body and I kissed her back. She moaned and pressed herself to me and kissed harder. We stayed like that until a girl walked by and whispered, "Jeez, guys, get a room."

We broke our embrace and Maggie started talking. She was one of those girls who figured that all silent moments were an affront to nature and took it upon themselves to fill them whenever they occurred.

"I just loved that move you made with your elbows," she said as she mimicked me by raising her arms and rocking her elbows into the faces of some imaginary combatants. "Those little shits needed to be taken down a peg or two. You should have seen them at the game. They were throwing stuff at our bench and being massive jerks." She looked up at me. I was moving my tongue over the area where she had nipped me with her teeth. "Did I hurt you? I am sorry. I like kissing and sometimes I get carried away. Here, let me kiss it better." She slid her hand behind my neck and pulled me to her. She kissed me again, but not as aggressively as before. She looked into my eyes. "Do you like me?" At the time, I was awash with strange and unfamiliar feelings. It was the first time that something overwhelmed my usual need to get back to the canvas. I nodded my head. "Is that a yes?" she asked and grinned at me. I nodded again. "Do you want to hang out together—you know—and do stuff? Fun stuff."

I had no idea what *fun stuff* entailed, but a big part of me wanted to find out. "Yes," I hoarsely whispered.

"Great." She grabbed my arm with both her hands. "Walk me home."

I simply nodded. We lived only a few blocks from each other, and I was on my way home. I walked in silence, and she babbled about everything that happened to her that week. I don't think I heard a single thing she said. My body was reacting in ways I had never experienced before. Once I got home, I was sure that I really wanted to do the *fun stuff* that Maggie wanted to do with me.

Now here she was—right in front of me, calling my name. My mind darted from the past to the present to Proofrock's overwhelming question. As I recall, his was something about peaches. Mine consisted of staying or running off in a panic or pretending I was not the Mattie Brown she remembered. I did none of those things.

"What are you doing here?" she asked and stepped right up to me and hugged me.

I surprised myself and hugged her back. I knew I did not need to speak. She would cover all those bases. I did respond with the obvious, "Maggie, what are you doing here?"

"I work here." She tugged at her green scrubs. "I'm a nurse. God, it has been forever since I last saw you. What have you been doing with yourself? I am heading out to get some lunch. I have been here since four this morning. Would you like to join me? There is a little place just down the block. I never eat in the cafeteria. They tried to poison me once, so I stopped going. Have you had lunch? It will be more like breakfast for me." She paused. Not because she ran out of things to say, but because she needed to take a breath.

I nodded. She grabbed my arm with both her hands and led me out. As we walked, she chatted, and I nodded, and I noticed my body start to react to the memories of all the *fun stuff* we did together before she moved away with her parents. Don't get me wrong—we were never boyfriend and girlfriend. We just used each other to explore what sex was all about. We were—to use modern vernacular: *friends with benefits.* It was one of the few times in my life when the canvas took the backseat to my thoughts and activities.

We sat in a booth in a hole-in-the-wall café. She ordered her breakfast while I sipped water. She reached out and held my hands. "So, get me up to date. Are you with anyone?" Maggie was always direct. I liked that about her. All of her intentions were clear. Our interactions held no subterfuge. She waited for my answer, as if the future direction of our conversation depended on it.

I looked at her. I was deciding whether to tell her I had to go or stay and become involved with her. There were no other options—at least none that I could see.

"I am not seeing anyone?"

"Good." She paused. "Neither am I, at least not since last month." A grin filled her face and her eyes sparkled.

I had a pretty good idea what that meant. Once again, thoughts of escape filled my head. Then she did it again. She gave no indication, and I was just as surprised as the first time she did it a dozen years before. She lifted herself off her seat, slid her hand behind my head, and kissed me on the mouth. She sat back down.

"I hope you did not mind that. I just wanted to see if it felt the same as it used to." My emotional roiling was starting to settle. I decided to go with it and see where it might lead. I also realized that it might be an asset to have a friend who worked in the hospital. Her food arrived, and she started to eat and talk. I settled into my old habit of letting her lead and doing whatever she wanted me to. "So, tell me what you have been up to for the last dozen years." I shrugged. "The same old Mattie. Do you still do that weird thing where your eyes roll back in your head and you disappear?" I shrugged again, but his time I had a wisp of a smile on my face. She caught it. "Ok. I will shut up. Tell me everything."

I decided it was time. I had never shared my new life with anyone other than my mother, and she didn't count. I looked at her for a moment. She waved her hands in front of her in a *'get to it'* motion. I started, "I think we should get together, and I will tell you about my life and you can tell me about yours. When is a good time for you?"

A huge smile filled her face. "I love that idea. I have three days off coming up. Let's get together on the weekend."

I decided to act more like my new persona and took control. "What is your number? I will call you. Right now, I have to go."

"Tell me yours and I will tell you mine," she said and grinned. She took out her phone, and I told her the number of the mobile I used for common household requirements. "Where is your phone?" I shrugged. "Ok then. Shall I write it down? No. You must still have that perfect memory." She told me her number. "You are not trying to blow me off, are you?"

"I would never do that. I will call you soon." I stood and touched her on the shoulder and headed out of the café.

ALTERCATIONS

THE next day, I was back at the hospital. I pushed all thoughts of Maggie aside. I made sure I did not run into her at the hospital. I needed to separate work from play. I did not have a lot of practice at that because, for me, they were the same thing. With Maggie back in the picture, they were no longer.

I approached the door to Beal's room. She was sitting up in bed, staring at the door. The moment she saw me, she called out, "Cervantes, it is about bloody time."

"They would not let me in any earlier. How are you feeling today?"

"Never mind that. Tell me again what happened."

I walked to her and sat in the chair beside her bed. "Well, you arrived at my office, paid me my fee, and took the watch. After a few niceties, you left. I saw you get into what looked like an Uber. Then you tried to get out of the Uber, but someone grabbed you from the inside while another man got out and shoved you back in. Then the car sped off."

Sandra Beal listened and at the mention of the man pulling her into the car, she rubbed her wrist. It was covered in bruises. "I think I remember more than yesterday." She touched her jaw. "I think that man punched me here." She touched her jaw. "I must have blacked out. I don't remember anything more after that." She furrowed her brows. "The watch is gone then." It was more of a question than a statement.

"If you no longer have it, then it would be logical that they took it. This brings me to the reason I am here. You asked me to find the watch. The reasons you gave were of an emotional nature. I questioned them at the time, but it was my job to find the watch, not question the reasons why you wanted it. Now that I have been visited by the police and am considered a suspect, I feel it is incumbent upon me to get to the reasons why someone is willing to assault you to get the watch." I paused and looked at her face. I suspected she was about to reveal something, so I decided to give her a nudge. "Who was the man living with you in your apartment in San Fran?" Her eyes widened. "I noticed a man's toiletries in your bathroom. You said you were living alone. I am curious why you lied."

"You are quite the detective, Cervantes. I don't appreciate you going around detecting things you were not hired to detect," she spat.

I decided to go on offense. I was going to take a chance, but I was pretty sure I was right. "And I don't appreciate you getting someone to follow me."

"What are you talking about?"

"His name was Kruger, if I remember correctly. The last time I saw him, he was floating in the Shannon River with a bullet in his head."

"Harry is dead?"

"So, you do know Harold W Kruger. Why did you send him after me?"

"After you? What are you talking about? Harry's dead." I could see that the information was new to her and was slowly sinking in. A tear ran down her cheek.

I still felt that the best path to the information I wanted was to be brutal. "Yes, he is dead. Now, why did you send him after me?"

"Harry was my friend, and I didn't send him after you. I did show him your card and told him what I had hired you to find."

"So, he decided to follow me to Ireland because you wanted to find a memento of your grandfather. I don't buy it. I think it is time you leveled with me. Tell me the real reason you want to find the watch and maybe I can help you."

She nodded her head. The tears were flowing. "I can't talk here. They are releasing me this morning, if I wish. I need to get a flight back to San Francisco, but the attackers took my phone, cards, and money as well as the pocket watch."

"I guess they were trying to make it look like a simple robbery. Come with me to my office. I will get you organized and a flight home. In return, I want you to tell me the whole story. Is it a deal?"

"It is a deal, Mr. Cervantes. Give me a few minutes to get dressed. I need to check out of here."

"I will wait for you in the hallway." I stepped out of the room and closed the door behind me. I stood leaning on the wall. It was an opportunity to check out the canvas. I slipped on my sunglasses and conjured the canvas. It burst open below me and I soared and dove for pure exhilaration. The mental freedom I felt after having been away from this place for some time excited me. I was not really looking, I was just experiencing. There was a flood of fulfillment as the colors and sounds and feelings swelled inside of me. I was home. I was without purpose. I felt like the *dapple-dawn-drawn Falcon.* If you get a chance, have a read of Hopkins' poem "The Windhover." That will give you a good idea of what it felt like. I heard a voice from the other side.

"… sir. Can I help you, sir?"

The canvas collapsed. I removed my sunglasses and looked at a young woman in scrubs. I smiled. I did not feel like smiling, for she had just interrupted an exhilarating moment, but I smiled. It might not have been an honest smile, but it did get the job done. It disarmed her. She smiled back. "I am just waiting for Ms. Beal. I believe she is getting dressed."

"I will check on her," she said and was about to turn around when three men strode up to the door. Two of them stood on either side, and the third man opened the door and went inside. The men standing guard displayed arm tattoos of various swirls and blurred images. They both had a tattoo of a snake with exposed fangs sunk into their earlobes. The nurse looked up at the guards and stepped forward to open the door. One of the men stepped in front of her and folded his arms across his chest. "Excuse me. I need to attend to this patient." The man did not move. He seemed to be looking out into space. "Sir—would you please move." There was no response. The nurse took out a small radio from her pocket. She spoke into it. "Security to room 406. Two men are blocking a patient room." She stepped back and waited.

I guessed that security would arrive too late, and I wanted to ensure the safety of Beal. I also wanted to know who these men were and what they wanted. I glanced around. There was a cart a few feet away. It held various items. The lower shelf held a stack of stainless-steel bedpans. I picked up one in each hand and stepped in front of the men. They looked at me as if I was an insect that they could swat away. They were mistaken.

I held up the bedpans to shoulder height with arms outstretched to the side. "Gentlemen—the lady asked you to move. Now I am asking you. Please move away from the door." The men did not respond. I quickly crouched down and swung the steel bedpans at the outer knees of the guards. There were simultaneous cracks and the men bent over, their hands reaching for the struck knee, each about to cry out in pain. At the same time, I swung the bedpans on a backswing and caught each man just above the temple. They both fell almost silently to the ground.

"Jesus fuck," whispered the nurse.

I used my foot to push one of the unconscious men aside and stepped up to the door. I listened. I heard Beal's frightened voice. "Whatever it is you want, I do not have it." She screamed.

I pushed open the door. The third man was standing over Beal. She was half-dressed, sitting on the edge of the bed. Her blouse was unbuttoned. He held her by the hair and the business end of his knife was hooked on the strap of her bra between her breasts. There was a drop of blood where it had nicked her skin. When he saw me, he turned with a surprised look. I assumed he was wondering how I had gotten past his guards without making any sound. I tapped the two bedpans together rhythmically and smiled. "It is time for you to leave," I said and continued to tap the bedpans together. The rhythm was gone. And the clanging volume increased. He looked at me holding two bedpans and then at the knife he now held out in front of him. It was pointed menacingly at my face. I was holding the sharp edge of each bedpan. I flipped them up and grabbed them so that the sharp edge was facing my opponent. I banged the bottoms together. The man laughed. "This is a first. Some dude brings a bedpan to a knife fight." He swept the air with the knife. I slowly crossed the two bedpans over my chest so the sharp edges in the front section were facing each other. He feinted a jab with the knife. I simply moved the bedpans farther apart. This would allow me to exert more force on my backhand swing. "You are a fucking idiot," he said and jabbed the knife toward my neck. I slammed the two sharp edges of the bedpans together, catching his knife hand between them. The realization of what was happening only dawned after it was too late. The sharp edges of the steel bedpans cut into his forearm and wrist. The knife dropped from his grip into one of the bedpans. Had I not turned the bed-pans ninety degrees as they swung past, I might have cut right through the bone. As it was, I cut deeply into his arm. The veins on his wrist side were pumping blood.

Security arrived at that moment. They assumed I was the reason for the call and headed in my direction, but the nurse shouted and pointed, "Not him. Them."

It took another hour to deal with the aftermath. Police were called. Both Beal and I kept our story simple. I was there to help her get back home and the men, obviously confused, had mistaken Beal for someone else. I had simply protected her. They took the men away and told us not to leave town. Beal protested. They wished to interview us the following day. I told her I would put her up in a hotel under an assumed name and would pick her up the following day. She was shaking with fear that some men would return. I finally agreed to put her up at my apartment. I knew I had a spare bedroom. Though I could not remember ever going inside it, I was sure I had ordered a queen bed.

I reflected on the snake tattoo on the attackers. I would use that to identify them. I suspected they were the hired help.

PROBING FOR INFORMATION

We entered my apartment through the lane entrance. I concealed the fact that I had to stick out my tongue to get access. Sandra, as we agreed I would address her, settled in the spare room. In my mind, I would always refer to her as Beal. A first name was reserved for a different kind of relationship. She slept most of the afternoon. I ordered takeout from the deli for supper, after which we sat in my living area. She seemed nervous in anticipation of my questions. I decided to start with some of my suppositions. If I got something wrong, she would point that out to me and hopefully volunteer the correct information. It was a good technique to ease someone to the truth.

We were sitting opposite each other drinking some lemon tea. "So, Sandra, I would like you to start from the beginning. Tell me everything about how you discovered that the pocket watch held clues to a secret and who you shared this information with. Maybe then we can figure out who is after you and what they want." She stared at me. I could see she was trying to make a decision.

"How do I know you are not one of those people hunting me while in the guise of the white knight?"

"I guess you don't, but remember, you came to me, not the other way around."

"You got the pocket watch for me, and I lost it again. Do you think you can get it back?"

"Maybe, but I do not see the point unless the watch has a purpose beyond telling time or as a memento."

'You are rather astute, Mr. Cervantes." She sipped her tea. "Well..."

"Please start at the beginning, Ms. Beal."

She wiggled back and forth in her seat. "Guess I need to trust you. Are you trustworthy, Mr. Cervantes?"

"Trust is a two-way street. I am deciding if I can trust you to tell me the truth—the complete truth without leaving anything out. If I feel I am being lied to or used, I will no longer be of any use to you."

"Alright. It starts with my grandmother. She is dead now. She gave my mother a letter from my grandfather. It was the last letter he ever sent. My mother kept it because my grandmother told her it was the first clue to a great treasure. Mr. Cervantes, I have read the letter. It did not say anything about a treasure."

"What did the letter say?"

"Well, it has been a while since I read it. I remember generally but nothing specific. He talked about missing my grandmother and my mother and how much he loved them. I do remember him saying that he could not disclose his location or anything about the war. Now that I think about it, the letter itself was odd."

"How so?"

"Well, there were several gibberish words crossed out."

"Perhaps he did not write it."

"No. My mother told me that Gran was sure it was from my grandfather."

"And it was damaged by the flood?"

"I am afraid so. My mother kept it in my grandfather's footlocker along with the other letters and some stuff that was returned to her after the war. She showed me all of his effects contained in the footlocker."

"Why did your grandmother say it was a clue to a great treasure?"

"I don't know. I assume there were other letters from my grandfather telling her about it. I think they had a special code, so anyone reading his letters would not be able to understand them. My mother believed there was something to the treasure thing but was unable to decode anything from the letters. My grandmother died before she passed down that information. She did tell my mother that she should look for his pocket watch, for it contained the clue to the location of the treasure."

"Do you have any indication of the nature of the treasure?"

"No. My friend, Harry, took the damaged letters to see if he could have the papers restored. On a whim, I decided to hire you to find the pocket watch." She sniffed. "Now Harry is dead." She looked up at me. "Do you think he found out something from the papers?

"I don't know, but he decided to follow me. Why would he do that if he did not find anything in the restored papers?"

She shrugged. "Harry and I were good friends. I can't believe he would cheat me."

I shrugged as well. "In my experience, the level of trust one can expect is inversely proportional to the size of the treasure. I don't mean to disparage your friend, but…" She started to weep. I stood and collected some tissues and handed them to her. "Do you know where Harry took the contents of the footlocker to be restored? That is a very sophisticated process and only an expert would be able to succeed without destroying the originals."

"I have no idea."

"Did Harry live with you?"

She nodded. "Yes. We were friends. No, more than that. I guess you could say we were sometime lovers. *Friends with benefits* is the modern phrase."

I could see her face flush as she admitted that she was Kruger's lover. "Did he use your address as his place of residence?"

"There is nothing wrong with that," she quickly retorted.

"You misunderstand. I am not interested in your relationship with him. I was just trying to determine if his mail was sent to your address. Restoration is an expensive process. If he used a credit card, we might be able to determine who he used. That might help solve the case." My thoughts went elsewhere, for it just might point to whoever was behind the attacks and the people who stole the pocket watch. There might have been a whole series of clues to the watch. My supposition, that the man and the woman I encountered in Ireland had followed me, might be wrong. They may have gotten that information from the restored material and went hunting for the watch themselves and tried to ensure I did not find it first. Harry must have gotten in the way, and they decided not to share. But who were they? I was sure that the restoration people would lead me to answer that question.

I stood up. "Can you find a way to have any of his new mail that arrived at your house as well as any he may have opened in the last month or so couriered to my address?"

"My neighbor could do that. Perhaps I should just go home and do it myself."

"Not a good idea, at least not until we figure out who we are dealing with. They obviously have no compunction in resorting to violence. They think you know far more than you actually do, and that puts you in grave danger. You will need to stay here. This place is very secure. I suggest you get a replacement ID, credit cards, some cash, and a new phone. Going home is really out of the question."

"Yes. Thank you, Mr. Cervantes. I don't feel very well. Do you mind if I have a nap?"

"Make yourself at home." I watched as she stood. She reached out for the arm of the chair to maintain her balance. She walked to her room. I settled down in my recliner and closed my eyes. The canvas opened up. I found my kestrel self sitting on a branch of a small dead tree overlooking a field. The landscape was desolate. It was raining. The ground was pitted with what looked like mud-filled craters that were slowly filling with water. Nothing living was anywhere in the desolation. The only motion was on the surface of the water-filled craters where the raindrops hit and the tiny wave interference patterns made the surface dance. The intensity of the rain increased and the sound from the torrent became an unbearable noise. I was being pelted. I leaped skyward in an attempt to escape. As I rose up, I could see the crater-filled landscape swell outward and overtake everything in its path. The higher I flew, the farther the desolation traveled, the harder the rain fell, and the louder the pounding of water became. I had to leave the canvas or be overwhelmed. The one thing I noticed before sitting up in my chair was the fact that I was always at the center of the desolation.

I reflected on my experience. I glanced at the clock and realized that many hours had passed. That was another anomaly. The flow of time was usually equal in and out of the canvas. This time, it definitely was not. Many hours had passed in the real world while it seemed as if I was immersed in the canvas for only a few minutes.

I was breathing as if I had just exerted myself. My pulse was above normal. I relaxed and reflected. What had just happened? The canvas had never displayed itself like this. It had always been a pleasant experience. I'll admit it was sometimes very cryptic, especially when it tried to tell me something. Not only was this last experience cryptic, it was dangerous. The fact that I was at the center and the more of it I observed, the larger it became, made it even more ominous.

The obvious answer was that I was being warned. Something serious was about to happen and I was at the center.

TRUST

I sat in my chair. I was restraining myself from falling back into the canvas. I knew I was addicted to it, but that had never mattered. It was like being addicted to water. It was a part of you. If you were thirsty, you drank. I was thirsty for the canvas, but my past experiences told me that too much of a thing, even if that thing was a part of you, could be dangerous.

I was sure that Beal would want to get Harry's body back to the States. I set my assistant, Billie, to that task. I knew it would take a while, given that he was murdered. I even expected the Irish police to contact me. I had disappeared, and that was suspicious behavior in the mind of any detective. I directed my assistant to contact them and apologize for not contacting them before I left. I hoped that would ease their suspicions. I did not want to go back, but I also did not want to make myself *persona non grata* in Ireland and probably all of Europe.

I also knew that it might be time to come clean with Beal regarding the microdot I found in the watch. Before I did, I needed to ensure she was what she purported to be. I emailed Billie and asked her to dig into Ms. Sandra Beal of San Francisco. I wanted her family tree to see if there was another member of her family who might also be interested in the pocket watch. I wanted the information before morning, so I gave Billie the go-ahead to use whatever services she might require.

I tilted back my lounge chair and, as I fell asleep, I reflected on my old self-defense teacher, Fritz. Waffen Zer Hand was his method of self-defense. He had taught me well. My use of bedpans earlier in the day would have made him proud. The mental stress was more tiring than the physical actions. Those actions made me smile.

I was awakened by my email alarm. It only signaled a critical message. I assumed that Billie had found something interesting about Beal. I opened the mail. It was from Billie, but it was not an answer to what I had requested. When I first started my detective company, it was recommended that I pay for a Search Flag Service. The internet is a good place to find information about other people but that is a two-way street. If someone is looking for me online, there are many traps that give out false information while, at the same time, blocking real information. I am also, through Billie, sent alarms. If possible, those alarms will tell me who was looking and what they were looking for. In this case, I got the 'what' but not the 'who.' Someone was doing an in-depth search on me. My service gave me a list of the false information they had sent out. Much of that information was deliberately perplexing, for one fake source would say one thing and another would say the opposite. Any real information was obscured in all the falsehoods. It only took money to get the false information sources to the top of a search list. It was an effective method of staying somewhat hidden. It was not a perfect system.

I started to make coffee. I was a bit of a connoisseur. I had several expensive machines, but I chose a simple process and made a pot of rich dark roast Americano. The smell filled the kitchen. I walked to the spare bedroom door and knocked. There was no response. I knocked and called, "Sandra. I have made coffee." There was no response. It suddenly occurred to me that she might have left. I did not have any alarms that would indicate someone leaving my building. After all, I had never had a house guest before. There was never a reason to check if someone had left.

I tried the door. It was not locked. I called her name and slowly opened the door. There was no one inside, and the bed was neatly made. Sandra Beal was nowhere to be found. I ran to my security monitors and watched the tapes. It showed her exiting the lane entrance thirty minutes earlier. I banged my fist down on the desk. It was not like me to react like that, but I felt, at that moment, betrayed. Where was she going? What had she not told me? I sat back to think. I was about to call up the canvas when I glanced up at the bank of surveillance monitors. There was Sandra with a bag in her hand. She was knocking on the lane door. I could hear nothing, as that door was soundproof. I did breathe a sigh of relief as I went to the door and let her in.

"I got us some coffee and a couple of Danish. I let you sleep. I hope I did not take your bed."

"No. I just fell asleep in the chair. It is very comfortable. You should have woken me. That door is soundproof. Had I not seen you on the monitor, you might still be pounding on the door." I turned and called casually over my shoulder, "I thought you might have run away."

"I considered that. I was going to write you a note, but I didn't have paper or a pencil. I made the bed. I figured a detective like yourself would figure I was coming back, otherwise why had I made the bed?" She grinned at him and then winced. The cut at the corner of her mouth cracked.

"Please don't go out again without me. Those people know where I live. They have been here before." Her eyes widened. "Don't worry. This building is like Fort Knox. You would need a bazooka to get in here, but out there alone, they could grab you. Who knows what they might do to you?

"I don't understand. They took the watch. I assume that is what they wanted. It must contain some clue to my grandfather's treasure. Why would they want me?"

I decided to play dumb. I was still not ready to tell her about the microdot for reasons that had nothing to do with anything but her safety. If she knew about it, she would be in more danger than she already was. I was also very suspicious of her motives in obtaining the pocket watch in the first place.

I led her to my kitchen, and we drank coffee and ate the Danish. I let her indulge in small talk while I nodded and listened. I wanted her to be as open with me as possible. When I got the information back from Billie, it would, hopefully, confirm she was being truthful.

We called an Uber to pick us up at the lane entrance. We were as cautious as possible. We bought her some clothes and a phone and visited her bank. I vouched for her identity. I hoped that would be enough. If it wasn't, I had other connections that the bank would have to accept as valid.

Things worked out as I planned. She canceled all credit cards and got new ones. I assumed she was not short of funds, given her ability to pay me. We returned to my building and settled inside.

Using her new phone, Sandra called her friend to ask her to courier all of Harry Kruger's correspondence. I listened to the end of the conversation.

"Mary, have you found the key yet? Good. Go in and gather up all of Harry's mail. He used one of the desk drawers in the office. Yes. The second down on the left. Gather all the papers you find in that drawer and any other new mail that may have arrived. He keeps a small laptop in that drawer, too. Yes. Package it up and send it to..." She paused and turned to me. "Your address?" I quickly wrote down my office address and handed the paper to her. She read it off to her friend. "Call me when it is on its way. Yes. Send it high priority. It should get here by tomorrow afternoon. Thanks, Mary. I owe you one." She listened to Mary. "I will tell you all about it when I get home. Must run. Bye."

"That is great. I hope we can find something from the papers. The restoration company's name would give us a place to start. I need to do some work in my office. Do you have anything to do? There is a collection of books in there," I said and pointed to the room off the kitchen. It is just a reading room. There are no windows, but I had it designed, so it appears like you are sitting in a spring meadow on a warm, sunny day. It is very conducive to relaxed reading."

"I will keep busy."

"Please don't leave and help yourself to whatever you want. The refrigerator is stocked," I said. I did not tell her that I had locked all the exits, so she couldn't even if she wanted to. "I will be in here if you need anything. Just knock. I will see you in the morning." She nodded, and I stepped into my office-cum-laboratory. I needed to review the information sent by Billie. There were notes on Ms. Sandra T. Beal, Harry Kruger, and the snake tattoo.

According to Billie, Sandra Beal was exactly who she appeared to be. She had never married but lived with a few men over the years. Harry Kruger was the latest. She was a retired teacher and had a meager pension, but she also had a rather large investment account she had inherited from her second common-law relationship. He had died of a heart attack ten years previous. There were no red flags that might suggest she was in any way involved with a criminal element. She was exactly who she appeared to be.

Harry, on the other hand, had been involved in several petty criminal activities over the years. Most of these involved gambling debts. Recently, he had changed his ways. Beal had paid his last series of debts and he had been on the straight and narrow ever since.

She must have told Kruger about a possible treasure, the clue in the watch, and her decision to hire someone to look for it. Her mother was not in any condition to have asked her to do anything. It appeared she was afflicted with dementia and was not long for this world. Kruger must have figured he could find it on his own. I assumed he had not told Beal he was going to look for it. When he found out she had hired me, he decided to follow me in case I beat him to it. Somehow, he ended up dead. He may have shared the information discovered from the letters with someone else.

The snake tattoo thugs had a very colorful past. I read through their history. It was a litany of gang crimes, including drugs, prostitution, and theft. There was more, but it did not improve my understanding of who they were. Their latest activities were in the area of *hired help*. They provided a service that was always unlawful and usually involved force. Someone had hired them, but Billie was unable to discover who.

The final collection of information was enlightening but very frightening. Someone had hired a hacker who was trying to get information on me, my business, and my home. They were looking for the architectural plans for my building. I knew those were not available. I was given the only copy, and it was in my safe. The hacker was trying to open my firewall and get into my computer system. I had hired the best to design and maintain it, but I was not naïve enough to think it was invulnerable. According to Billie, they had not been successful, and now that she knew they were attempting, she would stay ahead of their attempts. Billie's resources were considerable. It was unlikely they would ever be successful.

There was a thank-you note from a client. They had retrieved the emerald ring from the Persephone Players. They were able to trace its path from the original theft. The owner had inherited it and considered it to be costume jewelry.

The final piece was a collection of potential clients wanting to hire me to find a myriad of items. I considered choosing one to focus on rather than this microdot business. I knew I couldn't. The present puzzle was just too enticing.

In the morning my security system beeped. I looked up at a monitor and saw a package being dropped into my mail slot. Someone had been extremely efficient. The package of Kruger's correspondence had arrived.

I slipped into the front office through the washroom passage and retrieved it.

WILL THE REAL HARRY KRUGER PLEASE STAND UP?

I exited my front office and spread out all the material that was couriered from San Francisco on my kitchen table. Sandra heard me and came in and sat down. I smiled at her. "You can help me look through this. I know Harry was your friend, so if you would rather not, I will understand."

"No, I will help," she said and continued, "I do need to go back to San Francisco. I know it is a risk. My friend Mary will let me stay with her as long as this is going on." She swept her hands over the papers in front of both of them. I nodded. She had made up her mind. I was more than good with it. Having a house guest was difficult for me. "I have made arrangements and I have a flight at 6:00 p.m."

"I will provide protection to and from the airport. I have people on contingency." We both turned to the task in front of us. We focused on Harry's credit card statements and soon discovered a series of payments to a restoration company called "Perfect Paper." I opened the laptop and turned it on. The battery was low, but Sandra's friend was smart enough to include the power supply. I plugged it in. The login page appeared. I looked at Sandra.

She shrugged and then said, "Try 'iquit' all one word." I typed it in. It was rejected along with the message, *'Two more tries remain.'*

"I will send this to one of my specialist techs. They will be able to open it. The information it contains might be very valuable. You told me that Harry took the papers and the footlocker. If he sent the papers to the "Perfect Paper" company to be restored, what did he do with the footlocker? Do you know where he might have put it?"

"I never thought of that. He must have put it in his storage locker. He keeps one with some furniture that would not fit in my apartment. I have no idea where it is or where he keeps the key. He must have taken it with him when he followed you."

My thoughts went to Harry being pulled from the Shannon River. I had searched his pockets and there was no key. Perhaps he left it in his effects. I knew that his personal effects would not be returned until after the murder investigation was completed. I knew that I wanted to search the footlocker. It might hold a clue to what the microdot was trying to tell me. I turned to the papers spread out before me. "Storage locker companies send out bills. There must be an old one here somewhere." I looked up at Sandra. She was waving an envelope. I snatched it from her and removed the contents. I smiled. I now had the name and address of the company and the number of the locker. "Do you want company on your trip back to San Francisco? I am coming with you. If we want to find this elusive treasure your grandfather hid, I am sure the locker holds the clues we need. I would like to visit the restoration company as well. Pack your things. We can eat at the airport. I have to make some arrangements."

Beal smiled and touched my hand. "Thanks."

I knew we would get there late, so I decided to check into a hotel with Beal. I called Billie. She could organize this little trip far faster than I could. I wanted a plane ticket on the same flight as Beal. I wanted hotel reservations, and I wanted her to send someone to pick up Kruger's laptop from the lockbox in my office. She was to send the pertinent files to me once the computer was hacked. I also wanted something I very seldom needed. I wanted a gun—a Beretta BU 9 Nano was my pistol of choice. It was small and powerful enough to deter any attacker. She assured me it would be delivered to me at my hotel in San Francisco. The gun was to ensure I could protect Beal as well as myself if the need arose.

Thirty minutes later, we were on our way to LAX. Flight time was under two hours. The six o'clock flight would get us there a little after eight. We would stay at the hotel for the night, and I would drop Beal off at her friend's place in the morning. Then I would begin some real sleuthing. I knew I would check out the canvas in the quiet of my hotel room. I hoped

I would not see a desolate landscape once again.

All seemed to be going as planned. The flight was relaxing, mainly because we were not seated in the same row. The flight was not long enough to indulge in the canvas, even though the urge was strong. Once we were in our hotel, I heard a knock on my door. We had adjoining rooms and had agreed on a *knock pause knock knock* pattern on the door that separated us. This knock came on my room door. I stepped up and peered through the fisheye lens in the door. A man was standing a meter from the door with his hands up in front of him. There was a package in his left hand. It was my gun. I opened the door, glanced both ways, took the package, thanked the man, and closed the door.

I opened the package. It contained the Beretta in a small holster that would fit neatly on my hip. I checked the load and put the gun in my duffle bag. I ordered some room service and ate in the silence of my thoughts. I lay on the bed and let the canvas envelop me.

I was flying high above a landscape that looked nothing like anything I had ever seen before. The landscape below me was covered with sharp-edged objects of various sizes and colors. It was as if some giant had cleaved rocks into geometric shapes, painted them, and then discarded the regular ones. I landed on what looked like a misshaped octahedron lying on its side. I looked around me and realized that all the shapes strewn about the landscape were misshapen octahedrons. I was used to a normal kind of landscape. This one was very odd. I knew it was trying to tell me something. I was irritated at the obtuseness. I flew up and circled. The higher I flew, the less random the pattern below me became. The entire layout was center-orientated. I flew above the center of this landscape of imperfect geometric forms. There was something shiny there. I circled lower. Then it became obvious. The purpose of the entire landscape was to focus on the one object in the middle. I thought of the giant again. He had been practicing for his creation of the perfect shape. Here it was. A perfectly clear octahedron sitting on a small hill as if it had been put on display.

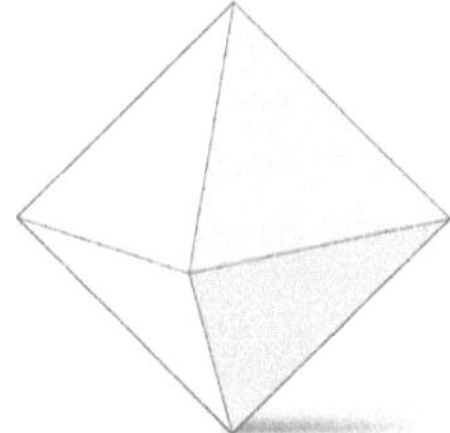

I heard a *knock pause knock knock* at the adjoining room door. The canvas faded. Sandra must want something. I went to the door. "Yes?" I asked.

"Open the door. I need to tell you something," said Beal. I opened the door. Beal rushed in. "I just talked to my friend, Mary. She called me. She lives in the apartment across the street. She said she was sitting looking out her front window when a man and a woman knocked on my door. When no one answered, they looked around to see if anyone had observed them. I left my porch light on. The man reached up and my porch light went out. He crouched down, and the woman stood in front of him. She was trying to conceal what he was doing. He must have picked the lock for the man stood up and they both went inside."

"When did this happen?"

"Just a few minutes ago. Mary just called and told me they were still inside. She could see flashes of light that she figured were from flashlights." She paused and gripped the door frame. She was shaking. "What are we going to do?"

"Call her back. Tell her to watch and see when they leave. I want to know if they are carrying anything with them."

"I don't have to. She is still on the line." She held up her phone.

"Please let me talk to her."

Beal handed me the phone. "Mary? This is Sandra's friend. Are you still looking out your window?" I paused. "Good. Make sure they cannot see you." I looked at the phone and switched on the speaker.

Mary responded, "I am in a dark room. They are still inside. Should I call the police?"

I shook my head, "Not yet, Mary. Can you describe them?"

"They were both quite tall. The man was skinny with dark hair and the woman was blonde. OH! They are coming out."

"Are they carrying anything?"

"I don't see anything in their hands. Wait. The woman has a case over her shoulder. I think it is Sandra's laptop. The bastards are stealing her computer. I am going to call the cops."

"Please don't do that, Mary."

Sandra Beal called out, "Do what he says, Mary. That computer doesn't even work anymore. I was going to get a new one, anyway. I get all my emails on my phone."

"Mary, thanks for the heads up. We will be by in the morning to check out the house." I handed the phone back to Beal. She smiled weakly and returned to her room. I closed the door behind her. Things were getting more and more ominous. This treasure must be much more valuable than I had anticipated. These people were getting increasingly determined. I knew that spelled danger. If she was the same woman I met in the watch repair shop in London, then she was very dangerous indeed.

A DIGRESSION: DRIVING LESSONS

I was in my early 20s when I learned to drive. My mother was insistent. She said that her son must learn this required skill for being an adult. All competent adults could drive and if I wanted to be competent, I would embrace the skill and take all the lessons. It was my mother's way or the highway. I had no idea what that meant until she explained away the literalness. I would learn to drive, or I would invoke her wrath. At the time, I lived in a basement apartment in her house. That was also one of my mother's plans to transform me into a competent adult. I was forced to cook at least one meal a day by myself. The rest of the time, I ate at her table. That is for some other chapter if I deem it necessary.

I know my mother was very afraid, much more than I was at the time, of her only son being viewed as being (horror of horrors) a dummy. This concern of hers was not really about me. It was about her. She was afraid my behaviors and predilections would reflect badly on her skill as a mother. In the end, I really did benefit. I can drive. In fact, I have all the license requirements of a professional driver.

My first lesson was pretty horrendous. I was not good at paying attention to things that were going on around me. I very nearly killed myself and the instructor. I stopped at a red light that was especially long. I decided to use the time to visit the canvas. I zoned. The light turned green. The instructor spoke to me. I heard him but there was something very cool happening right in front of me, so I ignored him. He shouted. Horns blared. He finally hit me on the shoulder. I turned to him. I was not used to being touched. I was angry. I shouted, "Why did you hit me? What do you want?" He stared at me with an aghast look on his face. I turned back to the task of driving. By this time, the green light had turned red again. I did not notice as I stepped on the gas.

There was a lot of honking and screeching of tires. Suffice it to say we both survived.

My mother hired a new instructor. He seemed to recognize my tendency to be easily distracted. He took me to a parking lot where I could make major mistakes without any consequences. We understood each other. I learned to drive. When I became a detective, I decided the ability to drive like a professional driver was a valuable skill. I took a lot more lessons.

HOME INVASION

WE needed a car. Leasing a car to do something clandestine was a tricky proposition. Any new rental car came stock with GPS. I was not sure of the reach of the people hunting the same treasure we were hunting, but I was not about to advertise where we were about to go. I was pretty sure that our pursuers didn't know about Kruger's storage unit, and I wanted to keep it that way. I texted Billie, and she was able to book a reliable car from a Rent-a-Wreck company. It was now parked in the hotel lot and the keys were at the desk. I decided we would go to Beal's home first, as it was the closer of the two.

We checked out of the hotel and picked up the keys. No fob, just ignition keys. Billie had ordered something compact and nondescript. Even the color was bland—a sun-faded gray. Following Beal's directions, I drove. The vehicle was not what I thought of as a responsive machine. It drove like a slug. Not that I have anything against slugs. They have their place. The real ones are very cool.

We pulled up in front of her home. It was part of a row house that held four units. The entire neighborhood consisted of these cute, well-maintained homes. She pointed across the street. "That is Mary's place. All the homes here are quad units. They are pretty much the same inside. Mine is this one." She pointed at number three. "I have to get my spare key from Mary. Won't be a second. I called her. She told me she was going out and would leave the key under the mat." A few minutes later, Beal was walking back with her key dangling from her hand. We walked up to the door. I looked at the lock. There were a few new scratches that were probably made by the lock picks used by the burglars. As Beal bent down to the lock, I caught some movement in the living room window. The curtain had shifted. I put my hand on her shoulder and reached out to my hip. I was about to pull the Baretta when the door swung open. A blonde woman stood in front of us with a gun pointed at my chest. It was the woman from the flight to Ireland and the watch repair shop in London.

"There is a silencer on this gun. I will shoot you and drag your dead ass inside if you try anything," she sneered at me. I could see a man approach from behind her. I raised my hands. "Put your hands down, you stupid fuck. You don't want any attention because I guarantee I will deal with it harshly." We both stepped inside. I glanced at Beal. Her eyes were as big as saucers. The woman backed up as we entered, while the man slipped behind us and closed the door. We were led into the kitchen at the back of the apartment. The curtain was closed, but one could see a tiny fenced-off backyard through a side window.

A woman was sitting at the kitchen table. She was secured to the chair. Beal rushed forward, almost in tears. "Mary! Are you ok?"

Mary nodded. She mouthed the words, "I'm sorry."

"Did these bastards hurt you?"

Beal was shoved to another chair by the tall man. The woman waved her gun. "Not yet, but that is always a possibility." She turned to the man. "Search him." The man approached me. I considered my options and decided that her gun trumped anything I could do at the moment, so I raised my hands. He patted me down and found the gun. "Her too," said the woman. We were both soon seated in our respective chairs.

Beal spoke, "Mary, what happened?"

"I put the key under the mat and was about to go to my spin class when this woman approached me and…"

She was cut off. The man slapped the back of her head. "Shut the fuck up." He turned to the woman holding the gun. "Let's get this over with."

"Be patient. I don't want to kill our only lead."

I spoke, "Lead to what?"

"You are the bastard who found the watch and screwed us around in London. I have something special in mind for you. We got the real watch from her after you had it for a couple of days. What did you find inside?" I shrugged. She walked up to me and grabbed my hair. She pulled my head back and stuck the gun barrel into one of my eyes. "There was supposed to be a clue inside to something. You must have removed it before giving it back to her." She pulled the gun from my face and pointed it at Beal. "Did you know that? You obviously wanted the watch for what was inside. We went through it with a high-power scope and found nothing unusual. We took it apart and inspected every cog and gear. Nothing. There was nothing." She moved the gun back to my face. "Where is it, Cervantes?"

I realized that they could not kill us until they got the answers they wanted. That put me in a position of power as long as they wanted something from me. "I have no idea what you are talking about. I found the watch in Ireland. In London, you assumed my pocket watch was the one you were looking for. I escaped your clutches and came back here. I completed my assignment for Ms. Beal here and gave her the watch she hired me to find." I paused and smiled at her. "By the way, how did you fare when you returned to the watch repair shop and found the London cops waiting for you?"

She looked up at the tall man. "Fuck him up a little," she sneered and stepped back.

As the man stepped toward me, I spoke. "Do you even know what you are looking for? I suspect you don't and therefore I assume you are working for someone else. He or she has obviously kept you in the dark." She raised her hand, and the man stopped.

"Are you telling me you know what is at the end of this rainbow?"

"I don't have any idea, but I do know that it must be incredibly valuable if someone is going to this extent to find it." I raised my eyebrows. "I think, perhaps, you and your friend here have come to the same conclusion. Are you still working for your client, or have you decided to do your own thing?"

"What are you suggesting?" asked the woman. She pulled out the last chair and sat in it backward with her gun barrel resting idly on top of the chair back.

Beal spoke to me, "Did you remove something from the watch before you returned it to me?"

I knew I had to do something very soon. I looked at the woman. I could see that she was feeling the weight of the gun with the mounted silencer. She had shifted it further forward on the chair back. It was still pointed at my chest. I glanced up at Beal. The tall man was behind her. I could not see a weapon in his hands. He was standing vigilant. I was running scenarios in my head like I was taught years before by Fritz. Events had sequences. First this, then that, unless this happens, then do that. The first step was critical. I had to get the gun out of her hand without having it discharged. The barrel stuck out so that the gun was balanced. If I flipped it up and it went off, no one would get hit by the bullet, but the grip would be much easier to hold on to as it would be forced back into her hand. She could quickly re-grip it and recover control. If I flipped it down and it fired, the bullet would hit the tiled floor and possibly ricochet, but the woman's ability to hold on to the gun would be severely compromised. The downward hit on the barrel would pull the gun out of her hand and into mine.

I decided on the latter. All I needed now was the slightest of distractions. Big distractions were often not good. They put people on guard. That was not what I needed. Mary supplied what I needed. She started to cry. The blonde woman turned to her and sneered, "Oh for fuck's sake, shut up or I will give you something to cry about." That slight turn of the head was all I needed. My hand darted out and swatted the silencer down. The gun came out of her hand. It flipped it in the air. I grabbed the grip, stood, and pointed it at the man behind Beal. He moved toward me, and I shot him in the foot. He collapsed and moaned in pain. Shooting someone in the foot is incredibly painful and debilitating but will not result in the kind of blood loss that a shot in the leg, or anywhere else, might incur. There were no large veins or arteries in the foot, just a lot of bones and nerves. I pointed the gun at the woman. She had turned and was about to run. Her actions gave me some insight into her relationship with the tall man. She was about to leave him and save herself. I ordered her to sit. She sat and stared at me.

"I should have shot you in London," she spat and lowered herself back into the chair.

It was at that moment I remembered a name they used in the London watch repair shop. Botox. Maybe he was an important direction of inquiry. I looked at the woman in the chair. Her defiance was palpable. I took out my phone and turned on the camera. I stood directly in front of her and aimed the phone camera and the silenced gun at her head. I watched her face. I took a course in microexpressions, but I wasn't very good at it, at the moment it was occurring. That is why I was taking a video of this woman. I would be able to study it later. "Who is..." I deliberately paused for effect. "Botox?"

She glanced up to the left and then scowled. "I have no idea, and get that fucking camera out of my face."

"Do you work for him, or does he work for you?" She did not respond. The tall man on the floor moaned. I continued, "Is he in the States or somewhere in Europe?"

"I told you; I have no idea."

"Why do you want whatever you think is in the watch?"

She smiled. "We want whatever you took from the watch before you returned it to Beal there." She looked at Beal. "You know he removed something from the watch. He wants it for himself." Beal glanced at me with a small measure of suspicion.

I decided to play along. "Ah, the treasure. What do you think the treasure is?"

She sat back in the chair. "I'm done," she said resolutely.

I shut off the camera and lowered the gun. It was obvious that she was not going to give me more information. I would study the video later.

"What are you going to do with us? If you call the cops, I am going to mess up your day." Her voice changed to a simpering tone. "Yes, officer. We were just bringing the Word of God to the neighborhood. When he opened the door, he pointed that gun at us and ordered us inside. Then, for no reason, he shot poor Walter." She sniffed, then returned to her normal voice. "How is that? Convincing."

I considered how to proceed with as little danger as possible now and in the future. I needed to get them locked up without involving us in any way.

WHAT TO DO? WHAT TO DO?

MY mind raced as to what I was going to do with my prisoners. Should I phone the police and have them arrested? That option was riddled with problems. As she pointed out, it could get messy. The police were nosey. They always wanted to take perps to court. I did not want to be called in to testify and be required to make this little treasure hunt public. That is, if they believed me. I might be the one that ended up in jail. Should I let them go? This option was inherently dangerous for obvious reasons. The woman would definitely return to haunt me. She might promise the moon, but that would just be a deception. I couldn't kill them. That is not my style. I don't like messes and that option was messy in several ways. I finally decided on an aggregate plan of freeing them and calling the police.

I spoke to Beal without taking my eyes off the woman. "Sandra, can you tie a good knot?"

"Of course. I was a Girl Scout. You want me to tie this bitch up?"

"Yes, I do. She is a weaselly one and I don't want to have to shoot her. Untie Mary there and use the ropes to tie her hands together." I turned to the woman who was sitting once again backward in the chair. "Put your hands together and hang them over the back of the chair." She responded. I could feel her searching for a path to escape. I walked behind the chair and poked the suppressed gun barrel to the back of her head. "I will not hesitate to shoot you if you decide to mess with me." I felt a shiver run up my spine. This was very cool detective work that was more than just looking for stuff people had lost and exploring the canvas. It was real.

Beal finished untying Mary. "Tie her hands together and loop the rope down the chair and tie the end to the rung at the front." I could see the satisfaction on Beal's face.

"Stick your hands out further, bitch," spat Beal. She tied the woman's wrists together tightly and then to the top rung of the chair. You could see the woman wince as the rope was cinched tight. Beal then looped the rope under the chair and tied the end to the front rung. "Hey, Cervantes, this is neat. If she tries to stand up, the chair will come with her." She grinned.

"Now check her pockets and put everything you find on the table. Then search him."

The man on the floor groaned. "I need a doctor."

I felt a rare cruel streak run through my mind. I glanced at his wounded foot. "You're not bleeding to death. A little bit of pain will help you understand the error of your ways."

"Fuck you," he half muttered under his breath.

Beal finished, and I looked at the collection of their personal items on the table. There were just a few items and some money. "Take the money and use it to clean up the mess once these two are gone." I turned to the man. "Where is your car?" I saw a glimmer of hope in his eyes.

The woman yelled out, "Don't you dare tell him anything!"

"Fuck you. You don't have any bullet holes in you, but I am in real pain. I need a hospital." He turned to me. "It is down the block." I indicated that I wanted more. He continued, "It is a black SUV."

"Surprise, surprise," I said and turned to Mary. "Mary, how are you feeling?"

"Ok," she said as she rubbed her wrists.

"Think you could go down the street and drive that SUV back here and park it in front of the house?"

"Sure." She grabbed the fob and headed out the front door.

I reached into my pocket and took out my phone. "Sandra, see those wallets?" I pointed to the table. Take out any of the IDs and credit cards and photograph them. Do both sides. Once you are done, return them and put them back in their pockets. I wouldn't want the police having difficulty identifying …" I paused and grinned, "…their bodies. And bring me their phones."

Beal did as I asked, and I slipped the phones into my jacket. I glanced at the pictures of their ID. The woman's name was Betty Bond. I laughed. "One would think if you are deciding on a fake name, you would come up with something better than that. How about 'Natasha Sokolova?' Well, Betty, I have decided to let both of you go."

"You're kidding," said Beal. I raised my hand to my lips. Beal stopped.

"I am keeping your phones, however. Now Sandra, untie her." I gestured at Betty Bond. Beal moved to untie the woman, and I placed the barrel of the gun to her temple. "Don't try anything." Just then, Mary came into the house. "Ok, Betty. Help your friend up and put him in the back seat." I picked up my gun that was on the table and clipped it to my belt. The two intruders limped to the door. Mary opened it and stepped back. The man moaned as he lifted his wounded foot. He limped forward and flopped down on the back seat. "Go around and get in the driver's seat," I said to the woman. As soon as she rounded the back of the SUV, I slipped her gun under the passenger seat. The man had closed his eyes and continued to moan. He did not notice. Once they were both ensconced in the vehicle, I handed the woman the key fob through the open window. "Now go. I don't want to ever see you again."

The woman started the SUV and revved the engine. She grinned and said, "Fuck you, asshole. You have not seen the last of me." She hit the gas and screamed down the block and around the corner.

Beal shook her head. "I don't think that was a smart move, Cervantes."

"I'm not done," I said and dialed 911 on the burner phone I carried for just such purposes. I put on the best Texas accent I could. "Yeah. I've just seen a shootin' Yeah. A woman in one of those big black SUVs, like government people drive. Yeah. License number 7BJT254. I saw them argue'n and then she pointed the gun at the man and shot him. She pushed him into the backseat and drove off. It was a big gun, and it didn't make any noise. He was still moving, so I don't think she kilt him. He kept screaming, 'You shot me, you f-ing B.' I don't like to use cuss words, but they was cuss'en at each other a lot. I think she was heading for the freeway. If you are quick, you might catch em. My name. No, sir. That's all I got. Bye now." I hung up the phone and looked at Beal. "That should keep them busy for a while." I grinned.

We walked back to the house. Mary set about making tea. I could see that they were both shaken. I made a decision. "You ladies rest while I go and check out the self-storage unit."

"You don't have a key. Let me check one more place that Harry used to put his stuff." She disappeared down the hall to her bedroom and reappeared a moment later. She was grinning with a single key dangling from her hand. "The bedside table drawer was where he put his pocket change and wallet. This might be the key. All locks come with two keys. This could be the spare." She tossed it to me.

"Great. If it doesn't work, there are other ways." I grinned. "Call me if you need me. I'll be back in a few hours." They both agreed, and I headed out to Harry Kruger's self-storage unit.

SELF-STORAGE

I drove to the self-storage building, constantly glancing in the rearview mirror to see if I was being followed. As far as I could discern, I was not followed. The building was a three-story structure with a very small frontage. I parked near the front of the building near the alley that ran along the side. The double doors led to a lobby with a stairway entrance and a large freight elevator. I stepped into the elevator and was confronted with a key panel that required a code. I did not have a code. I stepped over to the stairway door, but it was locked. It was a bit of a conundrum. I stood by the elevator, considering possible ways to get inside. I decided that bravado was my choice. I took out my private investigator's badge and clipped it to my belt. I stood at semi-attention just to the side of the elevator and waited. I did not have to wait long. A woman stood outside the doors. She was carrying a large tote and dragging a suitcase on wheels. She was struggling to open the door without putting either container down. I came to her aid. I opened the door. "May I help you?" I asked. She looked at me. The establishment did not provide help to its clients, and this woman was doubtful of my intentions, so I flashed my badge. "There has been a rash of vandalism of late and I was hired to ensure only clients with storage units were entering. Let me help you with that," I crooned and smiled.

She seemed to relax. "Sure. If you wouldn't mind taking this tote." I nodded and took it from her. We walked to the elevator.

I entered with her and said, "I will help you carry it to your unit. The building is under new management, and we want to ensure that our clients are happy." She turned to enter her code into the panel. I watched her carefully as she entered 31513 into the elevator panel. The lights on the buttons glowed yellow. She pressed the three. The elevator rose to the third floor. I carried the tote down to her locker. All the lockers on the third floor started with the number three. Her locker number was 315, the same first three digits she had entered into the elevator panel. Kruger's locker must be on the second floor—number 230. I smiled and headed to the elevator. I was pretty sure that the elevator code was the person's locker number with a 13 on the end. I punched in the number and the elevator buttons lit up. I pressed two and was deposited on the second floor.

I walked down the dim hallway, looking for the number 230. The hall jogged to the right. I followed it to the end. Locker 230 was the last one. Across the hall were two empty lockers with open doors. I tried the key in the lock. It was very stiff, as if it had not been open for some time. It finally gave way, and I entered the locker. It contained some furniture and a mattress, along with several liquor boxes stacked against the back wall. Front and center was a round dining room table with an old WWII footlocker sitting on the top. Beside it was a toolbox with its lid open. I was about to open the footlocker when I heard the elevator doors open with a ding. I could hear voices. I stepped out of the locker and quickly moved down the hall, and peeked around the corner. Three men were coming in my direction. They looked similar to the men I had encountered in the hospital. I quickly grabbed the footlocker and moved it across the hall to one of the empty lockers. I stepped back and grabbed a screwdriver from the toolbox on the table. I stepped out, closed the door, and slipped into the other empty locker. I hid behind the door and waited. I listened to the men talking to each other.

A gruff voice intoned, "Botox said this was the little mother fucker that put Freddie's crew in the hospital. I really hope he's in here because it will give me great pleasure to fuck him up."

"I agree, but not before we get what we want. The doctor wants him alive so he can ask him a few questions. That part will be fun cause I will be the guy who provides the persuasion..." He slapped his fist into his palm and grinned. "...If you know what I mean. Now be quiet. Jake said he saw him come in here. He wasn't on the first floor. He might be just around that corner." I could hear their footsteps. I peeked out the crack on the hinge side of the door I was behind. They moved to the front of Kruger's locker. "Look. The lock is off that one," The shortest of the three me whispered. "He might be in there." I watched as they opened the locker door. One at a time, the men entered the locker. I saw the door slowly swing closed behind them. The voices became louder. "He's not here. Check the boxes. Botox said to look for an old trunk. We find the trunk and we find him."

I opened the door slowly to avoid anything giving me away. I stepped up to Kruger's locker and in one smooth motion, silently closed the door, attached the hasp, and slipped the screwdriver through the "U." Then I unlocked the padlock to the storage locker, removed the footlocker, set it down quietly, returned to Kruger's locker, slid the screwdriver out of the hasp, and snapped the padlock in place. I walked quickly toward the stairway carrying the footlocker. These were fire doors that had to be opened from the inside. As I was about to step into the stairwell, I heard some banging and yelling from down the hallway. The stairway door closed behind me, muting the sound. I walked down to the bottom, opened the door and stepped out into the lane behind the building, then quickly turned to see if anyone was in the lane. Someone had tailed me without my knowledge. I made a mental note to improve my surveillance skills. I walked to the front of the building, scanned the parking lot and spotted an older model truck with a man in the driver's seat. He was looking down at something that I assumed was his phone. I slipped out of the alley toward my rental car and hoisted the heavy footlocker into the passenger seat. When I started the car, I glanced again at the man in the truck. He had not seen me. I drove slowly down the alley, out of sight. It was only then that I felt my heart beating double time in my chest.

As I neared the end of the alley, I realized I had overheard information on 'the doctor' AKA 'Botox.' The drug Botox blocks signals from your nerves to your muscles, preventing the muscles from contracting. In small doses, it can improve the appearance of fine lines and wrinkles. In large doses, it can be fatal. It is commonly used by plastic surgeons. I wondered if Dr. Botox was just that—a plastic surgeon. It would be a good place for

Billie to start searching. Right now, I could take a more direct route to his location and go back and attempt to follow the thugs. I was sure they would call the man keeping watch in the truck to go in and free them from the locker. I quickly turned around, drove to the lane opening to the parking lot and watched. I did not have to wait long. After the man in the truck held his phone to his head, he jumped out of the truck and rushed into the storage building. I took the time to reposition myself on the street just outside the parking lot exit. I planned to follow them to their destination. Knowing where they resided would be advantageous.

They came out of the parking lot in a large SUV, followed by the lookout in his old truck. The SUV screeched its tires as it drove past me. The old truck came soon after. It would be easier to follow, so I pulled out behind it. I assumed it would be going to the same place as the SUV. I soon discovered that I was wrong. The old truck turned off and headed in a completely different direction. It pulled into a Macdonald's parking lot. The man entered the restaurant. I watched the windows to see if he was going to buy something and leave. He sat at a table and took out his phone. I decided that I was not going to wait like an old-fashioned gumshoe. I drove through the parking lot and recorded his truck license plate. I would give that to Billie and find out more about these people a little more efficiently. I drove off and headed to the "Perfect Paper" restoration company.

PERFECT PAPER

I pulled into the parking lot of a six-story office building. The sign out front listed all the firms in the building. I could see "Perfect Paper" listed. I reached over to the footlocker on the passenger seat. The opening was facing away from me. I wrestled with it and got it turned around so I could open it. There was very little inside. I was not sure what I expected to see. Uniforms and some toiletries perhaps, but there were only a couple of large manilla envelopes. One was quite thick, while the other looked like it contained a dozen or so sheets. What caught my attention was the inside of the lid. On either side were small black-and-white pictures of a smiling woman with a child in her arms. They were in various poses and obviously taken at different times. The child was older than the ones on the right. They formed a sequence based on the child's age. I assumed this was Beal's grandmother, and the child was her mother. It was the middle of the lid that drew my attention. It appeared to be a picture of Adare in a graveyard for he was standing in front of a gravestone with one foot on a brass ball that was part of a small brass fence surrounding the grave. The foot had a cast, and you could see his bare toes sticking out. He also had one hand up, holding something near his ear. It was his pocket watch. I smirked. This was his way of telling her where the pocket watch was hidden. Standing in some graveyard was probably not enough information, so there must be more.

I looked at the envelopes. The thick one was marked 'Originals' and the thin one was marked 'Analysis.' I pulled a paper wad from the thick envelope and looked at it. It had suffered a great deal of water damage. Some of it was almost pulp powder. I carefully put it back, trying not to damage it even more. The 'Analysis' envelope held a half dozen sheets. The first page heading read "Perfect Paper Analysis of Water Damaged Paper Circa 1945 (approx)" and the date. I flipped through the remaining pages. They were transcriptions of letters. They were love letters from Adare to his wife. I was sure that Adare loved his wife very much. Most of the letters were incomplete. Some were merely fragments. I inspected the only complete letter. It was filled with what looked like typos that had been crossed out. I read it carefully.

My Darling,

I love you. I ~~nruwhlnimlt~~ miss you. I hope you ~~dpeafdero~~ are well. I am sorry that I cannot tell you about any of my adventures. I cannot even ~~lsadoiheotto~~ tell you where I am. The Krauts might intercept this message. All this spy stuff must ~~aermi~~ be kept secret. That does not leave much for me to tell you, so I will just ask ~~mscoinc~~ what you are up to. How is the house? Did you get the roof fixed? ~~cuts~~ I was worried you might try to do it yourself. How is Mrs. Davis? The last time I was home, she was not well. I hope you have ~~tiodo~~ made some new friends while I am ~~and~~ away. I don't want you to be lonely. This has to be a short letter as I am ~~kwh~~ heading out shortly.

Love,
Sam

P.S. Please forgive the typos. This electric typewriter has seen better days. It seems to have a mind of its own.

The crossed-out groups were odd-looking in that they did not seem to have any relationship to the word before or after. I remembered what Beal had said about a transposition cipher that the Adares used to communicate. I took a picture of the complete letter and the pictures inside of the footlocker lid and sent them to Billie with instructions to see if they contained a secret message.

I saw motion and looked up. A man and two women were exiting the building. They were all carrying cases. They walked to the parking area and got into their respective vehicles. As they drove away, I saw that the parking stalls were labeled Perfect Paper Staff Only. It appeared I was too late to see anyone. I closed my eyes. All that business with a heavy trunk made me tired. I slipped on my dark glasses. The canvas opened up, and I relaxed.

Falling into the canvas without a purpose in mind was, for me anyway, a religious experience. Don't get me wrong. I don't believe in any deity unless the universe itself is the actual body of a god. Imagine that we are just small parasites that have infested the body of some creature that is as vast as the universe; is the universe. The creature would have less knowledge and understanding of us as individuals than we do of one of the zillions of bacilli that inhabit our guts. All that drivel about some god watching over us is absurd. Would you watch over some nasty, disease-causing bacilli in the hopes that it might worship you?

If you read this and you feel I have slighted your religion, take some solace in the fact that I endeavored to slight all group delusions and fantasies that promote an all-powerful being that even knows of our existence, let alone loves us. Pure tripe. Sorry for the digression.

The canvas on this day was somewhat ethereal. It was fuzzy in some spots and clear in others, as if it was highlighting something. I found myself sitting in a field of grass that extended out into the distance all around me. I was staring up at the sky. I smiled. The canvas usually had me soaring bird-like, looking down at the landscape. The clouds were white rectangular shapes drifting down. As they got closer to the ground, I could see that the shapes were actually pieces of paper wafting back and forth. Each piece held a few letters that faded out just before it came to rest on the grass. I was intrigued by the message the canvas was trying to impart. As usual, it was cryptic. I heard a horn honk on a nearby street and looked through the canvas to the real world. I found myself staring at the sign for Perfect Paper while the canvas-generated paper floated past.

I sat up and removed my glasses. Maybe this was a sign—at least I decided it was. I got out of my rental car and lugged the footlocker out and put it in the trunk. I glanced around to see if I had been observed. All was quiet. I walked into the business tower lobby and scanned the list of companies in the building. Perfect Paper was on the third floor. I took the elevator up and walked down the hallway to the entrance to Perfect Paper. It was locked. The rooms were dark. I chastised myself for not putting more faith in real logic instead of following the canvas wherever it seemed to be pointing. The company was closed. I turned back to the elevator. I walked past a dental mechanic's office and a company called C-Nano-T. It was also closed. There was a poster in the window that caught my eye:

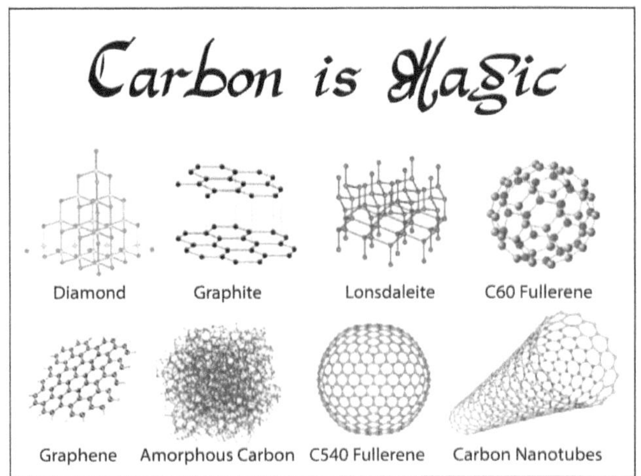

The poster seemed to be calling me. I stepped closer and stared at it. It was just a series of diagrams of various forms of carbon, claiming it was a magical substance. I felt a little overwhelmed. I felt like I was inside the canvas, and yet I wasn't. At least I had not deliberately conjured it up. It was more like the canvas demanded that I study this poster. I did just that.

I looked at each diagram in turn in an effort to bring whatever the canvas was trying to tell me into consciousness. I already had some background information on several of the forms of carbon depicted. I had read something about Nanotubes and Fullerene. I knew that the C60 Fullerene was named after Buckminster Fuller, who was the designer of geodesic dome structures that look similar. That is all I knew. The information was obviously not relevant to the problem at hand. I was trying to determine why so many people were trying to get the microdot. It held a secret to something that a lot of people wanted. I stared at each of the images once again. I looked from bottom to top and then from top to bottom. On this second pass, I stopped at the image of the molecular structure of diamond. It looked just like something I had recently seen. The canvas had shown me a lot of things since I started this quest. I started to sift through them. Then it hit me.

While in the canvas world searching for the lost emerald ring, a spider-like creature dropped down in front of me and joined with many more of the same creatures that formed a grid. It looked exactly like the diamond molecular image in the poster. The spiders were diamond molecules. A whole bunch of questions were suddenly answered. This whole business of the pocket watch was about diamonds. The Barbie and Ken couple, along with the shadowy figure called Botox, were obviously searching for a treasure of diamonds. I couldn't forget that Sandra Beal had set me on this quest. She must be after diamonds, too. Perhaps it was a treasure of diamonds. But where were they hidden? That was the question.

I quickly left the building with the intention of going home. I would stop at Beal's house on the way and have a brief chat about where this investigation was headed. I would ask her some questions to determine if we were working together or at cross purposes. I needed to grab Barbie and Ken's phones and send them to Billie. It was a long shot. They were burners, but it was worth a try. They might hold some information. After I planned to drop the car at the airport and fly home.

CLARIFICATION

A few hours had turned into more than four. It was late afternoon when I pulled up in front of Beal's house. I knocked on her door and waited. I could hear someone approach and stop at the closed door. I assumed she was looking through the peephole. The door opened.

"Where have you been? I was worried something happened to you." She swung the door open wide. "Come in. Did you find the footlocker in his storage cubicle?"

I nodded.

"Where is it?"

"The trunk of the car. I need to talk to you about a few things," I said and headed to the kitchen.

"Sure. I'll make tea," she said and walked past me.

Once in the kitchen, sitting and sipping the tea, I started my questioning. I did not want to make her defensive, so I started with, "How is your mother?"

"She is still hanging on, but I don't suppose she will be with us much longer."

"Good that she is still with us. Now, Sandra, you hired me to find your grandfather's pocket watch. I found it. It cost you a great deal of money for me to find what you said was an important memento for you and your mother."

"Yes, and I hope you can locate it and retrieve it once more. It is still very important to me."

"And your mother," I added with a hint of poignancy. There was a pause. We stared at each other. I set down my teacup. "Now, Sandra, please tell me why you really want the watch."

"That is a moot point now in that it was stolen and you haven't got it back," she stated sharply.

"I was not hired to get it back once you lost it," I replied flatly.

She sighed. "Alright. I will tell you the whole story. At least the parts that I know. I am going to trust you. Can I trust you?"

"You can trust me as long as I have your assurance that I can do the same. You have to tell me everything you know. Please do not leave anything out."

"Ok. But I need something stronger." She stood and poured a glass of tawny liquid from a bottle on the counter. She offered me a glass, but I refused. "My mother was told this by my grandmother. She told her that grandfather's final letter to her contained a coded message. The message explained that he had found a treasure of diamonds worth millions. It was pretty farfetched. My grandfather was prone to hyperbole." -

"Did the letter tell her where the pocket watch was located?"

"My mother was not sure. My grandmother said the letter suggested that a clue to the location of the pocket watch would be sent to her if he was killed."

"Was anything sent?"

"Nothing that I know of. We never even got his trunk until 1947."

"Where is this letter?"

"My mother told me that my grandfather was afraid someone might want the treasure, so he told her to destroy the letter. I don't think she did."

"Did you mention the contents of the letter to Kruger?"

"I might have said something about a treasure my grandfather had coded into one of his letters, but I don't think I told him about the clue that was in the pocket watch. He was .... oh god, I can't believe Harry is dead." She sniffed.

"He was what?" She gave me a puzzled look and wiped her eyes. I continued, "You were about to say something. You started, 'he was' and then you stopped. Please finish."

"Oh. He fancied himself a bit of a detective. He loved codes and things. He asked me if I knew where my mother put the letter. He wanted to see it. I guess he thought there might be more in it than my mother had told me." She looked up at me. I gestured for her to continue. "Well, I told him it might have been destroyed. I didn't want to get his hopes up. He asked if there were any other letters. I told him they would be in the footlocker but the contents were damaged when my basement flooded. He looked through the footlocker and pulled out a wad of papers. They were all mashed together. I guess that's when he decided to take them to that restoration company."

"Perhaps I should fetch it." I walked to the car and returned with the footlocker. I opened it and took out the envelope from Perfect Paper. I removed the letter I had read earlier. This is the restored letter from Perfect Paper. I have my assistant working on decoding it.

At that moment, my phone buzzed. It was Billie. The message was terse. "Here she is now."

Crossed out letters – nruwhlninlt␣dpeafdero␣lsadoiheotto␣aermi ␣mscoinc␣cuts␣tiodo␣and␣kwh

Keyword – The word "LOVE" was underlined so I used that

Translation - found treasure worth millions diamonds location hidden pocket watch

I read the text to Beal. I flipped back the lid and pointed the photo in the center of the lid. "Is this your grandfather?"

"It looks like him. I asked my mother about it a few years ago. She didn't know for sure that it was him, but she thought it must be."

I reached out and removed the photo from the lid of the footlocker and studied it again. He was standing in front of a gravestone with his broken cast-covered foot on the brass ball of the low grave fence. The fence was about 16 inches high. He was leaning over with his elbow on the raised knee. His pocket watch was attached to a short fob and was dangling from his hand. It was directly over the brass ball where I had found the pocket watch. This was too deliberate to be anything but a message as to where the watch was hidden. I automatically turned the photo over. There was a note on the back. It was something you might write on the back of a photo telling where it was and when it was taken. It said *"Killaloe Ireland St. Andrews church 1940"* I showed Beal. "This is how he was trying to tell her where the watch was hidden. Look, the watch is dangling over the brass corner ball right where I found it. I don't think this photo has ever been removed from the locker lid. That is why your grandmother never bothered to look for the watch. She had no idea where to start."

"But you found it without any clues. How did you do that?"

I looked at Sandra. I had no intention of answering her question. "Do you believe that there is a treasure of diamonds hidden somewhere by your grandfather?"

She looked down, as if considering her next move, then she looked up, having made up her mind. "Yes. I am sure of it."

"What makes you so sure?"

"I wasn't going to tell you, but I now believe that you are the only person who can find the treasure. You found the watch without using the clues my grandfather left. My grandfather told us about the watch, but we didn't figure out where to look for it." She went to a shelf with liquor bottles and took down a silver flask. She set it in the middle of the table. "This was in my grandfather's footlocker filled with brandy. I took it out when I tried to dry out the footlocker after the flood. I put it on the shelf …." She gestured to the kitchen shelf. "…and forgot about it. After my mother got sick, I started to reminisce about my family. I noticed it on the shelf and took it down. I opened it and took a sip. It was vile, so I started to dump it out. That is when I found something in the bottom of the flask." She pulled a silver locket on a long chain from under her blouse and flicked it open. She tilted it and we watched two large round cut diamonds spill onto the table. We both looked at them sparkle as they caught the light. "I got them assessed. They are a little over 2 carats each, are 'D' color, and 'IF' clarity. Not sure what that means."

"D color is the best and IF stands for internally flawless," I said. "I'd guess they are worth at least fifty grand each."

"Triple it," she said. I whistled and reached for one of the diamonds.

She quickly covered them with her hand and put them back into her locket.

"Did you tell Harry about them?"

"Not right away. I hired you to find the watch that, according to my mother, had a clue inside. Harry found your card, and I had to tell him the whole story."

"So, he followed me to Ireland and got himself killed. He must have told someone else. Do you have any idea who he might have shared this information with?"

"He was excited at the prospect of finding a fortune in diamonds. He must have been looking for more clues. He left on a "business trip" soon after. I guess that is when he went to Ireland."

"Did he mention meeting with our friends, Barbie and Ken?"

"No. He did ask me if he could take one of the diamonds to a friend to see if they were stolen. I gave him one, and he returned it the next day. I think he took it to a guy he knew who runs a pawn shop. I think they get lists of stolen goods. He told me the diamond came back clean."

"Did he go anywhere else before he left on his business trip?"

She looked down in thought. "No. Just the dentist. I dropped him off at the dentist's office a couple of days before he left."

"Where was this dentist's office?"

Sandra took out her phone and searched for the building. She handed me her phone. It was a medical building. I could see several signs advertising the various medical personnel in the building. I looked for the dentist. There was a list of professionals. Right under the dentist was a sign for a plastic surgeon and a list of procedures from breast augmentation to Botox injections. The story of how Barbie and Ken and "Botox" ended up chasing me around the British Isles was becoming clear.

I knew I had to visit the medical facility. I strongly suspected that Botox, Barbie, and Ken were connected to that building.

The doorbell rang. There was a brief pause, then someone knocked on the door. There was another brief pause and then someone called out, "Pizza. Delivery."

I turned to Sandra. "I am going to assume that you did not order piz za." She shook her head. My Spidey sense went off. "Grab your purse. Go out the back door and hide until you can get safely over to Mary's house." She was about to argue with me. I held up a finger to my mouth and pushed her toward the back door. "Shhh. Go." I heard the back door latch click softly. I felt for the gun that I was now glad I had obtained. I went to the door and called out, "Just a minute." I realized I had raised the pitch of my voice an octave. "I need to find my purse." I was laughing inside. I bet they didn't expect Sandra to actually want the pizza. I peeked out the window. I could see the back of a blonde woman standing off to the side of the door. A man was only partially visible. I guessed it was Ken. They wanted to get their own back, and they did not plan on being nice. I slowly went to the door, twisted the lock open, and quickly stood to the side. I slid down behind the sofa with my pistol at the ready. I called out, "Come in."

The door opened and everything went to shit.

PRISONERS

AN actual pizza delivery man entered. I could see fear in his eyes. I had guessed wrong about Ken being at the front door. Behind him was Barbie. She was holding a pistol with a silencer. She scanned the room. I peeked up from behind the sofa. "Cervantes, if you have a weapon, drop it on the sofa and stand up or I will make a mess of the poor pizza guy's head. Do you want his death on your hands?"

Then I heard a gasp behind me. I glanced over and saw Beal being forced into the room. A different Ken was behind her. I figured the guy I shot in the foot was still out of commission. This Ken was pointing a similar pistol at her head. "If she shoots the pizza guy and I shoot your friend, then we are both going to shoot you in some very painful places. We won't kill you until we know what you found in the watch. And you will tell us, I guarantee that," said Ken menacingly.

"Now drop your weapon," Barbie commanded. I released my grip on the beretta. It fell onto the sofa.

Ken poked Beal in the back with his gun. "Get it," he ordered. "Pick it up by the barrel."

She moved forward.

I saw the fear in her wide-open eyes. She picked up the gun.

"Now back up and hold it over your head."

She did what she was told.

He grabbed the gun from her hand and slipped it into his jacket pocket, then shoved her toward the sofa. "Sit. Both of you."

"Get her to tie strap his hands. He is a tricky fucker," said Barbie.

Ken tossed a set of plastic tie straps at Beal. "You heard her. Make them nice and tight." He watched as she slipped the tie straps over my hands and pulled them closed. "Tighter. I want them to hurt." Beal half-heartedly complied. "Now sit," he ordered. He walked over to Barbie and whispered something while facing away. He walked to the door and left the apartment.

Barbie sat on the chair opposite the sofa. She set the butt of the gun on her knee. It was pointed at me. She smiled. So, what is the treasure anyway? You might as well tell me now. It will be a lot easier on you in the long run."

"Ahh. So, Botox knows what the treasure is but you don't. He sounds like a trusting kind of guy." I thought I would tease her with what I suspected was the location of Botox. They might figure I knew more than I actually did and let something slip. "I assume you are taking us to his office." I turned to Beal. "Hey, Sandra what street is that medical center on? You know, the one that houses a dentist and a plastic surgeon. I don't remember."

"Shut the fuck up," she spat just as the door opened and the new dark-haired Ken entered. "Get up. We are going for a ride." She turned to Ken. "Anybody out there watching us?"

"Yeah. A guy is trimming his hedges, and a nosey woman is digging in her flower garden."

"Remove his restraints. I want us to walk out of here like we are all friends. Try anything, Cervantes, and I will shoot those two nosey neighbors and your friend here." Ken removed a knife from his jacket and cut through my restraints. She poked Beal in the back. Both she and Ken took off their jackets and tucked their guns out of sight. We all walked to the door with guns concealed. Ken went first. He stepped out with a smile on his face. We all followed. I saw that Ken had pulled a black SUV with the back seat windows tinted so dark they were the same color as the vehicle. It was sitting right in front of the house. We all walked, smiling, to the car. Beal got in the passenger side while Barbie and I got in the back seat. Ken was driving.

"Put these on," Barbie said and tossed a new set of tie straps at me. I slipped them over my wrists. She pointed her gun at my head, reached out, and pulled the tie straps tight around my wrists. I considered attempting to relieve her of the gun, but decided that the risk was too great. She reached into a bag at her feet and removed a black sack. She tossed it at me. "Put this on," said Barbie, and she held up the black sack. She tossed it at me. I glanced around at our present surroundings. I would use that as a starting point. Obviously, we were not going to Botox's office. I slipped on the hood, closed my eyes against the shifting shadows under the hood, and concentrated on the motion of the vehicle. I would memorize the time it took and the direction of every turn. The canvas opened, and I found myself transforming once again into a kestrel soaring the updrafts of energy. I was high above the city. Somehow, I no longer had to count the seconds or interpret the forces of motion into a direction. The canvas simply transformed it all into an experience. Once it found the final destination, the actions in between became moot. I could always locate it in the future. That is, if I had a future.

We rode in silence for twenty minutes. We stopped and the car engine was turned off. The canvas dropped away. I knew where we were and also had no idea at the same time. The Canvas works like that. If I wanted to find this place sometime in the future, I could, but I could not describe to someone else where we were. I am sorry for being rather obtuse, but I really have no choice. I have explained it as best I can.

We were pulled from the car. The sound of a door opening and closing, a slight change in air pressure, and an echo of our footsteps told me we had entered a building with a high ceiling, probably a warehouse. There were approaching footsteps. I could hear someone crying and assumed it was Beal. She shouted, "What are you going to do to us? Please let us go."

A new voice spoke. It was extremely raspy, like the person's vocal cords were damaged in some way. "That depends on you. Give me the information I want, and I will consider it." This was followed by a little laugh that mutated into a cough. I did not like the laugh. "Bring them up to the office," the voice rasped once again. The footsteps receded.

We were pushed and pulled forward. "There are stairs in front of you," said Barbie. I stepped up. The sound was an indicator that the stairs were metal. I instinctively counted the steps. There were thirty. Once at the top, I could smell a noxious odor. It was a mixture of rotten egg smell and something like nail polish. I tried to identify it as we entered a room and were slammed down into metal chairs. I felt someone putting tie straps around my legs and the chair legs. I instinctively cocked my heels up and pressed them against the chair legs. When they finished, I relaxed my legs. The tie straps were very loose. I could hear Beal weeping and then new Ken spoke, "Shut the fuck up or I will give you something to cry about."

That phrase caused a storm of memory to assault my senses. It happens to me sometimes. Something from the past that I suppressed comes charging back. In this case, it was my father shouting at me when I was very little. Even then, before I knew what the canvas was, it would intrude and dominate my senses. If it showed me something that frightened me, I would cry. To an outside observer, it must have looked very odd. One minute I was happy and smiling and doing whatever I was involved in and the next I was wailing in fear. He would approach me and use that phrase. He would also shout at my mother, "You better do something about this kid. He is not right in the head." In retrospect, he was probably right. I was not right in the head. I am still not right in the head, but I have decided that being *not right in the head* has its benefits.

I spoke, "Leave her be. It is me you want. She knows nothing."

I heard the raspy voice again. "She knows nothing about what?" I did not answer. "Yes, I suspected you might not want to tell me what I want to know."

"What do you want to know?"

"Good. Progress," he said and suppressed a cough. "I want to know what you took out of the pocket watch. Don't bother denying it. I know about the message in the watch. Kruger told me everything. It was too bad he got so nosey."

"Is that why you killed him?" I blurted. There was a wail that came from Beal at the mention of Kruger's death. I heard Botox tisk and somehow, I knew he was shaking his head.

"That is of no consequence. What did you remove from the pocket watch? It must have been very small. I have considered what it might be. It was during the war, and he was a spy, so I suspect it was a microdot." I did not answer. Suddenly, there was a wail of pain coming from Beal. I turned my head in her direction. I could see nothing through the sac on my head. I did notice that the sounds coming from her were different somehow. They were not coming from the same place as the first cries. Then it came to me. She was standing and was in a different location than I first thought. "This is a simple process. I ask questions and you answer. If you choose not to answer, then my employee will hurt Ms. Beal and will continue to do so with increasing severity until you do." I did not move or indicate in any way that I cared or even understood. I knew this lack of reaction would cause some response from Botox. He spoke, "Do you understand me?"

I nodded my sac-covered head. I needed to stall, so I asked questions of my own. "Why do they call you Botox? What is your real name?" I waited. Suddenly Beal screamed. "Hurting Ms. Beal is not the way to get me to talk to you. It is based on a faulty assumption. You assumed that I care what happens to her. Other tactics have a greater probability of success."

He rasped, "Such as?"

"You could hurt me, but that would not work and killing me will get you nowhere." I paused. "Have you considered a partnership? I am open to that."

A grating laugh filled the room. It was obsequiously supported by both Barbie and Ken number two. "You are quite the character. I want you to understand that I could operate on your face and turn you into a monster just for the fun of it. I am not a nice person."

"Just as I supposed; you are a plastic surgeon. That is how you got your moniker, Botox. Am I right?"

"Clever boy. Now back to this offer of a partnership—what could you provide that I could not get by simply tearing your apartment to pieces until I found what you have hidden? I bet it is in a safe. Am I correct?"

I smiled under the sac but did not react. I needed to cover up my surprise at how accurate his supposition was. "You are half right. It is in a safe but that safe is not in my apartment. It is in a much larger safe in one of the banks in which I keep safety deposit boxes. Hence, we are back where we started. To get it, you will need to torture me. I guarantee that will not work. So why don't you reconsider my proposal?" All went quiet and then someone pulled the sac off my head.

BOTOX

I blinked and squinted at the sudden burst of light. Standing on either side of me were Barbie and Ken. In front of me was a short stocky man with a massive head of curly black hair and a dark five o'clock shadow. I was sure that if he chose to grow a beard, he could have a full one in just a couple of days. His eyebrows were reminiscent of huge hairy caterpillars. They seemed to crawl in place as his face twitched in obvious anticipation of what he was going to do next. His hands were held in front, and he rubbed them together absent-mindedly. He reminded me of a hairy Dr. Evil, and I half expected him to lift his pinky finger to his lips, Mike Meyers style. I glanced at his shoes. They were tiny brown oxfords. He was wearing what looked like painter's coveralls. They were smattered with a dark reddish-brown stain that I knew instantly was not paint.

He noticed me staring at his coveralls and laughed and pointed at the stains. "This is my hobby. I have a small kitchen in the back where I make all sorts of delicious smoked meats. I am a purist. I butcher the animals myself." I scanned the room and stopped when a large cage came into view. He noticed me staring. "That is what the cage is for; to keep my animals. Maybe it will serve to keep you." He laughed again. "I would not wear this if I was to work on you."

I looked over at Beal. She seemed none the worse for wear. She was standing off to the side. I wondered why she had not been restrained. They had not even concealed this location from her. It appeared that all the moaning had been faked. Was she working with Botox? Had she betrayed my trust? I glanced up at her face. Her eyes were open wide. She did not look away. I made an 'I can't believe you betrayed me' face at her. I caught an almost imperceptible shake of her head. "So, what is your decision?" I asked. "I assure you that I can find what you are looking for." I paused. "… for a price."

"A price!" He laughed. "Just out of curiosity, how much?"

"Half."

He laughed again, "I'll say one thing, you are entertaining. Now Beal here, she only wants 10%. She has offered to turn over the location of the treasure as soon as she gets it from you. I have promised her 5%. After all, I am the one with the resources to retrieve it, wherever it is. As I understand it, you find things but do not retrieve them, the exception being the pocket watch. Correct?" I nodded. "So, tell me, how did you find the watch? Kruger scoured the contents of Adare's footlocker but found nothing, yet you just looked at a few photos of the watch and then got on a plane to Ireland and retrieved it. How?"

Botox nodded at Ken, who was still standing to my right. He reached up, grabbed my hair, and pulled my head back. I heard Beal gasp. Botox approached me, smiling. His hand slipped into the pocket of his coveralls and came out with a scalpel. He held it up so I could see it. Light glinted off the shiny surface as he waved it in front of my face. "Killing me will get you nowhere," I said with false bravado. I realized this guy was much more dangerous than I had originally thought. I needed to be less confrontational.

"Who said anything about killing? When I kill something, I usually turn it into some kind of sausage. I doubt you would make a tasty treat. Not enough fat." He patted my cheeks. He rolled the knife from side to side in his hand. I glanced over at Barbie. She had a macabre smile on her face. She was obviously anticipating something nasty. "I could stick the business end of this up your nose and simply flick out. Noses really bleed when cut."

A quick glance at Barbie showed her licking her lips in anticipation. I decided to appear to give in and play along with this psycho. I tested the tie straps holding my hands behind my back. They did not give a millimeter. "Tell Igor here to let me go. And while you are at it, please tell her to stop salivating …" I flicked my eyes in Barbie's direction. "… and I will tell you what I know?"

"I don't think so. I think you have to understand that I am a serious player in this little game." He nodded at Barbie. She smiled and stepped in front of me. She was wearing black leather gloves. All the fingers on her right gloved hand were covered with silver rings in the shape of various animals. She backhanded me across my face. I knew I had been cut. The pain was focused on my forehead and my cheek. I could feel the blood running down my face. Ken released his grip on my hair.

Beal rushed forward with a wad of tissues. She was about to press them to my bleeding cheek when she stumbled. She fell into me. With one hand, she tried to right herself and with the other, she surreptitiously reached behind me. She shoved something into my hand and pulled herself erect. She continued to daub my bleeding face with the tissue. I could see tears welling up as she turned and looked at Barbie. She stood with the blood-soaked tissue. "Leave him alone." And then to Botox, she said, "Why are you doing this? He would help you. Let me get a clean cloth and some bandages." Botox rolled his eyes and tipped his head at Ken. Ken walked to a cupboard attached to the wall and returned with some gauze and tape.

I explored what she had put in my hand. It was a small paring knife. She must have grabbed it when she went to the kitchen in her house. I slipped the blade between the tie and my wrist and started to saw back and forth. I covered the motion with movements of my head and facial contortions. I could feel the blood from a cut on my forehead start to drip into my eye. Beal daubed my forehead with some of the gauze and cleaned the blood. When she did, I winced, jerked, and moaned, all in an effort to cover the motion of the knife cutting through the tie straps on my left wrist. With a final jerk, the knife cut the strap. My hands were free. If I slipped my shoes off, I could easily pull my feet out of the tie straps that loosely bound my legs to the chair. Beal taped gauze pads to the two larger cuts and stepped back.

Botox stepped toward me and leaned over to inspect the damage done by Barbie's rings. "Come and see me when this is over, and I will fix those cuts. I don't leave scars." He stood up. "Unless you want some scars. Every detective worth his salt should have some battle scars. Consider this a fa vor." He grinned. "Now, where were we? Oh yes, you wanted 50% of the treasure. I am going to assume that you have reconsidered. I will give you a share equal to Beal here. 5%. Do you agree?"

I decided I had to prepare for what needed to happen. We must get away from this maniac. I let the canvas flood my consciousness. I felt my eyes drift back into my head. I knew I would look very odd, but that did not matter. The canvas was tightly focused. I could see an image of the small knife I held behind my back. It was sticking in the floor in front of me. I mentally reached out to get it, assuming it was an instrument that would aid in my escape. It would not budge. Every time I grabbed at it; it sank deeper into the floor. Around the knife were strewn pieces of cardboard. One of the pieces had blood smeared in the shape of an 'X.' 'X' marks the spot. I was distracted for a moment. Through the sieve of the canvas, I could hear voices.

Botox was shouting. I assumed he was talking to Beal, but I could not be sure. "What is wrong with him? Is he having a fit? Is it epilepsy?" He turned to Barbie. "Did you know about this?"

"No. I knew he was weird, but my research did not uncover anything like this. His eyes have rolled back into his head."

I stopped paying attention and refocused on the canvas. The piece of cardboard with the bloody 'X' caught my attention again. I pushed it aside. Suddenly, a small table grew out of the floor. On the table was a gun. It was identical to Barbie's gun with a silencer and all. I scanned my memory of the room. Barbie had set her gun down on a small table behind her. The canvas was telling me to forget the knife and go for the gun. Once I had the gun, I could escape. I slowly felt my eyes refocus on the real world. I stared at Botox.

"What the fuck was that all about?" he asked. I stared. Beal fell to the floor in a faint. It looked real to me, but after her previous actions, I suspected she was giving me an opportunity. Botox turned around to look at Beal. Both Barbie and Ken stared at Beal, who was now moaning loudly on the floor. That is when I moved.

ESCAPE

I pulled my feet out of my shoes and dove at Barbie as she turned back to me, alerted by my movement. I crashed into her, and she flew away from the small table. Her fall was stopped by Botox. He stumbled forward. I grabbed the gun off the table and pointed it at Ken. He was reaching for the pistol in a holster on his hip. I am very proficient with guns, but I am not good at pointing them at people, even people who wish me harm. I did what I had done to the previous Ken; I shot him in the foot. As he fell, I snatched his gun, which was half drawn from his holster. Beal stood up. I pointed the guns at both Barbie and Botox. Ken was moaning on the floor.

"My, my," said Botox as he slowly raised his hands.

"Fuck," said Barbie.

Botox looked over at Ken on the floor, moaning and clutching his leg just above his ankle. "I think my associate needs medical attention. May I attend to him?"

"Not just yet." I looked over at Beal. She was sitting up. "Are you ok?" I asked.

She got to her feet. "I am," she said, grinning at me. "What do we do now?"

"Good question." I turned to Botox. "I don't suppose you will just forget about this whole treasure hunt. After all, it is not yours to find in the first place. Whatever it is, it belongs to Beal here."

"I suppose you are right," said Botox. He grinned at me. "You will just have to kill us." He paused and a macabre grin slipped onto his face. "Killing is difficult, and I don't think you have the guts."

"You are right. I won't kill you, but it is not guts that I lack. That suggests that fear is stopping me from killing you and, by overcoming that fear, I would be capable of committing such a heinous act. Those are the emotions of an ignorant man. I assure you I have seen my 'killing you' future in its entirety. It does not look good to me. So, killing you is not on the table." I turned to Beal. "Get their phones." Beal patted them down. Barbie's phone was in her back pocket. She snatched it and stepped away. We both approached Ken, still moaning on the floor. "Check his pockets. I want his phone and the key fob to that Escalade we arrived in." I nudged his good foot. "Try anything and I will put a bullet in your other foot." Beal retrieved his phone. I turned to Botox. Beal approached him.

"Don't bother. I never use the things." He patted the large pockets of the coveralls he was wearing.

I glanced over at the large animal cage. I could see a lock on the door of the cage. "I want the keys to that lock," I said and waved one of the guns in that direction. He shrugged and stared back at me. I pointed one of the guns at him. I could see the defiance slowly fade as I lowered the gun and pointed it directly at his foot.

"All right," he muttered. The defiance in his voice faded, and he reached into the pocket of the coveralls and removed a ring of keys. "The red one opens the padlock on the cage." Beal took them from him.

"Thank you for your cooperation." I was unable to keep the sarcasm from creeping into my tone. "Now, let's help Ken here get up. I want all three of you to get into the cage." Barbie and Botox went to Ken and helped him to his feet and over to the cage. Beal opened the lock and the cage door. Once they were all inside, she snapped the lock closed and stepped back. "Now you may attend to your employee. I am going to assume that someone will find you soon." I sniffed the air again. The smell of rotten eggs mixed with perm solution reached my nose. It was a smell that likely came from a meth lab. I considered calling the police and then reconsidered. The knowledge of a meth lab on the premises might come in handy on some future date if Botox continued to be a problem.

"You fucker. I will hunt you down. You will regret messing with me," hissed Barbie.

I was not sure what got into me, but I felt really powerful at that moment. I was now more than a detective that found things. I was a detective, just like Phillip Marlow. I was trolling the underbelly of society. With that thought, a quote from Ramond Chandler jumped into my head.

"The private detective of fiction is a fantastic creation who acts and speaks like a real man. He can be completely realistic in every sense but one, that one sense being that in life as we know it, such a man would not be a private detective." – *Raymond Chandler*

I smiled. Obviously, Mr. Chandler never considered anyone like me. I looked at Barbie. "You are not taking me seriously. I will be very upset with you if I suspect you are planning to interfere with Ms. Beal or myself." With that, I pointed the gun at her foot and fired. There was a spit as the silenced bullet left the gun and a scream as it entered her foot. I walked over to the small table and wiped my fingerprints off of the pistols. I set them on the table and turned to Beal. I could see fear in her eyes. I was not sure if I liked it or not. I knew Phillip Marlow would see that as a positive. "Let's go," I said to her, and we both went to find the Escalade. I drove it back to the city and parked it across the street from my office. I sent Billie the location of the warehouse, just in case I ended up there again.

BACK HOME

I am not so naïve to think that my antics with Barbie, Ken, and Botox would deter them from going after a treasure in diamonds. There was just too much money involved. I did think that they would, at the very least, think twice about interfering with me. I knew they would not stop, but I hoped they would explore some other means to discover the whereabouts of the diamonds in question. That hope was squashed flat as Beal and I got out of the taxi from the airport. We were dropped off in front of my office. It was very late at night and there was no traffic. It was clear that someone had broken in. They smashed all the windows and trashed the inside. The file cabinets were turned over and the old files were strewn around the room. I looked at Beal and said, "Sandra, please wait here." She nodded, and I stepped through the broken window and went straight to the washroom at the back. The washroom paper towel dispenser had been knocked off of the wall. The fixtures would still function, but the cover on the back of the toilet was in pieces on the floor. I touched the sensor that would open the secret door at the back. It slid open. I returned to Beal and led her through the mess and into my apartment proper. It was untouched.

I spoke to Beal. "Make yourself at home. Please do not leave the apartment without telling me." I went straight to email Billie. I instructed her to hire a repair firm. I wanted them first thing in the morning, and I would pay double their usual fee. I also told her to send some protection to my apartment. I wanted 24-hour surveillance at both the front and rear entrances. I stressed that they might encounter some very nasty people and should be prepared. I checked out the surveillance tapes. It showed a couple of gang-member types breaking in and smashing stuff. They were only half-heartedly searching for something. It seemed as if they just wanted to inflict as much property damage as possible. The camera picked up a passing police siren. This seemed to cause them to pause. They waited for it to pass and then left.

I said goodnight to Beal and headed to my bedroom. I lay on my bed and closed my eyes. I was debating whether to explore the canvas or go to sleep. Neither happened because my mobile on my bedside table beeped. It was a text. I picked up the phone, expecting to see a note from Billie. It was not Billie. There were a bunch of texts in a row that had not been answered. The messages were all from Maggie. They went as follows:

Hi Mattie.
Text me back so I know you got this.
Hellllooоо.
Thinking of you.
Thinking of kissing you.
Do you want to kiss me?
Helllоооо again.
Thinking of doing other things. With you and to you.
Thinking of you doing things to me.
Yum.
And finally, the last one read:
I hope you have not ghosted me before we even got together. Please text me back.

I lay back on my bed. I remembered all the things we did together. I reminded myself that we were kids at the time. I needed to consider her motives. Perhaps they were not the same as they were when we indulged in each other's bodies. The thoughts caused my body to react. It had not done that in a long time. Sex with Maggie was the one thing that took precedence over the canvas. I realized that I wanted to experience that again. I didn't even mind her calling me Mattie. Motives be-damned. I smiled and texted her back:

Really sorry, but I was out of town. This is my "house phone," and I do not carry it with me. How about we meet for lunch on one of your days off? Let me know when and I will try to be available.

It was almost three in the morning, and I did not expect a response, but the phone buzzed almost immediately.

Oooh, I am excited. I don't know my new schedule for next week. I will text you. It is late. Nite Nite. 💋😍❤🤪

I smiled and got ready for bed. I could think of nothing but having sex with Maggie. Perhaps this was a good thing. It would relax me, and after my encounter with Botox and crew, I was stressed.

BEAL DEBRIEF

THE next morning was a little awkward. I woke to the smell of coffee. There was not much else in the way of food in my apartment, and I was about to suggest we go to the Deli for breakfast when I remembered the break-in. I called the Deli and ordered. I would exit from the rear of the apartment and pick it up. I entered the kitchen and Beal handed me a cup of coffee. She sat and stared at me. I could see her make up her mind as to what to say to me. She spoke, "I am on your side. I know it didn't look like it while we were at the warehouse, but I was. I visited that place with Harold. He took me there so we could find someone to help us locate the diamonds. I was not privy to any of the discussions, but Harry told me later that he did not want to work with Dr. Spencer…" I looked at her quizzically. She clarified. "…Dr. Spencer is Botox. Harry told me he had worked for him in the past doing odd jobs but decided not to tell him everything about the possible treasure."

"He must have told Botox something. How else would he have known to send his goons to follow me?"

"I just know what he told me."

"What kind of jobs did he do for Botox?"

"Harry never said. He just told me he had not worked for him in a long time. I am sorry I never told you this before. I was hoping it wouldn't come up."

"So let me follow the timeline here. You knew a few things about your grandfather. You had heard stories from your mother, but never really paid any attention. The treasure part was just a fantasy of your grandmother and told to you by your mother. You had your grandfather's footlocker in your basement but had never really looked at it. Your basement flooded and while you were cleaning up, you opened it and that is when you found the flask with the diamonds. It was then you decided that the stories of treasure just might be true and there might be more clues in the footlocker. How am I doing so far?"

"My mother really did want the watch."

"But not for the reasons you told me. How did she know that the pocket watch held clues to the location of the treasure?"

"My mother and my grandmother did not know that a treasure existed. My grandfather would send my grandmother secret messages in his letters. It was their thing. When I was little, my mother showed me some of the ways they would communicate. I remember sending notes to my girlfriends using a transposition cipher. It was pretty cool."

"A transposition cipher?"

"Yeah. My grandfather would make up a word search puzzle and send it to my grandmother to solve, but the whole thing was a ploy to get her messages about his location that the army would not allow. She said she needed to know where he was "so she could worry accurately." The first letter of the words she needed to find in the bogus word search was all that was important. Once she had the list of letters, she would use the agreed-upon transposition cipher to translate. They always used the word 'LOVE as their keyword." She smiled at me and sipped her coffee.

"I would love to see some of those. Knowing where he was located would be a great help."

"Oh. I have a series of those. My mother found them among my grandmother's things after her death and she gave them to me. They're in my desk at home. It's just a bunch of locations. Sometimes there was other information. I remember one that I thought was cool. It said something like 'Paris with resistance safe love you.'"

"Can I send someone to your house to collect those?"

"Sure. They are at the back of the bottom drawer of my desk."

"Did Kreger know about the letters?"

Beal turned her head to the side as if she were trying to shake something loose. "No. I never mentioned the letters to him."

"Good. That means Botox does not know they exist." I stood up. "I am starving. I am going to the Deli to get us some breakfast. While I am gone, would you please make a list of the groceries you will need to stay here for at least a couple of weeks?"

"Two weeks!" she exclaimed.

"I am afraid so. Right now, this is the safest place you can be. You will be protected 24/7. We will continue filling in the blanks in the timeline over breakfast." I left and headed to the Deli. I was careful not to be noticed or followed. The security team was not yet in place.

On my way to the Deli, my mind was racing. The letters would give me a timeline for Adare's assignments in Europe. I would study the microdot image in a new light. The canvas might have something to say about the coded letters. I was waiting to cross the street to the Deli when my spidey sense started screaming at me. My thoughts dissolved, and I looked around with forced casualness. The traffic was nonstop. I was trying to jaywalk, but it seemed impossible. I turned to walk down the block to the end and use the crosswalk when a black SUV pulled up beside me. The back door opened, a man stepped out, grabbed my arm, swung me around, and pushed me inside the vehicle. The back seat was empty, so I went with the forward motion, slid across the seat on my chest, and opened the door on the opposite side. I slid right out of the car and dashed between the traffic to the other side of the road. I looked back at a man sitting in the back seat. The door was open. Several cars had slowed to get past without hitting the open door. Horns were blaring as a large cube van could not get past and stopped. It blocked the man's view of me. I hustled down to the Deli and slipped into a seat beside the windows. I knew that I could not be seen by anyone outside, and I wanted to get the license plate of the SUV. I suspected it was Botox's men, but I wanted to make sure. Eddy, the owner of the Deli, approached me and asked me what I would like. I was about to order two breakfasts to go while waiting for the cube van to get past the SUV. Suddenly, the SUV sped away. I was unable to get a plate number.

"Are you alright, Mr. Cervantes?" he asked with a pencil poised to take my order.

"I am fine, Eddy," I said and turned to look at him. I ordered. I kept staring at the door, half expecting one of the men to enter the Deli. They did not. I kept an eye out and was rewarded as the SUV pulled into the parking lot of the Old Town Music Hall across the street. The driver got out and stood leaning on the fender. He was staring at the Deli. I immediately wondered where thug number two was lurking.

I looked back at Eddy and gestured for him to come over. He smiled back and stepped from behind the counter. The Deli door opened with a dingle of the bell on the top. Eddy glanced in that direction. He smiled at the new customer and said, "Would you like a table, sir?" The man turned quickly, and his jacket swung open. I saw a pistol on his hip. The smile disappeared from Eddy's face. The man turned and saw me sitting at the window. He moved in my direction. I reached out, picked up the saltshaker, and slipped it into my jacket pocket. I stood. I did not want to cause damage in the Deli, so I headed for the rear exit. As I walked, I removed the lid from the saltshaker and glanced back as I stepped out the door. The man had his gun in his hand and was moving toward me. As the door closed, I stepped to the side, filled my hand with salt, and waited. He opened the door. I threw the salt into his face. He yelled and lifted his gun hand to his face. I took advantage of the motion and slammed his gun hand into the closed door. He dropped the gun. I picked it up, pulled him forward, and kicked him behind the knees. He fell to the ground. I pressed the barrel to his head and said, "Who are you working for?" I pushed the gun barrel forward sharply to add stress to my question.

All I got was, "Fuck You."

"No, fuck you." I hit him hard on the back of his head. He dropped to the ground. I dragged him behind the green garbage containers and checked him for some sort of ID. All I found was a card for—what I assumed was—a strip joint. I could not conceive of any other type of establishment that would call itself "The Honey Pot." I took a picture of his face, then took all the bullets from his pistol and tossed it at him. Back in the deli, I got my order. Eddy asked if I was ok. I smiled and nodded, then slipped out the back exit and returned to my apartment.

I never mentioned anything about being followed. I decided it was better to keep that to myself. We ate the food I had purchased from the Deli. I sipped my coffee. "Did you make a list of supplies you will need for the week?" I asked. She handed it to me. I glanced at it and handed it back. "Looks good. Phone this in and get it delivered."

Beal took the note back. She frowned. "So, I have to stay here for two weeks."

"I really think that is a minimum. If Botox finds you at home, he will use you to get to me. You need to let me figure out what to do, so he either gives up the treasure hunt or realizes the whole thing is bogus and a waste of time. I need time to convince him of the latter."

"All right. What am I going to do sitting in your apartment all day?"

"You are a clever lady. I am sure you can find something to do. Just do not use your phone or use social media. That is likely to lead him straight here." She rolled her eyes at me and plunked down on the sofa. "I am sending someone to your house to retrieve the letters from your desk. Do you have a key?"

She shook her head. "I keep a spare at the back of the suite. There is a small porcelain frog in the flower garden. It is under him."

"Great. I have some work to do. I need to go into my lab. Just knock on the door if you need me," I said and left her sitting on the sofa. She looked a little lost, but that was a lot better than being a captive of the likes of Botox.

SOLVING THE MICRODOT

MY lab layout was fairly simple. Three sides had countertops and shelving above. There were no cupboards. Cupboards tend to conceal. My mother's kitchen was a case in point. She was always of the mind that an object in a cupboard with the door closed ceased to exist and needed no further thought. There was a problem with that theory in that the objects hidden were truly forgotten until you needed to use the cupboard space for something else. When this happened to my mother, she would start a cleaning frenzy. That meant that I would be commandeered to be her helper. Now, this was a job I hated. She would remove everything from the cupboards, clean them, and decide what to do with them. The cleaning part was my job. The deciding part was her job. Inevitably, she would return most of the things to the cupboards and remove just enough to allow space for the object she wanted to put into the cupboard in the first place. What did she do with the things removed from the cupboards, you might ask? Well, suffice it to say that the basement storage room was a horror to behold.

On the shelves in my lab were all the tools that my profession of finding things might need. All were in perfect working order and easily accessible. I did not need any of them at this time. What I needed was practically in the center of the room. I slipped into a large recliner and tilted it back. I let my eyes drift back into my head and watched the canvas open up. I was feeling like a drug addict in need of a fix, and I knew the canvas would improve my state of mind. I transformed into my favorite bird, a small brown kestrel, and soared on the updrafts. I simply hovered there. I was above a mist-shrouded landscape. Small clouds scudded by. I relaxed as the winds had their way with me.

I had always discovered interesting things when I was not purposefully looking. I hoped today would be like that. Suddenly, a downdraft caught me, and I spiraled lower until the clouds were above me. The ground was covered by lines in the shape of a web. My mind reproduced the image on the microdot. As I went lower, I could see the color of some of the lines change. The spokes remained black while the ones that curved became a blueish green. It was then I realized what I was looking at. It was a map. The black curved lines were roads, and the blue-colored lines were waterways. I did the canvas equivalent of sitting up straight and taking notice. I had to find the artifact that looked like a seven-legged spider. I flew lower and searched the area of the microdot map where I remembered seeing it. It was there, standing at the intersection of a blue line and a black line. The spider was definitely a picture of a diamond molecule. I was now sure this was where long-dead Adare had hidden the diamonds. A lot of questions flooded in. *Was the treasure still there? Was it worth all the trouble it was taking to find it? Maybe it consisted of just the two diamonds that Beal had found in the flask?* And the most important question of all: *What was this image a map of? Where was it?* I needed to determine the location if I was to make any progress in answering the posed questions.

I became purposeful and flew over the black and blue lines. Nothing revealed itself. It was like the canvas showed me a better view of the image on the microdot. It contained no details that might help determine where. I sat up and let the canvas fall to dust. I decided that old-fashioned detective work was needed. I got the microdot slide from my safe and projected it to the large TV screen on the wall and started writing down ideas that might get me closer to the actual location. I knew it must be in Europe. It must be a place that Adare the Spy was located during the war. I hoped the letters that Beal kept would give me some places to start. If I could track his locations, I might be able to connect the dots and get a little closer than Europe.

The letters would not arrive until tomorrow, so I moved to the computer desk in the corner and analyzed maps of Europe to see if I could find a place that looked like the image on the microdot. I started with Google Maps and zoomed in on where I found the watch. Killaloe was a good place to start. I knew Adare had been there, and I assumed he was the one who hid the watch in the graveyard. The map of Killaloe did not look anything like the microdot map. From there I went to Limerick. It was the nearest large city. I found nothing. I spent the next few hours jumping from major city to major city throughout Europe, to no avail.

My house cell phone buzzed. I plunked down in the lounge chair and answered it.

"Hello."

"Mattie, it's Maggie. Just wondering if you still want to get together. I have a few days off starting tomorrow. Maybe we could meet for dinner if you are free. I would love to see you. I would also love to *really* see you. So, are you free?" My mind jumped to a million scenarios. Going out to dinner with a woman was a completely new experience for me. Going out to dinner with Maggie filled me with dread and promise all at the same time. I chastised myself. I was no longer a boy. I was a full fledge detective as well as a man. "Mattie? Are you still there? I hope I didn't call at a bad time. If you want to chat later, I can call you back. Mattie?"

I cleared my throat. "Sorry. It is nice to hear from you."

"Were you in that outer space mode you sometimes go into? I thought you might have grown out of that."

"No. I was working on the computer. I have a case."

"So, you are not free. It is just that I get my days off starting tomorrow. Then I have to work for two weeks straight. I am afraid you might forget about me, so I called."

"I am glad you did."

"So do you want to go out with me or not?"

The phrase *I really want to see you* echoed in my head. My mind flashed back to some of our previous adventures, and I decided it would be good for me. "Maggie, I would love to go out with you. How about tomorrow night? Maybe we could meet. Let me know where. Perhaps you can make a reservation at your favorite restaurant."

"Great. I will text you. I have one question."

"What is that?"

"It is about your mother. Is she still running your life?"

I laughed. "Why would you ask that?"

"It is just that I remember the last time I saw her. She was screaming at me that I should leave her son alone, as if I was bullying you or something."

I laughed again. "Don't worry about my mother. I must get back to work. Send me a text with the where and when you want to meet."

"Ok, Mattie. I am looking forward to it. All of me is looking forward to it if you catch my meaning." She laughed.

"Bye," I said.

"Bye, Mattie," she replied in a seductive voice.

I hung up the phone. I heard a pounding noise. That sent me to the security monitors. At least four men were working on repairing the broken windows of my office and cleaning up the mess. By the look of their progress, they would be done in a couple of hours. I knew I was not going to get anything else done, so I went out to chat with Beal and see what she had bought for dinner.

FUN WITH MAGGIE

I was sitting in the waiting area of the restaurant Maggie had texted to meet me. I was early, so I considered visiting the canvas but decided against it. There were just too many people milling about. My mind drifted back to our time together. My mother took center stage in this memory.

My mother was pragmatic about most things. All problems could be solved with her practical sensibilities. All problems but one. That problem was Maggie. When she found out that Maggie and I were "friends," she grew concerned. That concern turned to apprehension when she discovered we saw each other every day after school. I would walk Maggie home and spend the next hour in her bedroom. Her parents were not home until after five. By then I was gone. To this day, I don't think they ever knew that I was there.

My mother discovered our meetups. Knowing how she would react; I told her a half-truth. I am not a good liar. I told her I was helping her, and she was helping me. I refused to elucidate the nature of that help, except to say that it was critical to our education. For a while, she let the whole thing slide. I think she was hoping it was a phase and I would soon start acting weird again. She understood my weirdness. When things did not change, and I became more normal and spent nearly every day after school with Maggie, her apprehension increased. She started acting fearful that I was going to ruin my life. That is when she tried to stop our meetings by scheduling things after school. She would never actually talk to me and ask straightforward questions. She left that to others. Once, she scheduled an appointment with my psychiatrist. That appointment did not go well. I remember it clearly.

I sat down in his office. I was filled with a suspicion that my mother had set this up. I soon discovered that I was correct.

Dr.: Hello, Mathew. How are you?

Me: Fine.

Dr.: Good. Is there anything you want to share?

Me: No. Can I go?

Dr.: Where do you want to go? You just got here, and you haven't told me anything about what you have been doing lately.

Me: I want to go to my friend's house.

Dr.: Who is your friend?

This question confirmed my suspicions that my mother had set this up. I was now anticipating questions about sex and contraception.

Me: Why do you want to know?

Dr.: Your mother is concerned. She thinks you are having relations with a girl and that you are spending all your time with her. She is afraid you might get too (he paused) … involved.

Me: We are just friends. We have sex. It is fun. I like it. She likes it. I don't see the problem. She is on the pill.

Dr.: Are you in love with this girl?

Me: No! I told you. We have sex. That is all. I am going now. (I stood up)

Dr.: One last thing, Mathew, are you still looking at (he paused and shuffled through some papers) ...the canvas, or have you stopped?

Me: No. Why would I stop? What has that got to do with this little sex talk that my mother set up?

Dr.: Nothing, I guess. I was just curious to see if you had outgrown that habit.

Me: or your information, anyone who has spent time with the canvas would not want to stop. It is the coolest thing ever. Are you finished with your dumb questions?

Dr.: Yes, Mathew.

Me: Can I go now?

(He looked up at me.)

Me: I am going.

I turned and left his office. My mother was waiting for me. I walked to the door and called over my shoulder, "You can go in and snoop in my private business with him. I am going to see Maggie. I am late for our meeting." I left.

My thoughts were interrupted to see Maggie standing in front of me. She was not dressed in scrubs anymore. I don't know why I expected her to be wearing her work clothes. I guess it was because in the past we never paid attention to that. We mostly just spent our time together naked. We would go into her bedroom and take off our clothes. We would kiss, touch, probe, pinch, and then have sex. Once we were finished, we would get dressed and I would leave.

I really looked at her. Her light red hair was up, with a couple of curly wisps hanging down on either side of her face. She had makeup on. The eye shadow was a light pink, and her lips were mauve with black highlights around the edge. My eyes fell to her dress. It was emerald green. She was fuller than I remembered. Her breasts were bigger. She approached me and bent over to kiss me. I found myself staring at her breasts as her dress fell open. She kissed me on the top of my head. I stood up. I guess I must have looked lost, for she did what she always did and took control.

"I made the reservation for seven. We are a bit late," she said as she led me to the reservation desk. She caught the eye of the man behind the desk. "Cervantes. Two for seven." She looked up at me, expecting a reaction. She had made the reservation in my name. I smiled, even though I was unsure of the reason she had used my name and not her own. We were shown to a table near one of the large windows that ran across the front of the seating area.

As usual, she started to talk. I found myself falling into the old habit of nodding and smiling. I liked listening to her voice. It had a pleasant lilt and relaxed me. Maggie was not one to talk in riddles. If she wanted something, she always came right out with it.

"Ooh, I'm starving." She opened the menu. "Why don't you order us some wine? I like red. Some merlot, I think. This is a steak house and merlot always goes well with beef. I think they specialize in prime rib. Are you going to have steak?" She paused. I nodded. She set down her menu and glanced around the restaurant to see if anyone was paying any attention to us. Seeing no one, she bent forward and continued, "Are you up for some fun after dinner?" She did not wait for an answer. She wiggled her chest back and forth. "…Cause I am." I simply smiled in response. "Good." She said and picked up her menu again.

We both had the filet mignon medium rare, with two glasses of merlot. I had never seen her eat before. She stayed in perfect form. It was obvious to me that eating, to her, was not much different than having sex. It was filled with murmurs and actions of appreciation right down to the last bite.

I asked her a question. I knew she would have to answer in such a way so as not to have the conversation come around to me. And I did want to know. "So, Maggie, what have you been doing for the last 10 years?"

She started at the time her family moved. She told me that she missed me terribly. She studied to be a nurse. She met several men and had married none. She moved to Venice Beach after she got a job at the hospital and had been here ever since. She admitted to scouting out a doctor or two but decided that doctors were not the great catch they were purported to be. Uptight was the word she used. I laughed and said that I was probably the most uptight of anyone she had spent time with.

We ended up at her apartment. We fell into our old ways. We drank brandy in the nude and had delightful sex. I took a taxi home with the promise not to take another ten years to do a repeat performance.

DISCOVERIES

I woke clear-headed. The sex the night before was wonderful and had also served to clear away the effects of alcohol. I am not a big drinker, and it would not take much to give me a headache the next day. Beal had prepared a big breakfast from the groceries she had delivered the previous day. We ate without much conversation. The house phone rang, and I was informed by Billie that the repair crew was finished and I could avail myself to the front office. It had been re-keyed. The keys were to be left in the drop box. She also told me that the letters that Beal said were from her grandfather should already be in the drop box in the office. I sat and turned to Beal. "I have work to do today. Do you have something to entertain yourself?"

"I bought some books yesterday. I think I will snuggle down with a good romance novel and while the day away."

"I will be in the lab. If you need me, just knock."

"Same," she replied. I looked questioningly at her. "If you need me. I assume you are going to be studying my grandfather's letters. I just thought you might need me to explain something. Do you have a plan on finding my grandfather's diamonds?"

"I have no plan yet. It is too soon." I paused. "You do realize that the diamonds, if they actually exist, were probably stolen from somewhere, and the *powers that be* might want them returned. That includes the two you found in the flask."

Her face became hard, and her teeth clenched. "That is not up to you. You are under contract. Find the diamonds and I will decide what to do with them."

"You are mistaken. I completed the contract when I gave you the pocket watch. At this point, I am just trying to keep you safe. If you do not wish to stay here, you can leave at any time."

"In that case, I wish to engage you once again to locate the diamonds."

I could tell I had hit a nerve. In truth, I wanted to find the diamonds almost as much as she did. It was the mystery of a lifetime. I didn't want the diamonds after I found them. "No. I do not wish to start a new contract. I do wish to enter into a partnership."

"A partnership? What kind of partnership?"

"Well—you have supplied the information and the clues. It is a treasure your grandfather hid. I, on the other hand, will be doing all the work, so I figure a 90/10 split is more than generous."

"Ninety for you, I assume."

"Of course."

"This is bullshit. Those diamonds rightfully belong to me."

"Here is my logic. I figure that ten percent of the diamonds, if they are anything like the ones you found in the flask, will ensure you can live a very comfortable life. The remaining diamonds will be returned to the rightful owners if they can be found. I am guessing they were taken from Jewish people during the war. I am also going to assume that your grandfather would have wished for something like that to happen." I figured the last part would make her think. I was right.

"I agree, but only because it would be impossible for me to find them on my own. If Botox were to find them, he would take it all and probably kill me to keep me quiet."

"Thank you. Please don't leave. Botox is a real danger to both of us, and you are safe here. If you need to go out for some reason, please call 314. The person on the other end will ask you for a 15-minute window of time that you will return, during which your fingerprints will work to unlock the back door. If you do not arrive during that time period, you will be locked out. Understood?" She nodded. At that moment, I had a thought that I hoped would keep her on my side. "This could make an interesting novel about how your grandfather got the diamonds. You might consider writing it all down as we discover more of his story. It could be a best-seller, especially if it follows the publicity that returning the diamonds would bring. We can always keep your cut secret. Something to think about."

I left her to her own devices and went to fetch the puzzle letters from the drop box. I could tell she was interested in my suggestion. I retrieved the puzzle letters and the one complete letter that had been rescued by Perfect Paper from Adare to his wife from my lockbox. I took them to my lab and spread them out on the long counter, sorted by date. I set the open lockbox beside the papers.

There were about eight of them. They consisted of a few sentences expressing his love and then a 20 x 20 word-search with a themed list of words below. None of the puzzles were solved, but all had been decoded from the word list. I sent this information to Billie hoping it would help her decode the letter. The true message was written on the back of each letter. It was just a matter of determining the location he wished to communicate. I sent this information to Billie hoping it would help her decode the letter.

Mar 17 1940	*nn␣k␣␣ttIonrgrin␣dwifB␣eLoonorIl*
	In London working for Brit Intel
Apr 21 1940	onagtpah␣i␣Lolnisipou-nn␣y␣heloepfdpiw␣c␣tq␣u
	playing with special photo equip - fun
May 5 1940	agialor␣c␣itnhwotueelsk␣ple␣osiagis␣p␣eppasn
	taking ship Walpole to Europe special assign
May 10 1940	ninpr␣bwiohimemr␣t␣p␣sdhoans␣ataarig
	on ship in Amsterdam harbor waiting
May 26 1940	aiono␣t␣nwyb␣lornoK␣␣rcnn␣kf␣dook␣dbeoOotr
	back in London broken foot OK do not worry
Aug 25 1940	ned␣tapi␣eirnoor␣sei␣l␣popobssiathghslp
	in Ireland to photograph possible spies

I wished I had seen these earlier. He must have put the watch in the graveyard ball while he was in Ireland. The photo of him in the lid of the footlocker seemed to confirm this. He was trying to tell his wife where he had hidden the pocket watch. I checked out the two remaining locations, all occurring in the next six months. The first was sent from southern France and then three were sent from Spain. The last one was from London. It mentioned the Blitz. I wondered if he had been killed in one of the German bombing raids on London. My list of locations was:

London England

I guessed his photography skills were needed.

HMS Walpole

Had to look this one up. It was the ship sent by Churchill to rescue a huge cache of industrial diamonds that the Germans could use to build weapons. These diamonds were recovered. Adare was on that ship.

Amsterdam Netherlands

Adare was there when the industrial diamonds were taken from the Diamond Mart. Interesting.

London England

With a broken foot. Something must have happened in Amsterdam. I wondered what?

Limerick Ireland

No info

Vichy France

No info

Madrid Spain

No info

London England

During the Blitz. Perhaps he was killed there because there was no further contact with his wife.

I sat back and rubbed my eyes. They were burning. My sleep the previous night was not restful. I kept waking up. I assumed it had to do with a relative stranger sleeping in my house. I sat in the reclining chair in the corner of the office. I was going to try to nap, but that was not to be so. The Canvas wanted attention. I did not mind. I found the canvas very restful. I soon found myself riding the canvas-created updrafts. I was purposeless, just like the youthful me when I first discovered the canvas. It was exhilarating.

Suddenly, I felt the need to dive with my kestrel avatar. I swooped down, gaining speed until the ground loomed. I turned a single wingtip and the hawk I had become swooped out of the dive and rocketed over the landscape. I approached a small medieval-looking town. The wooden buildings were all single story. Some had thatched roofs. Inside, I could see a man. I alighted on a nearby tree branch and watched him. By the look of the tools, he was a carpenter. He appeared to be building a small shed. All the walls were in place, and he had just finished thatching the roof. Beside the shed was a large pile of bundles. He carried the bundles into the shed. He stacked them against the back wall until all the bundles were inside. They reached the top of the wall. He then carried lumber into the shed. I could see him clearly as he built a wall in front of the bundles. Once he finished, he stood back and inspected his efforts. There was a crack between two of the boards near the top of the wall. He removed the top three boards and reseated them so the crack was gone. He carefully inspected the wall for cracks. Once he was satisfied that there were none, he locked the door.

It was times like these I hated the canvas. I knew it was trying to tell me something in its most cryptic fashion. What, I had no idea. The worker didn't stop. Just a few meters away, there was another shed that had obviously just been completed. I could have sworn it was not there when I first arrived. There was another pile of packages stacked in front of this shed. The carpenter repeated his previous actions. He moved all the packages to the back wall of the shed and constructed a wall to conceal them. He checked for cracks. This time, the cracks were nearer the bottom. He removed two bottom boards and replaced them so there were no cracks, inspected the wall, and closed and locked the door. I flew up a few branches. I glanced over the area. Something had changed. The first shed was gone. I looked back at the carpenter. Only to discover that the second completed shed had also disappeared. To the right was a third shed with another pile of bundles stacked in front. The carpenter was calmly walking toward it.

If the canvas was trying to tell me where the diamonds were hidden it was not successful. It was unlikely they were hidden in some old shed. The bundles were much too big to be filled with diamonds. Perhaps they were hidden in many different places. That did not make sense. He wanted to tell his wife where to find the diamonds in case he was not able to retrieve them. This must be the case. He was most likely killed before the end of the war. The simplest scenario consisted of telling his wife where he had hidden the watch with the clues to the treasure's location inside on a microdot. She had deciphered the message in the last letter. He told her that there was a treasure, but not how to find it. She had missed the clue in the photograph inside the lid of the canvas.

I turned my attention to the inside lid of the footlocker. I looked at the pictures. I pulled the tack, holding the picture of Adare in the graveyard, and turned it over. The back held the information that his wife needed to find the pocket watch. It said, "Shot in Killaloe Ireland at St Andrew's church." He had given her enough, but she had not found it.

I had the only clue that mattered, and that was the microdot. I abandoned the letters and the footlocker and projected the microdot image on the screen. I glanced over at the list of cities where he had spent time in 1940 and decided to see if the microdot map was for any of those cities. It only took a few minutes to overlay the image on the microdot on various city maps. I decided the most likely city must be Amsterdam. That is where the Diamond Market is situated, and he was there on May 10, 1940. I remembered the seven-legged spider was an exact match for a diamond molecule I had seen on the poster. The diamonds must be hidden there.

I expanded the image further and inspected every line. If this was indeed a map of Amsterdam, there was one particularly wide one I guessed was a canal. There was something odd about it. Then it jumped out at me. The black line representing one of the large canals was covered with gray letters. It looked like this:

GELEDHHDTEWBNCACARTEHUORIERORISIRPUNLSNCGINET

The letters still held no meaning. I sent them to Billie. Perhaps the same transitional code would work here. I stressed to Billie that I needed her to drop everything and try to use the same method to decode this message. I needed it ASAP. She did not disappoint. She returned this:

BRUG NINE CELLAR
SECOND ARCH
RIGHT SIDE
IN THREE
UP TWO
Augustus

I looked up a couple of things, and I am pretty sure that a brug is a bridge. When I Googled brug nine, I discovered it is a bridge in Amsterdam, also known as the Torensluis. I don't know how a bridge could have a cellar. I will leave that to you as well as the arch business.

Yours,
Billie

I thanked her and laughed out loud. I was about to call out to Beal and share my discovery, but something told me not to. Her agreement to work together with me seemed to be contingent on my usefulness. It was obvious that she wanted all the treasure and might decide to double-cross me. She did not need to know, and if she did not know, then she could not strike a deal with someone else. I shut down the projector and pushed the open footlocker to the side. In doing so, I thought of Adare's complicated plans to get the treasure, even if he might not be alive to enjoy it. He must have loved his wife very much to go to these lengths to ensure she was looked after when he was gone.

I knew I had to go to Europe and investigate the clues. I did not want anyone to enter my lab. I seldom secured it to its maximum level, but something, a mistrust perhaps, made me engage all the security devices before leaving. The lab was now impenetrable. Even if the entire building burned to the ground, my lab would still be pristine inside. I turned to see a section of wall slide out and conceal the steel door. The impenetrable entrance was now hidden.

OFF TO GERMANY

THE next morning, I awoke early. I had a late morning flight. I left a simple note on the table for Beal - *Gone to find the diamonds.* I packed a few items I knew I might need: a knife, a small powerful flashlight, and a lock-picking set. I put these in my luggage. I didn't think they would cause any problems at the airport. If they did, I was sure I could replace them if needed. The airport process was very efficient for once. Perhaps it was because I was totally immersed in what I was about to embark upon. It was giving me a bit of a rush. I was remembering.

When I decided to become a detective, I knew my mother would flip out and probably try to have me committed if I told her. I remember the day I told her that I wanted to be an undertaker. I was still in high school. I had become enamored with death. It fascinated me. Not that I wanted to work with bodies. Yes, I knew that is what an undertaker did. It was more like I wanted to see some dead bodies, so I knew what to expect when I encountered one. Again, not that I expected to encounter any. My thoughts on the subject were a little fragmented. We were in the kitchen when I told her that was what I wanted to be when I left school. She did not say anything to me directly. She simply walked away. The next day, I had a new appointment with my psychiatrist. She told me she would take me personally instead of having me go by myself after school. This should have set off my alarm bells, but I must have been preoccupied with something on the canvas. The next day after school, she picked me up.

"I could have walked myself."

"No, I think I want to chat with the doctor before you go in."

"Why?"

She did not answer. The car was filled with a chilly silence. I had learned long ago that she was not going to answer me, and I was not going to ask again if I knew *what was good for me*. I never really understood how the phrase *what is good for you* indicated that something really bad would happen if you did what she did not want you to do. Anyway, we ended up in the doctor's office and she went in first. I simply conjured the canvas and floated away on some fascinating updraft. I was not too concerned about how I looked because I was the only person in the office. I guess my eyes rolled back in my head when my mother exited the office. When she returned to the waiting room, I heard her screech, "Mattie, Mattie—snap out of it!" I sat up. "The doctor wants to talk with you. I will wait out here."

I went in and sat in the chair opposite his desk. I nodded at him. He nodded back and opened his top drawer. He removed two KitKat bars and tossed me one. I smiled. I was thinking that I had him trained and not the other way around. It was a delicious thought.

He nibbled on one of the fingers of chocolate. "Your mother is concerned."

I nibbled on a finger. "My mother is always concerned," I said and stared at the ceiling as if there was something incredibly interesting up there.

"She is concerned that you are going to waste your life."

"Everyone wastes their life from someone else's viewpoint." My response was because of my recent philosophy course. There were only six of us in the class. The latest discussions revolved around 'Reality vs Point of View.'

"She tells me you want to be an undertaker when you leave school. She is concerned that you will be wasting a brilliant mind. She wants you to become …" He paused here. "… something more intellectual." I bit into another finger from my KitKat bar. "She asked me if she should have you committed. To protect you."

"Protect me? From what?"

"Yourself," he responded bluntly.

"What does "committed" mean?"

"Well, it means she would have more control over what you can do. You might be kept in a hospital or other medical facility."

"She can do that?" I sat up with an incredulous look on my face.

"Not without a doctor's order," he smiled. "Don't worry. I would never have you committed. You are one of the sanest people I know. Your mother howe…" he stopped. He did not have to continue. I knew what he was about to say. "How old are you, Mathew?"

"Seventeen"

"You have one more year before you are legally an adult and can pretty much become whatever you like. You could go to an undertaker's school if there is such a thing."

"I don't want to do that anymore. Please inform my mother that you have cured me of the notion."

He nodded. "I am glad we had this little talk. My advice is that you keep some of your more …" Again, he stopped. He was choosing his words carefully. I kind of figured that the series of words that went through his head were *weird, odd, strange, bizarre, macabre, nutty, etc.* He finally settled on, "out of the ordinary ideas to yourself." I nodded. He continued, "How is the canvas these days? See anything cool?"

I knew he was trying to lighten the mood, so I went on for a bit about a new landscape I was exploring. He smiled until the timer on his desk dinged. He stood up.

"See you soon, Mathew. I will chat with your mother now." He winked at me. I left the office and my mother entered. I never heard any more about the visit. I did learn to keep my thoughts to myself. No more sharing with my mother. Once I had my own apartment, I was able to take a series of courses that would benefit any detective. Lock-picking was one of them. Actually, it was a course on Locksmithing. It had proved invaluable on many occasions.

My seat was once again in first class. I had decided to fly to Frankfurt and take the train to Amsterdam. If anyone was following me, it would be easier to spot them on the train. On the flight, I did not attempt to see if anyone looked suspicious. No one bumped into me, so I was sure no tracking devices had been surreptitiously placed on my person. I settled in my seat, chatted with the flight attendant about my needs, slipped on my night mask, and conjured up the canvas.

TRAIN TO AMSTERDAM

I arrived in Frankfurt, Germany, at 8:00 a.m. none the worse for wear. First-class seats are a must if one is to travel on any long flight. I have flown coach but only on short hops. They could never be described as pleasant. I'm a first-class kind of guy. (I'm giggling at my comment.) I'm just ordinary, but I can afford first class, so that is how I fly.

I took a taxi to the train station. I entered the car and put my case in a locker. I was soon settled into my seat. The first-class seat configuration was two seats, the aisle, and then a single seat. I was in the single seat. I settled in and waited for the train to leave the station. I paid little attention to my fellow passengers, for I donned my dark glasses and closed my eyes. I was about to open the canvas to explore what it knew about Amsterdam. I suspected that the canvas did not know anything about anything. It was just a container of all things at all times that I was somehow able to access. Once inside, it became a matter of directed exploration. I never got the chance.

"Excuse me," said a voice in front of me. I opened my eyes. A woman was leaning around her seat. She was 30-ish, attractive, and smiling. I lifted my glasses in response. "I hate to be a bother. I know that these seats will turn but I cannot for the life of me figure out how. Do you know how they work?"

I smiled at her. She had an accent, but for some reason it was wrong. At first, appeared to be what can only be described as "posh English," but it was wrong. I dismissed my thoughts about her accent. "How can I help?" I asked. I kept my tone neutral.

"I wanted to spend the trip looking out the window at the sights. I was told that I could turn the seat and lock it in that position. But it won't move." I looked down at my seat and spotted a lever. I lifted it and attempted to turn my seat. It did not move. She was watching me. "Yes, that is what I did, but I couldn't move mine either. I looked again and noticed a toggle just to the side of the lever. I flipped it and tried again. The seat turned smoothly. I returned my seat to its original position. "How did you do that?" she asked as she stood and put her palms together as if she was about to pray. She smiled again. "Show me, please."

"It appears that you must flip this toggle before it will turn. I guess it is a locking or safety feature." I pointed at the mechanism on the side of my seat.

She turned back and her seat quickly turned toward the window. "Thank you," she said.

I pulled down my glasses and resumed my canvas connection. I was the kestrel lazily circling.

"Excuse me," the woman said. I could only assume that she could not see my eyes through the dark glasses I was wearing. She thought I was just sitting, staring into space, and could interrupt me. In a way I was. I removed my glasses and looked at her. I can only guess that my expression was one of irritation, for she quickly said, "I'm sorry. Were you resting?"

"No. I was just thinking." I forced a smile onto my face. "What can I do for you?"

"I was just wondering about our destination. I have never been to Amsterdam before. Have you?" I shook my head in the negative. "Oh." She paused. "Well, I was wondering if you have booked a hotel room. If you have, can you tell me if it is expensive?"

"That depends on your financial situation."

"Is it right downtown?"

"I think so."

"Which hotel?" this question was followed by her chair rotating around to face me, a smile, and a lean forward, allowing me to see a good portion of her ample breasts.

My hackles jumped to attention. I love that word. *Hackles.* It was obvious that she wanted to know my hotel and allay any suspicions as to why by distracting me. I must admit, I was distracted. I had only seen Maggie's naked breasts, but these were voluptuous and my base self wanted to see more. Because I was motivated in a couple of ways, I decided that I would play along to see where this was going and what she would be showing. (I know—too cute by half or by two.) This thought caused a smile to slip onto my face and my eyes to focus on her breasts. I looked up at her and said, "I'm not sure what it is called. My itinerary is in my suitcase. It is locked up over there. I don't think it was super expensive. A few hundred Euros a night, as I recall. I take it you have not booked a room yet."

"No, I have not. Not yet. Do you think there might be a room available at your hotel?"

I was about to put her off when the phrase "Keep your friends close and your enemies closer" jumped into my head. I was on my way to find a treasure in diamonds. Perhaps this young lady was following me. I wanted to know what she knew and who sent her. If she was just being honest, then I might cater to my baser motives. The thought of bedding her was not unattractive. A third option jumped into my head, and it sobered my thoughts a little. Perhaps she thought of me as a perfect mark. She needed a place to sleep and someone to pay her tab for a few days. She saw me as harmless, easily manipulated, and easily robbed. If I allowed my teenage ego to take over, I might have put a stop to it. Instead, I let my super sleuth ego have free rein. I answered her, "I don't know, but given the time of year, I am pretty sure this is their slow season."

"You think so. I read the reviews on a hotel that my friend recommended. They were not great." She stood and turned around. She bent over to pick up her handbag. Now she was being overt with the sexual teasing, for her short skirt did little to conceal her ample derriere. She turned back, opened the handbag, and removed a piece of paper. She read the review. It was not flattering. She sat down and leaned forward again. "Do you think we could share a taxi so I can check out your hotel?"

I scrunched up my forehead. My mind raced. "I must drop something off before I go to the hotel, so that does not work for me."

She put on a pouty face and sat back in her chair. Suddenly, she stood up. "I have an idea. I'm going to give you something. I hope it will convince you to take me with you," she said and jumped up. She grabbed my hand and dragged me out of my chair. "Follow me."

I was not sure where this was going, but I knew I was already uncomfortable. I withdrew my hand and sat back down. "No thanks," I said and managed a weak smile.

Her demeanor changed suddenly. My body tensed. My thoughts went to Botox. Maybe she was in his employ? "Look, I will level with you. I find myself in financial difficulty and I cannot afford a taxi." Her body language changed with her tone. She was no longer trying to seduce me.

"All right, you can come with me as long as you don't mind waiting for me. I have a short meeting to attend. I just need to drop something off." I had made up my mind not to take her to my hotel. I did not want her to know where I was staying.

"Thank you," she said. We sat in silence for the remainder of the trip.

Once out of the train station, I called a taxi. I kept my suitcase with me as if it contained something valuable. I asked the driver to stop near a street corner where other taxis were waiting. I got out. "I will be just a few minutes," I said and paused as I realized that I did not know her name. "I must deliver something. I grabbed my bag and got out of the taxi. I walked into a corner office building. I looked for another exit and quickly left the building. I glanced back and saw that she was still sitting in the taxi. I wondered how long she would wait before realizing that I had ditched her.

HOTEL DIE PORT VAN CLEVE

I arrived at my hotel soon after. I knew I had to keep this woman, whose motives were unclear, out of my business. I ordered an early dinner from room service and relaxed. The woman's motives were still front and center. I remembered our conversations. I heard her accent again and realized what was wrong with it. It was American trying to be English. Why would she fake an accent? Did she not want to be identified as American? She wanted to know where I was staying, to the point of suggesting sexual favors. Only someone with knowledge of why I was here would do what she did. A treasure of diamonds can make people do just about anything.

I lay down on my bed and slipped into the universe of the canvas. I was surprised at what I had become. I was not a hawk flying high above the landscape. I was tiny and definitely earthbound. I was not sure what I was. As I scampered about in what appeared to be a rather desolate landscape, I came upon a shiny piece of tin. It caught my reflection as I passed. I was a rodent. I was either a rat or a mouse. I stepped back to the reflective tin and studied my new body. I was neither a rat nor a mouse. I was something else entirely. My face had attributes of a human and my front paws were more like hands. I shrugged. The canvas obviously had something to tell me. It was weird sometimes. I had to assume this body was the best choice to ensure I could discover whatever it wanted to tell me. Past experience with the canvas told me two things: one, it always spoke in riddles and two, sometimes what happened had no relationship to anything in my world. If I viewed it as an entity, then I thought it might just be trying to fuck with me. This was definitely in that category.

I was in a junkyard or garbage dump. Masses of rusted metal and piles of rotting wood were all around me. I could smell the decay. I scrabbled around the piles of debris. I was looking for whatever I was supposed to find. I had no idea what to look for. I was just about ready to call it quits when I heard a rattle and a crash of metal. I scampered to the top of a particularly high pile of trash. I was trying to ignore the smell. It was almost overpowering. Then someone or thing called out to me. This was a very rare event.

"What are you doing up there? Get down or you will never be able to get the stink off of you," yelled a voice from somewhere. I looked around but could not see who might have called. I ran down the trash pile in the direction of the voice. There was no one there. I heard the flap of wings and a bird landed beside me. It was a very familiar bird. It was my usual avatar. It was a sleek kestrel. It bobbed and weaved and stared at me. "You need to take more care if you want to stay clean," it said. I felt like I was talking to myself, then I realized that perhaps I was. Suddenly, the canvas collapsed.

I sat up in bed. My alter ego was trying to tell me something. Perhaps I had changed. This particular case had changed me. I had smashed a man's nose with my elbow, battled with chamber pots in the hospital, shot two people in the foot, and left a strange woman without money on the hook for taxi fare. These actions were out of character. At least I hoped my image of myself as a person with integrity was true. My time with the canvas was suggesting that I might want to reassess some of my actions. Perhaps the woman from the train was just what she stated. Maybe I should have taken her to the hotel as promised. I was getting better at company. I thought of Maggie and our teenage relationship. That had changed me for the better. That improved my people skills. I stood up too quickly and felt a little dizzy. I recovered quickly and shook my head to clear the fog. A new thought entered my head—*any future liaison with this woman will be dangerous.*

I realized I was exhausted and retired for the night. The next morning, I left the room and headed down to the lobby. I kept my eyes peeled for anyone who might take undue interest in me. No one did. I approached the hotel desk and requested to speak with someone who could help me with a little sightseeing. I had some very specific places in mind. The receptionist smiled and said she would have someone meet me in the lobby. She directed me to the bar. "I will send Filip to chat with you. He will be a few minutes. Yes?" I agreed and sat at a small table in the bar. I ordered a coffee and a croissant and looked around in as casual a manner as I was able.

After fifteen minutes, no one had arrived. I thought of donning my dark glasses and spending some time in my favorite place. I reached for my pocket when a man came and stood beside me. "My name is Filip. I understand you would like a guide to take you around Amsterdam."

I looked at a very tall and lanky man dressed in jeans and a jean jacket. He was blond and sported a ponytail that stuck out of the back of his baseball cap. I guessed he was in his early forties. I stood. "Please have a seat," I said and sat back down with him. "I would like someone to take me to some very specific spots and explain some of the history of those spots. Are you knowledgeable of the city and its history?"

"I was born here. If I do not know, I can surely find out. I charge 200 euros for 4 hours, plus the cost of petrol. When would you like to start?"

"Now, if that is possible."

"Yes, I can do that. What places would you like to visit?"

"I have two in mind. I am writing a book and need to do some research. I would like to start at the harbor and travel to where the industrial diamonds were kept in 1940. I don't think the building is still there, but I would like to experience going from the old harbor to where it was located. Can you do that?"

"No problem. Are you writing about what happened in 1940 when the British came and took the diamonds back to England before the Germans could steal them?"

"I am not writing about that specifically, but my character was involved in another theft during that time and I want to see the path he might have travelled. After that, I would like to go to the 'Tor en slu is'. Is that how you say it?"

"It is pronounced like Torensluis. *Tour-is-slag*," he said slowly. "Brug 9. Bridge 9 in English. Yes, I can take you there. Brug 9 is very close by. We could walk there."

"Great. Let's go there first," I said.

We stood and left the hotel. I was still concerned that I might be followed and glanced at the passers-by. No one paid the least attention to us as we walked. My guide told me about the bridge we were going to visit. "It is the widest bridge in Amsterdam. It spans the Singel Canal. It was completed in 1648. The name Torensluis means 'tower lock.' There used to be a tower that stood on the bridge but was torn down in 1849. I suppose that is the reason it was so wide. The foundation of this tower is under the bridge." We walked onto the bridge. He pointed at the bridge deck. "See these bricks. They are different from the other deck of the bridge. This is where the tower stood. Below these bricks is a room that was the cellar for the tower. It is still there. It was used to house prisoners at one time."

Upon hearing the word cellar, I knew I was in the right place. "Tell me more about this cellar."

"It is an interesting room that can be accessed by going down those stairs." He pointed to an opening with a chain across two posts.

"Can we go down and see?"

As an answer, he looked around and then stepped over the chain. He helped me over. We walked down some stairs to a wooden platform. A brick archway led to a locked door. He rattled the door. "It appears to be locked. I guess you could apply to visit. They sometimes have events down here. There was a jazz club here at one time." I reached out and inspected the padlock. It was large, round, and made of hardened stainless steel. It would require more than a smack with a hammer to open it. I noted the brand, hoping to see if I might be able to pick it. It was a German-made Abus 20/80. I frowned. It would not be easy to pick.

My guide turned and started up the stairs. "The only other thing is the statue of a famous Dutch writer Multatuli. I think that is his pen name. His real name was Dekker. I don't remember his first name." He pointed to the other side of the bridge at a statue. There were several tourists taking pictures in front of it. We turned and walked back across the bridge on the other side.

I wanted to spend a few minutes just observing the bridge and the people on it. I needed a sense of it if I was going to break into the cellar. I saw a café on my hotel side. The sign said, 'Café van Zuylen.' It had an outdoor terrace and would be a perfect observation spot. "Do you mind if we stop for a coffee at that café?" I asked.

"No, of course not. It is your money." He grinned at me. "And I assume you are buying."

COFFEE AT CAFÈ VAN ZUYLEN

WE were soon seated at a table. Our view of the canal and the bridge was perfect. I sat facing the bridge and my guide had his back to the view. I watched him continually glance up at any new patrons entering the café. He would watch them for a few seconds and then dismiss them. I asked, "You keep checking out the entrance. Are you watching for someone?"

He smiled. "No. It is an old habit. Forgive me." He glanced up at a couple being seated near us. "I used to be a police officer. I am retired."

"Any particular reason?"

"For what?" he asked. I could tell he was distracted.

"For retiring."

He looked at me. "I just had enough. Being a cop has a lot of stressors. Showing tourists around the city is a lot easier and, surprisingly, it is more lucrative. What other job could I make 200 euros in four hours, some of which involves sitting in a café drinking free coffee?" He smiled.

I watched as his smile morphed into a grimace. I heard very loud footsteps behind me. My thoughts were of someone that Botox might have sent. The footsteps sounded like a rather large person was making them. I was about to turn to see who was stomping toward us when someone walked right past me and turned to face me. It was the woman from the train. I could tell she was angry.

"You bastard. How could you leave me sitting in that taxi? I barely had enough money to pay the fare. You realize that we waited for a half hour with the meter running. I had to pay him and get out." She leaned into me and lifted her right arm. She was about to slap me when Filip reached out and grabbed her arm. She turned. "Get your fucking hands off of me or I will scream bloody murder!"

My mind raced. I needed to defuse this situation. I stood and pulled another chair up to the table. The waiter approached, sensing that things were about to escalate. I held him at bay with a hand gesture. "The lady would like a cup of herb tea," I said. He nodded and left. "Please let me explain," I said to the woman and gestured to the chair. She sat and stared at me. The waiter returned with the tea. I guessed he thought that expediency was the best way to keep the situation calm. She looked at it with disdain. I continued. "My meeting took a lot longer than I expected. Time flew by. When I realized that I had been a lot longer than planned, I sent someone down to pay for the cab and inform you I would be longer than expected. I told them to tell you to wait in a nearby café if you still wanted to come to my hotel. The messenger returned and said that the taxi was gone and there was no sign of you."

She reached for her tea. "You owe me for the taxi."

"Right. How much?"

"200 euros."

"Expensive taxi," I retorted.

"I don't believe this bullshit story. You need to pay for being a bastard. All you needed to say was that you did not want me to come with you and I would have been fine with that. But no, you led me on and took advantage of me."

"Pardon," I said incredulously.

"You took advantage of a desperate woman by coming on to me on the train." She sipped her tea. I glanced up at Filip. He raised his eyebrows and grinned. I looked back at the woman and made a decision. I reached for my wallet, took out two 100-euro notes, and set them on the table in front of me. I looked at her. "That is for the taxi," I said as I opened my wallet again. I took out two more 100-euro notes and placed them on the pile. "And that is for the inconvenience and having to suffer my thoughtlessness." There was no point in arguing with her about what really happened. It was now obvious that she was running a con and that had netted her 400 euros. She reached and covered the banknotes, but my hand slapped down on her hand and held it in place. "There is one caveat." I stared at her.

"What?" she spat out at me.

"That you go away. Do not contact me again. If you see me, go the other way. Make sure I never see you again. Understood."

"Yes, I get it."

I was about to raise my hand from her hand when I thought of something I wanted to ask her. "One more thing—Why the English accent? You are American, are you not?"

She stared at me. "Get your hand off my hand and my money." There was no trace of an accent. I lifted my hand. She took the bills and left the café.

"My, my. What was that all about?"

"Nothing really. Just a crazy woman I met on the train. Let's go for a drive. I still want you to show me the routes from the harbor to the location of the Diamond Mart circa 1940. Make sure you are not taking a route that did not exist in 1940."

"Not to worry. The roads and canals in this city have not changed very much in 500 years."

We took our drive. I was not attending to any of the routes. I wanted to see if I could figure out how Adare got the diamonds in the first place. I soon realized that it was an impossible task. Maybe Adare would find a way to tell me the whole story. It did not seem possible that he could have taken the diamonds at the same time the English agents had taken the cache of industrial diamonds to England. That took place on a Sunday and the Diamond Mart was closed. The vault had been opened for the two Englishmen by some bank employee.

I ended our ride. I asked him to stop at a building supply or hardware store. I wanted to purchase a few items. I did not tell him what I wanted to buy, and he did not ask. I purchased a cold chisel, a small hammer, a small container of plumber's putty, and a small flashlight. I returned to the hotel. I thanked Filip and crashed in my room. There was no trip to the canvas. There were only lurid dreams of the woman in the washroom on the train intermixed with my latest encounter with Maggie. I hoped I would see her again once this mystery was solved. I needed the kind of simplicity she offered.

DINNER: BRASSERIE DE POORT

I slept the afternoon away. It was not like me to have erotic dreams, but my encounter with the woman from the train was finding its way into my sleep. I woke up and tried to dismiss the dreams as unfortunate and entirely due to recent events in my life. I had always considered myself as being somewhat immune to sexual distractions, but after my encounter with the woman from the train, I was not so sure.

I wanted to become more single-minded. I needed to focus on the diamonds. I thought I was very close to getting them. Once I found them, I would have to find a way to get them back to LA. I was pretty sure that taking the diamonds through a commercial airport would cause problems if they were discovered. I could not take the chance. I would leave it to Billie to come up with a solution.

I decided that I would have a nice dinner out, as it might be my last night in Amsterdam. I called the front desk and requested to speak to the concierge. I asked them for a recommendation for a restaurant. After some discussion, the woman suggested Brasserie De Poort. It was within walking distance and served 'bites.' I was confused, but I was enlightened by the concierge that it was similar to Spanish tapas. They served a variety of dishes that were just a few bites each. I decided that was where I wanted to eat dinner and asked if they could make a reservation for me for 7:00 that evening. She would call and confirm.

I lay down and drifted to the canvas. It opened into a large room that looked more like a warehouse. There were stacks of boxes and old furniture set out to look like a proper furniture store. Everything had a large tag attached. I was sitting in a dusty old reclining chair that was tilted as far back as it would go. I could look up at the ceiling without moving my head. The dust-covered beams were dripping with strands of web that looked more like the fake web used at Halloween. I reached down to look for the handle on the side so I could bring the chair to its upright position. I found it and pulled it. The chair snapped upright and threw me forward onto my feet. I was in human form. I was me. That did not happen often. The canvas commonly created an avatar so I could better deal with the location I found myself.

I wandered and looked at the furniture. None of it was modern. None of it was new. It had all been well used. The material and wood were worn. Some even had holes. I don't know much about particular styles, but it all looked like it was circa 1930 Art Deco. It reminded me of a second-hand shop. No, it was shabbier than that. I walked farther into the warehouse. I came upon a large workbench. Beside the bench was a large stuffed chair clamped to what could only be described as a furniture lift that was able to turn the item in its claws in any direction from upside down to sideways to right side up. The chair had undergone an upgrade. The wood inlay looked new, and the body was in the process of being reupholstered. Perhaps this was an antique shop.

On the bench was a series of small cabinets, decorative boxes, and trunks. They were in various states of disrepair. One of the cabinets was opened to reveal a series of hidden compartments. I approached this one. I noticed a little drawer that popped out of one side. On a whim, I pushed it in and heard a click. I tried to open it again, but I could find no way to do so. It was firmly shut. I wondered if this was the canvas' way of telling me that my quest was going to be unsuccessful.

The phone rang. The canvas dissolved. It was the front desk, confirming my dinner reservation. I still had an hour before I had to leave. I took out my lock picks and chose the grouping that would most likely be of use on the padlock to the cellar at Brug 9. I checked out the best way to pick the Abus 20/80 padlock. A couple of YouTube videos later, I figured I could neatly pick the lock. I glanced at the time and headed out to the restaurant.

The walk was pleasant. The city lights were just coming on. Along with the lights came some evening pedestrians. I kept my eyes peeled for anyone following me. I saw no one who was paying me undue attention. I was soon seated with a glass of wine, scanning the menu. I felt a little like an old-time gunslinger. I was sitting at a table with my back to the wall. I ordered the four-bite meal and gave the waiter instructions to choose what he considered to be the four best items on the menu. The food came with about five minutes between dishes. It was delicious. I wanted to see the dessert menu. I was scanning the selections when I felt someone approach. I assumed it was the waiter and looked up. It was the woman from the train. She quickly sat down. She appeared to be frightened of something.

"I thought I told you never to come near me again," I whispered sharply.

"I know. I will return your money, well, most of it." She pushed some banknotes at me. "I need your help. Someone is following me. They stopped me on the street, grabbed my arm, and ordered me to go with them. I pulled away and ran. They ran after me, but I lost them in a crowd."

I was very suspicious. The woman had changed her story several times. "How is that my problem?" I picked up the menu. "How did you know I was here?"

She shrugged. "Just lucky. I was checking out restaurants near where you had lunch. I figured your hotel must be close by so… anyway, I found you and I need your help."

I signaled the waiter for my bill. He brought it over, and I put some cash on the table to cover it. I looked at the money she had dropped on the table. I nudged it toward her, "Take it. I have no idea how I can help. Where are you staying?"

"I am staying at a hostel. Not my favorite but it is a bed, and I can afford it." She smiled at me. "Where are you staying?" I ignored her question. "I figured I would take a shot. I think I would be safe in your hotel room." She reached over and put her hand on top of mine. She smiled weakly. "I can make it worth your while."

"What is your name?" After asking the question I realized I had not even told her my name.

"Nora, Nora Braithwaite."

"Well, Nora, what do you think these people who are chasing you want?"

She shrugged. "I am just trying to see Europe on a shoestring. The book I bought says you can, but after spending six weeks here I don't think that is possible. On the train, I thought you looked like someone I could spend time with and…"

I interrupted. "And you could con," I finished her sentence.

She flushed red. "Just so you know, the business on the train was a first for me. I was feeling desperate. I arrived in Amsterdam with less than three hundred Euros and no place to sleep."

"You haven't answered the question. What do these supposed kidnappers want from you?"

"I have no idea. Nobody paid me any attention until I met you. Perhaps …." I could practically see the wheels turning in her head. She shook off the thought. I did not. *Perhaps the men chasing her were trying to get to me.* "Sorry for asking. I am going to take a cab back to the hostel, and I don't want anyone grabbing me. Will you at least walk me out?" I nodded. "Great. I have to go to the ladies' room. Will you wait for me?" I nodded again. She got up and walked in the direction of the washrooms. I considered getting up and leaving, but I was still trying to make up my mind about what was going on. My Cervantes persona wanted me to avoid her completely while Mattie Brown was intrigued. I was torn as to which path to take.

Nora came out of the washrooms. Her face was set. I assumed she was sure that I would not invite her to stay with me. "Some cabs are waiting. Can we take one? Drop me off at my hostel and I will not bother you anymore. I promise." We walked out onto the sidewalk toward a taxi waiting in a line of taxis. As we approached, the leading taxi pulled away and the next taxi in line took its place. I reached out and opened the back door. Nora walked past me and got in. She was in the process of sliding over when a man stepped out of the shadows, grabbed my left arm, and twisted it behind my back. He shoved me into the taxi. I heard Nora scream as the man who pushed me slid onto the seat beside me. I was practically lying on Nora's lap. I reached out with my right arm and opened the far door.

I drew my legs up to my chest and kicked out. My feet made contact with the man who had pushed me into the vehicle. One foot hit his chest and the other slammed into the side of his face. I turned as he fell out of the taxi, pulled myself up and pushed Nora out of the now-open far door. I quickly followed. I slammed the door behind me and I started to run with Nora in tow.

We ran for a couple of blocks and then hailed a taxi. We got in. The driver requested our destination. "Please drive around for a few minutes. I have to talk to my friend." I turned to Nora. "Give him the name of your hostel." She spoke to the driver, and he nodded. I turned to her. "Well, that was interesting and a little frightening."

"To say the least. Who were those people? Were they the same ones that tried to kidnap me?"

"I don't think they were trying to kidnap you. I think they are interested in me."

"Why?" For the first time since I had met this woman, she looked frightened. "Are you a criminal? Or a spy?"

"Neither. I am a detective."

She looked up at our location. "My hostel is on the next block. Are you going to just leave me there?"

"No. I am going to provide you with something. Where are you from?"

She leaned forward and gripped the seat in front of her. "LA."

I grinned. "Perfect. Now listen. You are going to get your luggage from the hostel as quickly as you can and then come back out. We are going to go someplace."

"Are you taking me to your hotel? I promise I won't be a bother." She reached out and placed her hand on my knee. The action's purpose was obvious. I removed her hand. "You are going to ghost me again, aren't you? Just tell me now so you don't get my hopes up just so you can crush them."

"No. We are going to the airport. I am going to buy you a one-way ticket to LA. You are going to go home. I assume you have a place to stay in LA." Her brow crunched up. "If you don't, I will arrange something for you. In two weeks or so, I will fly to LA. That is where I live. I will come and see you and we can decide if we want to be friends…" I paused. "… or whatever."

"Why are you doing this?"

"I don't want to frighten you any more than you already are, but I think some very bad people saw us together and figured they could get to me through you. Let us just say that I feel responsible for your safety and leave it at that.

"So you are not going to dump me in LA? Fuck, I don't even know your name."

The taxi stopped. "Go and yet your belongings. Quickly."

She put her hand on the door handle and stared at me. She made a decision and left the taxi. She returned 10 minutes later. "I am sorry I took so long. I had to check out." She was smiling. I assumed that was because I was still waiting for her.

The process of buying her a ticket for a flight to LA went seamlessly. Before I sent her into the departure lounge, I handed her one of my cards. "Cervantes," she read. "That is an odd name."

I nodded. "I am going now. I trust that you will board the plane. I will have someone meet you at the airport and take you to your lodgings. They will report to me if you do not arrive. I will not be happy. I will then assume you are not who you purport to be. I will make sure we never meet again. Do you understand?"

She nodded at me. I was about to turn to leave when she dropped her bag, threw her arms around my neck, and hugged me. She pulled back and whispered, "Thanks."

I left the airport and headed back to my hotel. It was late, and I had to talk to Billie and make arrangements. I planned to sleep for a couple of hours before I headed out to Brug 9 and the cellar.

BRUG 9 CELLAR

I had just settled into my room when I received a call from Billie.

"Hi, Billie. Nice to hear your voice. How is everything?"

"Good, boss, but there is something I need to tell you."

"I'm listening."

"You got a threatening message with a picture attached. Normally I would handle it, but I figured you would want to know. I will send it to you so you can decide what to do. I made sure it was clean. Call me back if I need to address it."

"Thanks, Billie. Take care." I hung up and waited for the threatening message to arrive. My phone beeped, and I opened the message.

I looked at the photo. It was clear who had sent the message; the picture was of a foot with an obvious bullet hole. It looked female. I smirked, "You deserved it," I said out loud, thinking it was Barbie's foot. I read the message. *Hey, asshole, just so you know, we have Beal and that is not my foot. If you want to see her again, then you had better deliver the diamonds to me. I will let you know where once you have them. You have one week before we start removing bits and pieces. You know how Botox likes to practice with his knives. Hurry up. He is getting impatient.*

I read the message over a few times. Something about it was odd, but I could not put my finger on it. I texted Billie.

Please check to see if Beal is still in my apartment. She responded *I will have someone check on her this afternoon.*

I reread the message and studied the picture. I had a strong feeling something was amiss, but I could not see what it was. I lay back and closed my eyes.

It was a little after midnight when I woke. I left the hotel with a small tool-filled backpack slung over my shoulder. I was wearing a jumpsuit made of polyester woven with a Polyurethane Laminate. It was comfortable and completely waterproof. It also did not reflect light. I knew I might need to conceal myself. This jumpsuit would make it hard for anyone to spot me. I did not go directly to the bridge. I started walking in the opposite direction and slowly circled, all the while keeping an eye out for anyone who showed an interest in me. At one point, I came upon a woman standing with her back to the wall of a building. She was in dark shadows and suddenly stepped out into the light of a street lamp. I was startled at first and turned to walk in a different direction. She called out something to me in Dutch. I shrugged my shoulders and signaled that I did not understand her. She spoke in English. "Hey, mister, would you like to party with me?"

I breathed a sigh of relief upon realizing she was a 'lady of the evening' to use a polite term. I spoke as I passed her, "Sorry, but I do not have any money."

"That is too bad. Maybe some other time," she purred and sent me a kiss. I smiled back and turned toward Brug 9. At this time of night, there were very few people about. There were a few couples on the far side of the wide bridge. I stood in front of the chain that was in front of the stairs that led down to the cellar. I scanned the area, looking for anyone suspicious. I felt like a real detective about to cross the line separating the legal from the illegal. A shiver shot down my back. I chastised myself for being a silly romantic. I calmly stepped over the chain and strolled down the stairs. There was a small light above the archway leading to the cellar. I reached up to extinguish it and noticed that was not going to be an easy task. It was not a bulb that I could unscrew or smash. It was a small panel of LED lights powered by a solar panel stuck to one of the bricks. The sunlight charged the batteries during the day and maintained the light at night. I glanced around once more and seeing no one, I took the hammer out of my pack and hit the lamp. It came loose from the brick and splashed into the canal. I watched as the light settled into the murky water. It stayed lit as it winnowed down. The canal couldn't have been more than three meters deep, as I could still see the glow where it hit the bottom.

I quickly entered the archway and crouched down in front of the lock. I took out my picks and set to work on the padlock. I opened the plumber's putty and removed a large wad. I stuck it to the back of the lock and pressed it to the door. The lock was now held in place and would not move. I could now use both hands to pick the lock. I put my flashlight into my mouth and aimed it at the lock. It took only a few minutes—thanks to the YouTube video I watched on opening that specific padlock. I removed the lock and pressed it to a brick on the side. I entered the cellar and turned on my flashlight. I recited the directions left by Adare.

BRUG NINE CELLAR
SECOND ARCH
RIGHT SIDE
IN THREE
UP TWO

I scanned the room in front of me. It was quite deep with what looked like a stage at the far end. The ceiling was curved the same way the arches that supported the bridge were curved. On either side was a raised shelf about a meter from the floor and a half meter in width. Every three or four meters along the walls above the shelf were curved arches a meter wide with a depth of a half meter. There were several light fixtures set into the arches. I pictured jazz patrons sitting on this ledge with their feet dangling and tapping to the beat of a band on the stage.

I walked over to the second arch with a base about a meter from the floor. It was deeper than the first. I stood in front of it and tapped the right side. I counted in three and up two bricks. I tapped on the brick. The sound was the same as all the other bricks. I took out my tools and set the flashlight, so the light lit the brick. Using the cold chisel and the hammer, I soon freed the brick. I pulled it out. As I reached for the flashlight, I felt a chill run down my spine. I might have just found a treasure of priceless diamonds.

I reached into the space behind the brick. It was much larger than I had anticipated. Someone had hollowed it out. I felt nothing but bits of masonry and sand. I leaned forward and shone the light into the space. I could not see anything. I waved the light back and forth. It glinted on something shiny. My heart jumped in my chest. I reached in to grab the shiny object and pulled it out. It was a small metal container. I shook it. There was a tapping sound with each shake. It reminded me of a bead in the bottom of a can of spray paint. "Tink – tink – tink" I opened it and turned it upside down in my hand. My flashlight showed me a single diamond. I dropped it back into the container and replaced the lid. I shone the light into the hole once again. There must be something more. I felt all around and scraped the mortar with my fingernails and the chisel. There was no indication that there was anything else in the hole.

"Shit," I said to no one. I turned and looked around the space. My mind was racing, trying to see where I went wrong. At one end, there was a short wall covered with blue and white tiles with images of children playing. I went over and tapped a few. Perhaps there were other hiding places. I knew it was a waste of time. I had found what Adare left for me to find. Perhaps someone had beaten me to it. I reflected on the brick I had removed. It had not been touched since Adare put the canister here sometime during the Second World War. He must have removed the diamonds at that time. That was about 80 years ago. I walked back to the archway. I set the brick back into the hole and swept away the bits of mortar. I licked my fingers and rubbed some dirt over the sections of mortar I had chipped out. I wanted to conceal my handiwork just in case I needed to return and have another look into the space behind the brick.

I rattled the container once again and shone the light over its surface. I suddenly realized that the container was a film canister—an old-fashioned film canister. I opened it up and peered inside. I could see the small diamond as it reflected the light. Something else was also reflecting light. The inside of the canister shone on one side. I put my finger over it and slid out a piece of celluloid. Once again, my heart jumped. I shone the light over the celluloid and realized that it was a negative. I could not make out what the negative would reveal. There were many straight-angled shapes. I would need to get a positive made. Adare, for some unknown reason, had moved the diamonds. He had left a clue where, by leaving a diamond and a negative. I hoped that the negative would finally indicate the location. I was feeling a mixture of disappointment and elation. I put the negative and the diamond into the canister and placed it into one of the waterproof pockets of my suit. I did not want to leave any evidence that I had been here. I checked that all my tools were in my pack and headed for the door. I quietly slipped out and closed the door behind me. I removed the putty from the lock and snapped the padlock in place. I glanced down to see if the light that had fallen into the canal was still visible. I could see nothing. I turned to go up the stairs when I heard voices above me. I stepped back to the platform and leaned against the railing at the far end. I listened. I could hear some voices nearby that slowly faded. I was about to move out of the shadow and return to the bridge surface when two hands gripped my arms from behind and pulled. I flipped over backward, expecting to fall into the canal. Instead, I hit something hard. My head snapped back against a board. I was stunned. I realized I had been pulled over the banister and into a small boat. The boat floated under the bridge. I was suddenly in pitch darkness. I could see nothing. I shouted, "What the hell are you doing? Let me go."

A voice of heavily accented English spoke just above a whisper. "Shut the fuck up." I felt a boot hit me in the stomach. I groaned and passed out.

OVERBOARD

I opened my eyes, but I did not move. I took stock and realized that I was still in the bottom of a small skiff with a large boot on my chest. I could not see any lights above me. I squinted and realized the skiff was still under the bridge. I must have been out for only a few seconds. The boat was quiet except for the whine of what I assumed was an electric motor. The motor stopped. The foot on my chest lifted and a set of hands hoisted me up to a sitting position. I was trying to decide if I should feign unconsciousness. I heard a voice. "Wake him up."

I got the feeling that the wake-up call they intended was probably a slap, so I opened my eyes. "What do you want?" I whispered meekly, not wanting to incur another foot in the gut. A light hit my face. A second man was in the bow of the boat. He shone the light on my face.

"Sit him up," the man with the flashlight ordered. I was grabbed by the front of my jumpsuit and sat in the center seat of the boat, facing the prow. A gun was pressed to my temple by the man behind me. It was illuminated by the flashlight. He spoke. "Give to me."

I started to protest that I had nothing to give to him. The gun was poignantly pressed into my temple so that my whole body leaned to the side. "Give to me!" he demanded. I removed the backpack and dropped it in front of him. It clanked on the bottom of the boat. I knew that both of the men would glance toward the backpack as it hit the deck. The noise it made might have raised their hopes that it contained something valuable. I used that distraction to my advantage and kept on leaning. I kicked my legs out straight. The man holding the gun fell backward. The gun went off. I heard the bullet whine off the bricks above as I dove into the canal. I went as deep as I could and then looked up at the bottom of the boat. The best thing for me to do was to hide behind the aft section of the boat. I came up near the motor and sucked in some air. There was a rope dangling, so I grabbed it and slid under the water again. I could hear the muffled sounds of the men shouting. They were talking in Dutch.

"Jij verdomde idioot! Waar is hij?"

"Hij moet snel komen."

I did not understand, but I caught the drift. I stayed beside the motor with most of my body under the boat while holding onto the rope. All was quiet. I knew I just had to wait. I heard the clink of the tools in the backpack and then it was tossed on the floor of the boat with a thunk. There were more voices. I could hear a police siren in the distance. It seemed to spook the two men in the boat. I heard a new voice. It was slightly muffled. I realized it was coming from a phone. The man in the bow was talking to someone on the phone.

"Stuur Han's bemanning om de kust te doorzoeken. Hij moet ergens uitkomen." He paused. "Gaan!" he commanded.

Then the motor started. I was well away from the spinning prop, but I had difficulty maintaining my position under the boat. I reached up and held on to the gunnel. The two men never looked back. We soon approached a small dock. I slipped away from the boat and hid behind a pylon. They got out of the boat and tied it up. They climbed a ladder attached to the side wall of the canal and disappeared. I climbed out of the water and up the same ladder. I observed the two men walk across the street and into a bar. I crossed the street and stepped into a narrow passageway beside the building. I looked down the street in the direction of Brug 9. Several men were walking along, peering down into the canal on both sides. I had to assume they were looking for me.

I shook my head in an effort to dry my hair. I was only partially successful. I took off my boots and shook the water out. The jumpsuit had repelled a lot of the water. I appeared to be dry from the outside, but the water had leaked in at the ankles, wrists, and neck. I neglected to seal those areas. I did not expect to be jumping into the canal. I glanced at the entrance to the bar. There was no one about. I boldly walked inside and scanned for the men's washroom. Two signs with some Dutch words were above a hallway leading to the rear of the bar. They said HEREN TOILET and DAMES TOILET.

I figured that "*heren*" was for men. I quickly walked down the hallway to the men's washroom. It appeared to be empty. I washed my hands and then tried to dry my hair by rotating the nozzle of the drier to point at my head. After a few minutes, I began to feel respectable. I now needed to get back to my hotel without being intercepted by anyone who wished to take what I had concealed in the waterproof pocket of my jumpsuit. My mind started to wonder about my attackers. Who were they? Who sent them? And most importantly how did they find me? If I was compromised, I needed to be much more careful about what I did and where I went. These and other thoughts were swirling in my head. I stepped out of the washroom and felt the door close behind me. I was looking down at the floor to conceal my identity. I saw a shadow on the floor in front of me. A man had walked down the narrow hallway toward the washroom door. I looked up. He looked down at his phone and then back up at me. I saw his eyes light up and knew he recognized me as the person whose picture was on his phone. He started to turn around. He opened his mouth to yell at someone behind him. I used that moment to reach out and grab his arm. The phone he was carrying clattered to the floor. I backed up to the washroom door, shoved it open, and violently pulled the man into the washroom. He spun around and hit the edge of a sink with the small of his back. His head bounced off the mirror behind him. He opened his mouth to yell. I reached for his head with both hands and slammed his skull into the mirror. His eyes glazed, and I let him slip to the floor. He hit the back of his head on the sink as he fell. A part of me felt I had gone overboard with the head smashing and allowing him to hit the sink on the way down was a little beyond the pale. I reached down and felt his neck pulse. It was strong. He was not dead. I searched him for ID and took it. He had a few Euros in one of his pockets. I took them to make it look more like a simple mugging. I dragged the unconscious man to the nearest stall and lifted him onto the toilet, locked the stall door, and crawled out.

Once again, I left the washroom. I needed to get out of there as quickly and quietly as possible. I did not bring any identification with me to the cellar of Brug 9, especially not a phone. As luck would have it, I noticed a phone on the floor of the hall. It belonged to my assailant. I smiled, not so much for finding a phone by which I could call a taxi, but my description of the man I had left unconscious in the washroom. He was more of a victim, and I was the assailant. But these bastards had started it. I rubbed my stomach and remembered the boot that had slammed into it. I knew I would have a big bruise and, with that, my empathy for the man in the stall vanished.

I was about to call a taxi from the phone in my hand when I realized it was locked. I needed the fingerprint of the owner. Since getting it would require that I return to the scene of the crime, crawl under the stall, get his fingerprint to unlock his phone, and crawl back out, I decided it was not worth the effort. Keeping the phone was a risk. Perhaps it could be pinged and show my location. I set it carefully down on the floor near the wall. It was my way of apologizing to the man I had hurt.

I boldly walked out of the bar and took in my surroundings. I was not that far from my hotel. I could see a busy street and I walked in that direction. I had a few Euros I had taken from my victim. I hailed a taxi and was soon back in my room. My clothes stank of canal water, so I stripped, had a shower, and called Billie. I explained about the negative and the need to get a print so I could discern the locale of the image. She said she would locate a photography shop and send the address in the morning. I thanked her and went to sleep.

CANVAS DREAMS

I woke a few hours later. It was still dark. I had been dreaming twisted dreams and could not find sleep again. The cellar under Brug 9 had added to the mystery instead of solving it. It did provide another clue and reassurance, in the form of a diamond, that I was on the right track. The question of why Adare would provide a clue to the treasure's location in the form of a microdot in the pocket watch and then snatch it away made no sense to me unless he felt that the treasure would not be secure in the cellar. There was a war going on. Perhaps leaving the diamonds in the middle of an occupied city was not something he was willing to risk. The canvas beckoned, and I followed.

I was back as my favorite avatar. The kestrel I became was powerful and skilled. I hovered high above the landscape the canvas presented to me. It reminded me of an old WWII map of Europe as seen from space. The colors were muted for most of it except for a small section of Ireland. I dove and was filled with the exhilaration of speed. With the slightest movement of a single wing feather, I banked and zoomed level over the landscape. I alit in a familiar place. In real life, I had been here. I was on the steeple of St Andrews Church in Killaloe, Ireland. I could see a group of people leaving the church. I noticed that several of them were soldiers. One had a cast on his foot and walked with crutches. His uniform was different than the others. It was American. He had a couple of cameras around his neck. He stopped and appeared to be resting. Once the other churchgoers had left, he hobbled into the graveyard behind the church. He took a couple of pictures. He set the larger camera on a gravestone, set a timer, and hopped on one leg until he was in front of the grave where I had located the watch.

He smiled. I assumed the picture was taken. He glanced around as if he was checking to see if he was alone. He sat on the ground beside the grave fence, twisted off the brass ball on one corner, took something wrapped in cloth out of his pocket, stuffed it into the ball, and replaced the ball on the decorative fence. He stood and retrieved his crutches and camera. I considered what the canvas had shown me. I realized that there was nothing new. I had figured out the general actions, and the canvas had filled in the details. Maybe they were accurate, and maybe they were just a likely possibility. In any case, the scene faded, and I was once again high above a map of Europe.

I was suddenly over water. I could see a ship steaming toward the continent. It was dark, so I swooped low. The designation "D41" was painted in large letters on the side of the ship. It was the Walpole. That was the ship bringing Jan Smit and Walter Keyser to retrieve all the industrial diamonds from the Diamond Mart so the Germans could not get them and use them in their war machine. Adare was on that ship.

Now I must interject the telling of this story. Upon seeing the Walpole and remembering my own research I realized consciously, for the first time, that the canvas was not some omnipotent source of all information. Since it was happening in my mind, all the information it was imparting was coming from me. This was the opposite of what I had always assumed. I reflected on this realization. Yes, it was true most of the time. For instance, the Walpole was a ship mentioned in one of the notes decrypted by Adare's wife. I must have had some previous knowledge and my brain made some connections. But this was not always true. Take the lost emerald ring that was worn by an actress in the play in the park. I had no previous knowledge of that situation. The thought dissolved with the conundrum unsolved along with the Walpole.

I was now in a large square surrounded by old buildings. There were a couple of automobiles circa 1935 parked up a small side street. I settled on a statue and looked around. It was eerily quiet. I saw movement across the square. A man carrying a leather pouch exited a building by a side door. He looked furtively about, climbed on a bicycle that was leaning against the side of the building, and peddled away. I was about to follow when I looked up and saw three paratroopers fall from the sky. They were wearing Dutch uniforms, but I knew they must be German. They had seen the man peddle away and started shooting at him. Behind me, a car started up and roared up to the three disguised German soldiers. The man at the wheel was vaguely familiar. The soldiers raised their rifles. He raised his hand in the usual Heil Hitler salute and roared past. The soldiers lowered their rifles and took up positions near the building where the man on the bicycle had exited. I followed the car that was following the bicycle. The streets look familiar. The man on the bicycle dismounted on a bridge. It was Brug 9. He glanced around and then he ran down some stairs to what I knew was the cellar where I had found the canister behind a brick. The man in the chase car arrived and observed the man running down to the cellar. He quickly pulled onto the bridge, exited his vehicle, and followed him down the stairs. I flew to the cellar entrance and lit on the railing. I could see the man from the car peering into the cellar. I was close enough to make out his features. The man was Adare. Somehow, he knew the contents of the pouch the man had hidden. A few minutes passed. I saw Adare back away from the cellar opening and press himself against the wall. The exiting man did not see him as he ran up the stairs. I flew up. He mounted his bicycle and peddled across the bridge. Just as he got to the other side, shots rang out. The man flew off the bicycle and crashed into a barricade. I watched as a small group of disguised German soldiers stepped up to the fallen man. They shot him again and searched him. They had not seen him come out of the cellar. They continued on their way without hesitation. Adare looked over the top of the bridge parapet and saw that the man he followed had been killed. He entered the cellar. I waited for Adare to exit the cellar. A few minutes passed. When he came out, he was empty-handed, but the knees of his dark suit were covered with grey dust. He must have decided that the hiding place was a good one for whatever was in the satchel.

The canvas swirled, and I opened my eyes. I had no proof that what I had just witnessed was what actually happened. It could be that my mind just took what I knew and extrapolated to a possible scenario. Suddenly it occurred to me that all the business of sending his wife clues was just plan 'B.' Plan 'A' was to get the diamonds out of Amsterdam and back to the US. Since the treasure was no longer hidden in the cellar, he must be executing plan 'A.'

I got out of bed and retrieved the canister. I carefully opened it and dumped out the diamond. It dropped onto the desk. I nudged it with my finger. I slipped out the negative and held it up to the light. It was difficult to make out what it was. At first, I thought it was a building of some sort, but the words in the middle gave it away. It was a gravestone with someone's name embossed on the front. I could not make out the words. I would need to get it enlarged and printed if it was to be of any use. Adare had moved the diamonds to some grave. I hoped it was nearby.

I checked my phone. There was a text from Billie with addresses of some photography shops nearby that still had the equipment to develop black and white prints. I replaced the diamond and the negative back into the canister. I put it carefully into my grab-and-go bag, along with my passport, cash, and credit cards. Fatigue overtook me and I went to sleep.

HACKED

IT was late morning when I woke to a ringing phone. It could only be Billie. I put it to my ear and said, "Hello, Billie." She was the only person who could call this number. I heard only one word, "Phantasmagoria," and then nothing. I quickly turned the phone over in my hand and opened the back. I removed the battery and set the pieces on the desk. I knew I would need that phone to work again, but not until I spoke to Billie. I shut off my laptop. The hotel IP it was attached to might also be known to, who I assumed was, Botox and crew. I plopped down on the bed. I swore, "shit—fuck—shit." This was a wrinkle I did not need. Our communications had been compromised somehow. Please understand that I pride myself on being unhackable. Even so, there were contingencies in place just in case the unthinkable happened. Now it had.

The first of those contingencies was to get out of the hotel and find a new base of operations. I quickly packed and headed to the front desk. Even using hotel phones was out of the question. At the front desk, I was handed an envelope I knew must be from Billie. I checked out using one of my preloaded charge cards, walked out of the hotel, and hailed a taxi. I told him I needed someone to print a black-and-white negative for me. He took me to a block that had two shops and told me to take my pick. I entered the first and explained I needed a print and also a blowup of a particular section. I asked if they could do it immediately. I held up a hundred euro note. The proprietor smiled. He could do it in a few minutes. I sat down and waited. I took this opportunity to open the envelope. It was indeed from Billie. Inside was an address of a photography shop. It was not the shop I was presently in. I was not sure of the timeline, so I assumed the worst. Botox knew about the shop in Billie's note. After a few minutes, the proprietor of the shop returned and handed me an 8x10 envelope. I glanced inside. The negative was in a small package at the bottom. It was indeed a photo of a grave and a blowup of the section I had indicated. I held up the 100 euro note and said, "I was never here. Understand?"

He replied in English with a smirk, "No, sir, I have never seen the man you are describing." He slipped the money into his pocket.

I nodded and left the shop. I hailed another taxi and requested he find me an inexpensive hotel with adjoining rooms. I would like it as close as possible to the address of the photography shop Billie had sent to me. A plan was forming. I had the blowup of the negative. Now I needed to get rid of my pursuers.

My driver dropped me off at a Best Western. I was surprised that the chain was in Amsterdam. I checked in and requested two adjoining rooms. I told the front desk that I was expecting my brother and his wife soon and they would be staying in one of the rooms. All I needed to do now was to get this information to Botox's minions so they would come to the hotel where I could waylay them until I had checked out the graveyard. I hoped I would not have to travel to another city to find it. I hoped I could retrieve the diamonds and be home before they knew I had left.

I really wanted to inspect the photograph, but time was of the essence. I took a taxi to the photography shop that Billie had originally organized. I knew I might have to leave in a hurry, so I hired the driver to wait in a spot just down the block. I paid him an exorbitant amount with the promise of more when I returned. I would be returning to the hotel from which he picked me up. I knew that Botox's crew would go there in the hope of capturing me. There was a small café nearby and I could watch the entrance for anyone that might arrive. I hoped that I was not too late. I entered, ordered a coffee, and took a seat by the window. I did not have to wait long. A large black vehicle pulled up to the curb in front of the shop. It caught my attention immediately. The side windows were tinted. Seeing inside was impossible. It sat idling. It occurred to me that the occupants might be scanning the area for me. I leaned back in my seat so my face was concealed by the window curtains. Nothing happened for at least 10 minutes. Then the door opened.

A man stepped out of the vehicle and turned. A woman followed. The man helped her onto the sidewalk. She was carrying a large bag on a long shoulder strap. Her right hand was inside the bag. I looked at her and realized that it must be Barbie. She was blonde and had a walking cast on one leg. Her face was set in a grimace. She limped purposefully to the door. At one point, she started to lose her balance. The man put his hand on her elbow to help her. She reacted violently and pulled her arm away. They both headed to the door of the shop. The man stopped outside. I could see her through the shop window. She was speaking to someone out of sight. Suddenly, I saw her lift a large silenced gun from her bag. She was pointing it at someone. It was then that I decided to leave. Barbie was not messing around, and I did not want to be anywhere near the business end of that gun. I was rapidly reassessing my plan. I looked at the man watching the door. At that moment, I realized that I had not remained hidden. Our eyes locked. He lifted his hand and looked at something. It occurred to me that he was looking at a photo of me and, by his reaction, he recognized that I was in the café. It was definitely time to go. I dropped five euros on the table and ran to the door. The man stepped inside the shop and called to the woman. I heard him yell, "He is out here! Hurry!"

I had to run a couple of hundred meters to my waiting taxi that I prayed was still waiting for me. I turned to see Barbie come out of the shop and look in my direction. The man was trying to hurry her into the black SUV parked on the curb. She pulled her hand away and yelled, "Follow him for fuck's sake. Don't let him get away." The man turned and started running in my direction. I had a big enough head start. I arrived at the taxi and yelled at the driver to leave quickly. He stepped on the gas. I looked in the back window to see the man running back and climbing into the SUV. It turned to follow us.

I knew I did not have time to change my plan. I would have to modify it to account for the gun that Barbie was toting. The man might also have a gun. In the original plan, I was going to 'way lay' them. But now that they had guns, waylaying them was not only harder, it was a lot more dangerous. I had to disarm them without getting shot. I spent the trip trying to remember the layout of the floor of the hotel. The elevator was in the middle of two hallways that were at right angles to each other. In the corner was a small settee with a table at one end. There was a large vase on the table. I tried to remember the shape of the vase. I think it was an abstract nude. I decided it would be my distraction. A crude plan was forming just as we arrived at the hotel. I could still see the SUV behind us. I paid the driver and told him to drop me off at the front doors and then leave quickly. I did not want him to get hurt. It was just like Barbie to do something nasty to him if he was still around.

The front desk receptionist was a young girl. She smiled as I entered. I gave her my name and told her to send the couple who were about to enter up to the room I had booked for them. I gave her the room number and rushed to the elevator. Once on the floor, I grabbed the vase from the table and opened the door to the first room. I entered, leaving the door open a few centimeters. My luggage was open on the luggage stand. I pulled down the sheets and messed them up a little. Then I went through into the adjoining room. I locked the adjoining door in the second room and waited by the door that led to the hotel hallway. I put my ear to the door. I waited for them to both go into the room.

I could hear Barbie. "Check the bathroom. He has to be here."

"Het is duidelijk."

"English."

The voice responded with a heavily accented, "It's clear."

I waited. The plan was to separate them. I could hear their voices in the room. I stepped out of the room next to the one they were searching and threw the vase down the hall. It shattered against the table in the corner. I quickly ducked back inside and went to the adjoining door.

"What was that?" shouted Barbie.

"Dunno," her partner answered.

"Don't be an idiot. Go and check for fuck's sake."

I heard the man leave the room.

I decided that she would be waiting just inside the room with that big gun of hers pointing at the door to the room. I quietly opened the door between the adjoining rooms during one of her frequent calls to the man who had left the room. I was standing behind her. I tiptoed closer until I was just a meter away. She held the gun in her right hand. I moved to her left. If she decided to turn around, she would turn to her right. It was the shortest distance. I would knock the gun from her hand and push her over. I reached out and poked my finger into her neck. "Drop it!" I ordered. She froze. I could almost feel her thoughts tangle in her search for the best response.

"You going to shoot me?" she asked. I responded by poking my finger hard into her neck. "I don't believe you."

"Where this gun is pointed, the bullet will tear through the muscles at the back of your neck. The bullet won't kill you, but I wouldn't want to be you afterward. I poked hard again. "Drop the gun. On second thought, extend your arm out and point the gun at the right wall. She slowly moved her arm. I slowly slipped behind her. I reached around and smashed my hand down on her wrist. Her hand opened, and I caught the gun before it hit the floor. I pushed her toward the bed. Her walking cast was like an anchor, and she fell awkwardly backward. I pointed her silenced gun at her head. I could see her seething. I had bested her once again.

"Are you going to kill me?" she shouted.

I realized her purpose was to warn her accomplice. I turned and shot a bullet into the bed. The gun spit a silent bullet. The bed cover spewed stuffing beside her hand. She looked at the hole in the cover and closed her mouth. My intent was clear. I walked to the side of the bed and dragged her to her feet. I pulled her to the side of the door and stood behind her. I rested the barrel of the gun on her shoulder and waited. A few minutes later, her accomplice came back and walked into the room. He turned to Barbie and stopped. He was about to reach for his gun when I smiled and shook my head. He could see Barbie's gun in my hand. I considered shooting him in the foot like I had the others, but decided against it. It would be far too messy. "Take it out slowly and toss it on the bed," I said.

He looked at me questioningly. I was not sure he understood. I gestured with the weapon in my hand. I said, "The gun. Toss it." He reached into the side of his jacket and tossed the weapon on the bed. I did not know what this man actually did for a living, so I decided to err on the side of caution. "Take off your jacket and your pants and toss them on the floor over there." Once again, it seemed as if he did not understand. I spoke to Barbie, "Tell him to strip."

"Strip nu," she said.

I gestured to the far side of the bed. He took off his jacket and hesitated for a second. I grinned and raised the gun. "If you think you can distract me by throwing that at me, be assured that I can shoot you at least three times before that jacket touches me. Now take off your pants." He seemed to understand. I now assumed he knew more English than he had let on.

Barbie spoke. "Do it." I felt her head nod. Something had been communicated between them. I wasn't sure what, but my plan to take their clothes with me required he take off his pants while I had the proverbial 'drop' on him. He bent over and was about to crouch.

"What the fuck are you doing?" I spat.

"Taking off shoes. The pants won't fit over them," he said.

"You wouldn't happen to have a gun strapped to your ankle, now, would you?"

He shook his head. I watched as he took off his shoes and kicked them aside. He stood and undid his belt and pants. He unzipped his fly and started to push the pants down past his thighs. I felt some tension in Barbie's body. I was still behind her with one hand on her shoulder. The gun was pointing at the man as he lowered his pants. It was at that moment I felt something was about to happen. It was my early warning system. It was something I learned from old Fritz, my defense teacher. I could hear his voice, *'In a standoff, don't?'* At the time, I didn't understand but, like a lot of the things he said to me, time brought clarity and understanding. I had been standing in one place for far too long and I instinctively stepped to the side. At that moment Barbie ducked down, and in a whirl of movement, the man grabbed at the back of his calf. He spun around at the same moment I chose to step to the side. Then everything stopped. The two were on the floor and I still had the gun. There was a knife sticking out of the wall behind where my head used to be. I watched the man on the floor glance at the bed where his gun was nestled. His pants were still around his ankles.

I no longer wanted to continue this little confrontation. It was getting too unpredictable for my tastes. I picked up the gun from the bed and pulled the knife out of the wall. "Strip down to your underwear." They both looked at me. "Strip to your underwear now!" They took off their clothes. "And the walking boot. I don't want you walking anywhere." I watched her struggle to get the boot off. Her foot was covered with a flesh-colored sock. There was a bloody stain on the top where I had shot her foot. "Must hurt," I said casually. "Oh, by the way, was that a picture of your foot or did you shoot Beal in the foot to get revenge on me?"

She sneered. "You obviously don't know who your enemies are."

At that moment, I gained some insight into why I felt that the picture of the wounded foot was odd. It wasn't real. It was supposed to be Beal's foot, but it was a very good fake, like the kind used in movies. Probably created by Botox. As a plastic surgeon, he would have those skills. The logic followed that Beal was no longer on my side. She did not like the deal I had offered her and wanted more. I also reflected on the way she reacted when we were prisoners of Botox. Perhaps she was working with him even then. I said nothing in response to her goad.

"Move the clothes over beside the door." They both looked at me questioningly. I pointed at her. "You. Take the clothes over there." She followed my instructions. I took the zip tie sets from my jacket pocket and handed them to Barbie. I gave her a set of instructions that resulted in the man's hands zipped behind his back. Barbie was facing his back with her hands looped through his and zipped tight. I ordered them into the bathroom and into the tub. It took a few minutes for them to coordinate their steps. I directed them to sit in the tub, facing away from the faucet.

Barbie hissed at me, "You fucker."

I turned on the cold shower and glanced behind for a moment to see them struggle to shut off the faucet. I smiled, quickly left the room, and closed the door behind me.

THE CEMETERY

I tossed the two guns in and snapped my suitcase closed and stuffed their clothes into a hotel laundry bag and entered the elevator. I stopped one floor down, propped the elevator door open with my suitcase, and stuffed the bag of clothes behind the settee in the hallway. I got back on the elevator and left the hotel. The rooms were prepaid so stopping at the front desk was not required. rooms, I got into a taxi and started to inspect the photograph in my pocket to determine my next move. next, I needed to contact Billie to find out about Beal. A quiet hotel room and a new prepaid SIM for my phone were required. I spoke to the driver and communicated what I wanted. He soon dropped me off in front of a hotel that was near a mobile phone store. I entered, secured a room, walked out to the phone shop, and purchased a new SIM.

Once back in the hotel, I removed the photos and inspected them. The main image was of a gravestone. Adare obviously had a thing about graveyards. I guess they were one of the things that stood the test of time. The dead don't move around much. The gravestone was a double. Looking at the dates, I assumed it was a father and son. Paul and Eduard Diamant—Architect. The youngest died well before the second world war. There was nothing in the photograph to indicate the location of the graveyard. I smiled at the name. It was rather à propos. Diamant was Dutch for diamond. The second photograph was a blowup of one of the bricks inset in front of the graves. A circle had been scratched out on the negative. It appeared as a black dot on one of the bricks. I had to assume that the diamonds were hidden under that brick. I would need a tool to excavate it. I would need Billie to find the graveyard.

I was suddenly overwhelmed with fatigue. I needed to sleep. If I didn't, I would make a mistake. I knew I was close. If I was not at my best, I could miss something important. I lay down and fell into a deep sleep. I did not dream or, at least, I didn't remember dreaming anything. I slept for ten hours. I woke famished. I looked around the room. It was a two-star hotel and ordering food was not even a possibility. I remembered a small café on the main floor of the hotel. I went down and ordered a huge breakfast. That might be the only meal I would have time for. I ate, then sat drinking coffee while I made a mental list. Phone Billie and get the location of the graveyard, and maybe the actual location of the grave. Also, have her book a flight home for the next day. If the treasure was not there and I had to solve another one of Adare's riddles, she could cancel it.

I headed back into my room and inserted the new SIM into the phone. I called a number that I had memorized for just this situation. Billie answered.

"Augustus. Are you ok?"

"I am good. I have deterred my pursuers for the time being. I need you to find the location of a particular grave. I am hoping that the graveyard is nearby. If you cannot find the actual grave, I can go and look for it. I also want you to book a private flight from here to LA tomorrow afternoon."

"Why the private plane? It will be expensive."

"If all goes well, I will need to transport some items that might arouse the interest of law enforcement. If things don't go as I hope, you will have to cancel. I would like to cover all contingencies, so book a first-class flight for me to LA. If I am on it, that means things did not go as I had hoped, and my search is over."

"Well, good luck. I will text the information you want to this phone as soon as I am able. I don't suppose it will take very long. There are a lot of databases dedicated to grave location. By the way, I did a deep dive into that computer you gave me belonging to ..." she paused, "...Harold W Kruger. There wasn't a lot on it. He did a few searches into missing diamonds circa WWII and a particular plastic surgeon's office. That was all. He didn't use it for email, so nothing there."

"What about Beal? Is she still in my apartment?"

"I don't think so. I have called and there is no answer. Where do you think she might have gone?"

"Interesting. That's great, Billie. Thanks." I hung up and went back to my room. Beal was the least of my problems. I prepared for an overnight in a graveyard. I laid out the jumpsuit I had used earlier. I took the knife and small gun that once belonged to Barbie's friend and put them in my backpack. I was not sure I would need the gun, but the knife would be a good tool to lift the brick and dig under it. The weather was reasonably warm, so I did not expect to get too cold overnight. My phone buzzed. It was the text from Billie:

> *Zorgvlied Cemetery*
> *about 20 minutes by taxi*
> *open from 9 – 5*
> *map of graves available*
> *Flights booked—itinerary attached for both possible flights*
>
> *Good luck.*
> *B*

I planned to enter the graveyard, find the grave and hide out until dark. Once I was alone, I would dig up the diamonds. If possible, I would try to sneak out that night. If not, I would wait until the morning and just walk out. At least that is what I hoped.

I had a few hours to kill, so I decided to visit the canvas. I lay back on my bed and drifted. I was soon smiling, at least smiling in my mind as opposed to actually smiling. The canvas seemed to be much more unspecific—if there was such a word. It didn't seem to attempt to impart information to me. Like when I was a kid, there were soft colors and warm sounds and delightful smells all around me. It was wonderfully relaxing. It was just me. No avatar. I seemed to float down to a meadow filled with flowers. I was lying on a blanket. My eyes slowly closed. I could feel a warm breeze on my face. The canvas did not want me to open my eyes until something special happened. I was in anticipation as to what it had in store for me. I felt a hand touch my cheek. I controlled the urge to open my eyes and look. The hand traveled down. The fingers tiptoed over my chest. The hand began to undo the buttons on my shirt. I could no longer contain my curiosity. My eyes opened. Laying beside me were two women. One was Maggie and the other was Nora. They were both smiling. They looked at each other and nodded. They began to undress me.

I sat up suddenly. This had never happened before. I was aroused by the canvas. Understand that the canvas is much more real than any dream. It was very much like two real women about to take my clothes off. All I could think was that these two ladies held real potential for some interesting and dynamic sexual adventures, but I would need to culture them. I felt a powerful urge to go home. This damn treasure hunt was stressing me. It made me do uncomfortable things, and I needed to stop. I was the kind of detective that found stuff. I did not have enemies who wanted to wish me harm. At least, that is how I always saw myself.

I looked at the clock. It was time I was on my way. I would find the treasure and get away before Botox sent someone else. Barbie and her friend might have gotten out of the tub and had someone bring them some clothes. I didn't think they would have found the bag of their own clothes. I also doubted Botox would trust them after their epic failure to capture me. I figured I was safe. The only way they could find me now was if… A thought suddenly occurred to me. The guy at the photoshop was very easy to convince with a few euros. That meant he might also give me up for the same thing. The bad guys would have to go around to all the shops that had the equipment to develop black-and-white photos from negatives. There were not that many. It was a great term, *bad guys.* It encapsulated all those who wished me harm. The shop owner could have easily printed another copy of the grave clue and made even more money.

I went to my suitcase and took out Barbie's big, silenced gun and added it to my backpack. A silenced gun would come in handy if making noise was an issue. I called the front desk, requested a taxi, and went down to the lobby. I sat and waited. No one appeared to be looking for me. The taxi arrived, and we set out. It was a little after four when I arrived at the Zorgvlied Cemetery. I entered and went to look up Paul and Eduard Diamant's grave. I snapped a picture of the map of the graveyard and noted where the Diamant grave was located. I might need to find a place to hide, and a map would come in handy. I strolled as if I was a tombstone tourist. I took the odd picture but always with other people in the pictures. If I had to wait, I would check out the photos for *bad guys* who might be looking for me. If they got a copy of the grave photo, they could just as easily find the grave's location as Billie. I soon found myself passing the Diamant grave. I casually looked around and, seeing no one suspicious, approached it. I stared at the brick that was marked in the photo. As it was near closing time, I found myself alone. I knelt down, concealing myself from any casual glance in my direction. Maybe I could do it now. I quickly decided that I could. I took the knife out of my backpack and slid it into the soft earth beside the brick. I soon dug away the earth around the brick and levered it up. I set it aside and stuck the knife into the earth. It slid in easily. For a moment, I thought that there was nothing and then the blade hit something hard. I glanced up. I was still alone. With a few quick flips of the knife blade, I cleared the earth away from a small rusty metal box. I was disappointed. I replaced the brick. The box was far too small to hold a fortune in diamonds. I shook it. There was something inside. I opened it and saw that it contained another film canister, like the one I found in Brug 9 cellar. All my hopes of going home were shattered at the sight of the canister. I picked it up and shook it. It also rattled. I was about to remove the screw top when I looked up. I saw two men purposely striding in my direction. They had not seen me yet as I was mostly concealed behind the gravestone. If I stood, they would see me. If I did not stand, they would see me in a few steps, for the path curved and I would be obvious. They would also be closer. I looked at a small thicket off to my left. There was a large oak tree beside it. If I could get there, I could hide behind it. I was not sure if they would resort to shooting, so the oak tree seemed like a good choice. I slipped the metal film canister into my pocket and casually stood and strode toward the tree.

One of the two men called out to me. "Meneer, de begraafplaats is gesloten. Vind je weg naar de uitgang." I relaxed a little. Perhaps they were not bad guys after all. I did not understand and shrugged. He repeated in accented English, "Sir, the cemetery is closing soon. Please find your way to the exit." He pointed behind him and the two men continued on their way. I breathed a sigh of relief, nodded politely, and walked in the direction they indicated. I hailed one of the many taxis parked in the cemetery lot waiting to take the tombstone tourists back to their respective hotels. Suddenly, a large black SUV swerved into the parking lot. Two men got out and ran toward the gate. I turned in an effort to conceal myself. The men ran past me. I heard a voice coming from the SUV, "Stop. He is there!" The two men turned and started back in my direction. At the same time, the taxi I had hailed drove up beside me. I opened the door to the taxi. I heard the spitting sounds of a silenced weapon and saw two holes in the taxi's door. They were shooting at me. I considered getting the gun I had with me and shooting back when the choice was taken from me. The black SUV driver gunned his engine. At the same second, another taxi moved to pick up his fare. The SUV slammed into the side of the taxi and another taxi moved behind it, effectively blocking it in. My taxi pulled away. The driver was oblivious to the mess that was forming behind him. I looked out the back window and saw a police car drive up to the SUV. I was concerned that the bad guys would go "all-American" and start shooting. They did not. I saw the two men slip their guns into their jackets and disappear, leaving the SUV driver to sort it out. I smiled at the driver and told him the hotel I was staying at. He nodded. Twenty minutes later, we arrived at my hotel. I tipped the drive far more than was necessary, but I figured it would partially cover the cost of getting the two bullet holes in his door fixed.

PLAN 'A'

I sat at the desk in my room, opened the film canister, and tipped the contents onto the desktop. Once again, a diamond skittered across the surface, followed by a rectangular piece of metal with the letter 'A' embossed. There was nothing else. I slapped my hand on the desk and cursed, "Fuuuck." I seemed to be right back where I started. I inspected the metal letter. There was nothing that might be considered a clue to where Adare had put the treasure. Maybe there was no treasure, and he was just a crazy man. The diamonds left in the canisters said otherwise. Even they were worth a lot. No one would leave them as clues unless they actually meant that the searcher was on the right track. Their value would pale in comparison to the anticipated cache of diamonds, especially if they were anything like the two that Beal found in the metal flask.

The letter might mean something, but I could not get the concept of Plan 'A' vs Plan 'B' out of my head. If this was Plan 'B,' then the metal letter must mean something and lead to the treasure or the next clue to the treasure. If it was Plan 'A,' then the treasure was already back in the US and the letter was a clue as to where.

I considered the clue. How could the metal letter 'A' be a clue to anything unless it was part of something larger, like a name? Then it hit me. Adare's initial was 'A.' I had no idea what the 'A' stood for, but I remembered his initials on the pocket watch: SAA. Samuel A Adare. What did that mean? Maybe it was the first letter of some place like Amsterdam or America? That did not help much. If it was a clue, it was just too obtuse. I prided myself as a good detective, but if this was a clue to the next hiding place, I was at a loss. I decided to trust myself, so I concluded that Adare had succeeded with Plan 'A' and this clue was to inform his wife that the treasure was somewhere back in the US.

With that decision, I need to pack up and go home. I texted Billie and requested that she cancel the private plane. Since I did not spend the night in the cemetery, I had a whole day to rest up before my first-class flight left for LA tomorrow. I would use the flight to explore the canvas. Maybe I could glean some understanding as to where the treasure was hidden.

I lay on the bed and remembered my last meeting with the psychiatrist. At this point, he was no longer someone my mother made me visit. He called me personally. He stressed that it was not an appointment about my mental health, at least not entirely. He simply wanted to talk with me and make me an offer. I was twenty at the time and living in my own apartment. Mind you, I was still being supported by my mother. I hated that. She still figured she had some say in how I lived my life. After this visit to my old doctor, things would change. For me, they changed for the better. For my mother, not so much.

It was an odd day for an appointment. It was Saturday. I entered an empty waiting room. His receptionist was not at her desk. No one was there. I heard a shout from his office. "Mathew. Mathew, please come in." He was standing at the open door to his inner sanctum. I went in. I was still very confused about why I was there. It was not my favorite place. I stood and stared at him.

"Mathew. I am really glad you could make it. I know how you value your time. Please sit." I sat. "Please relax. I want to make you an offer."

I was really confused. "An offer? An offer for what?"

"Well, I am writing a book and I want you to be a main focus."

"I don't want to be the focus of anything, much less a book." I stood up. "Now that is decided, may I leave?"

"Mathew, you may leave any time you wish. I cannot stop you, but I think you might want to hear me out."

"Why?"

"Well, I know how you hate being controlled by your mother. She controls your finances. How would you like to be able to control your own finances?" I sat down.

I remembered how he had run interference when my mother tried to control my sex life. I decided to listen. "Ok. I will listen."

"Well, I am writing a book about a number of my patients who came to me via their parents or some institution. They came to me to be modified in some way so they would fit better into the world that others had chosen for them. All these patients did not need to be modified in any way. In fact, modifying them would be a horrible outcome. They were just different. All I needed to do was to help them cope better with a world that was not going to play fair. They all had skills that gave them power. My job was to get them to understand and use their power to live positive and dynamic lives. "

"Am I one of those patients?"

"Yes. In fact, you are the most important patient of all."

"Why do you need me? You could just write whatever you want."

"Well, Mathew, I need you because I do not understand you. Now that you are an adult, I would like to explore your mind a little more to get a clearer picture of what makes you tick."

"You make me sound like a machine."

"I'm sorry. That was not my intent. You are fascinating, and I want to understand you. Will you help me?" I looked at him and then I looked at the door. "One more thing. No one will ever know it is you in my book. Your real identity will be kept confidential. You will be Patient X or whatever you like."

I relaxed. "I want to be Patient Q," I said. "What do you want to know?"

"We need to complete some paperwork first." He took a file from the drawer of his desk. He handed it to me. "You need to read this and if you agree, sign it."

I opened it and started to scan. I am a very fast reader. I stopped when I got to a section titled 'Remuneration.' I stopped. "You are going to pay me!" I exclaimed.

"Yes. The amount is contingent on how well the book sells. I am also going to write a series of screenplays. If they get produced, it could mean a lot of money."

"Cool," I said.

Well, I signed the contract and spent a couple of months trying to explain the canvas to my psychiatrist/partner. I even submitted to more sessions of hypnosis. I do not know if he truly understood. After the ten sessions I was contracted for, I shunted the project aside. I received many cheques and still do to this day. They helped me with my independence from my mother. My psychiatrist approached me recently to see if I would like to identify myself as the "Canvas" guy and do some TV interviews. I refused. I no longer needed the money, and I did not want the publicity. Some of his other patients in the book accepted his offer. I suspect they regretted it. I watched one that was on a late-night comedy show. He was made fun of like he was a circus freak. I was glad I refused.

SURPRISE ENCOUNTER

UPON packing my bag, I realized I had to get rid of the firearms that were still in my backpack. It was very early, so I wandered around the hotel looking for a place to stash them so they would not be found until well after I was gone. I did not want to end up in a file in some police force database as a potential owner of the weapons. The weapons needed to remain hidden for at least a month after I was gone. Longer would be better. I ended up in front of a locked door that led to the roof. I returned to my room and took the weapons, wrapped in a pillowcase, and my lockpicking tools back to the door. I picked the lock in a few minutes and stepped out onto the roof. I wandered about, looking for the perfect hiding place. Several vents might work, but I decided to remove a couple of screws on an access panel of an air conditioner/heat pump. I stuffed the pillowcase of weapons around the back of the works inside the metal housing of the device and replaced the screws. I left the roof and relocked the door.

I headed for the airport and arrived three hours before my flight. I planned to eat in the first-class lounge and organize my meals for the flight. I checked with the departure desk and discovered that Billie had organized everything. I ate a full breakfast and moved to a lounge seat. I was about to slip my dark glasses on when I noticed someone observing me. It was a woman. She smiled. I could not imagine a woman smiling at me unless she had an ulterior motive. I smiled back. She stood and walked over to me and sat in the chair beside me.

"Hello," she said. I nodded in response. "I have two hours to kill, and I thought it might be fun to spend that time with an attractive man. I hope you don't mind me being forward."

"Not at all," I responded. My mind was rushing to see if I recognized anything about her that would shed some light on who she was and what she wanted. She was thirty-ish, dark-skinned, with stunning blue eyes. I assumed she was South Asian, but the blue eyes suggested something else. She had a British accent that was, as the Brits say, 'posh.' She was a complete stranger. "I have never considered myself attractive."

"I guess 'attractive' is an attribute that resides in the eye of the beholder. Perhaps 'interesting' is more accurate. You look interesting. Where are you going?" She did not wait for a reply. "I am flying to New York."

"LA," I said. I was trying to decide if I wanted the conversation to continue or not. If she was going to New York then she would be on a different plane. I decided that it was safe to chat with her and I took the lead. "New York. Do you have business there?"

"No. Not business, per se. I have to find someone."

I smiled. "Finding things is my forte. It is rather serendipitous that you found me interesting." My suspicions rose up.

"Really?"

"Yes."

I took out one of my cards and handed it to her.

"Cervantes? Like the writer. He wrote Don Quixote, I think."

"You are correct, but I do not joust with windmills." I looked into her eyes. They seemed to sparkle ice blue. I could not see any sign of deception. "I don't usually find people."

"Just things?" I nodded. "Your card says you can find anything. That is an incredibly bold statement." I shrugged. "Do you think you could find my sister?"

I decided this was some sort of game she was playing with me. I had time to kill, so I played along. "I guess that depends on whether she is actually lost. A lot of people disappear from their families, but they do not consider themselves lost. I am very expensive, and I wouldn't want you to waste your money searching databases, etc. That is something a third-rate investigator could do just as well."

Her eyes flashed sharply with anger. She was irritated by my candor. "My sister did not just forget to leave a forwarding address. She is gone. I have already gone through all the third-rate investigators, as you call them. They were of no help. Something has happened to her."

"What are you planning to do now?" I asked casually.

"I am doing it. I have been doing it for almost a week now."

"What is that?" My curiosity was piqued. Then she did something I did not expect. She reached into her purse and took out a card. She snapped it on the table like she was playing poker and had four aces. It was one of my cards. For a moment, I thought it was the one I had just given her. It was not. I looked up expectantly and waited.

"I have an apology to make. I have been hunting for you. I sent multiple letters to that address." She tapped my card. "I was not contacted, so I took things further. I hired a detective to find you. They told me you were in Amsterdam. I have been sitting in this airport for a week, hoping I would run into you. I decided that my plan was silly, and I would never find you, so I bought a ticket." She slapped the table. "Here we are." She reached out and placed her hand on mine. I was about to pull it away but decided, for some reason, not to. This surprised me. I was obviously taken in by this woman.

"So, are you actually going to New York?

"Yes. That is where my sister was last seen. But if you take my case, I can meet you in LA at your convenience." She looked down at her watch. "My flight leaves in 30 minutes." She looked at me with those incredible eyes.

I took out a pen and wrote my mobile number on the back of my card. "I have some things to finish first. Give me a call next week and I will set something up."

She squeezed my hand. "Thank you." I smiled inwardly. The case was not all that intriguing, but her incredible eyes had me infatuated. I would hear her out. She turned and left the lounge. As she walked away, I realized I did not know her name, but it was too late.

THE TRIP HOME

ONCE again, my flight gave me the opportunity to visit the canvas. The only thing that might take priority was a plane crash. I did not worry about plane crashes. I was without a focus. The whole pocket watch diamond mystery was on some sort of hold. I had spent a great deal of energy and time searching for a treasure I did not find. All I had was a couple of small diamonds and the letter 'A' embossed on a piece of metal and no clue where to look next. I made arrangements with the flight attendant so I could have hours of uninterrupted time. I slipped on a sleeping mask and was soon engulfed by the canvas.

Once again, my high-flying avatar had abandoned me. I was a small creature scurrying around a littered landscape. At first, I thought I was in a junkyard, but once I climbed up on a pile, I realized it was just garbage. I was in a garbage dump. The wonderful sights and sounds I had come to expect from the canvas had been replaced by gray-brown rot and stink. I was alone and lost in this disgusting landscape. I was about to extricate myself from this nasty place when I heard a ping and saw a rusty can jump up and nearly land on my head. That was followed by another ping and the mess at my feet exploded and rained disgusting ooze down on me. At that moment I realized that the pings were bullets being fired at me. I ran. I was smattered with rotting goop. It was in my mouth and eyes. I knew I needed to hide. If I left the canvas, I would never find out what was happening. I had never been attacked before. There was a large boulder sitting precariously on the edge of a pit. A small hole had been dug beneath it and I scurried inside. I shook myself and, as if by magic, the goop that had covered me disappeared. I stuck my nose out and glanced around. There was an immediate ping on the rock above me. I felt some small shards of stone sting my snout. I pulled back and rested. My heart was pounding just like the heart of this avatar. There was usually a disconnect. At least I thought there was, but I had not experienced this kind of stress in the world of the canvas before. It was new to me.

As long as I stayed in the canvas, I was at an impasse. There was nowhere to go. But I was also safe. Maybe that is all the canvas was trying to tell me. The real world was going to try to hurt me, and I needed to go to my safe space and wait it out.

I felt a touch on my shoulder from the real world. "Mr. Cervantes. This is your wake-up call."

I removed my mask and smiled. "Thank you." I looked at my watch. Time had flown by. It felt like I had spent only a few minutes in the canvas world, but nine hours had passed. The flight was just over eleven hours. I needed to use the facilities, have a snack, and organize my thoughts. I decided I might as well heed the warnings from the canvas and go directly to my office/apartment in Venice Beach. I thought about Beal. I had not gotten any information on her location from Billie. It completely slipped my mind. I did not know if she was still in my apartment. I didn't even know if she was still on my side or if, as the faked picture of her foot with a bullet hole suggested, she was now my enemy. All I knew was my apartment would be a safe place, just like the large rock in the canvas. I knew Botox would want to chat with me as well as torture me for information. Information that I did not have.

I was sure that they did not know my flight. Billie would make sure there were no more successful hacks. Our communications were secure. All I had to do was get from the airport to my apartment without alerting them. I figured that Barbie would be back in LA soon if she were not already. She would be especially nasty if she could lay her hands on me.

I cleared security and was picked up by a limo driver that Billie provided. As an extra precaution, I called Billie.

"Augustus?"

"Billie, thanks for the limo. I am a little concerned about someone grabbing me. Can you track this phone?"

"No Problem. Better yet, just leave it on. Put it in your pocket. When you are safe at home, you can hang up. That way, I can hear what is happening to you. It might give the time to be proactive."

"Great. I don't think I will give them an opportunity. The driver will drop me off at my door. If you think it wise, I will leave the line open."

"Can't hurt. Talk soon."

"Thanks, Billie."

If I was taken, she could, at the very least, send the police to rescue me. It was a thirty-minute drive. I had the driver drop me off at my back door. I intended to get out of the limo with my bag and quickly slip inside. I asked the driver to keep the limo as close to the door as possible. I scanned my tongue, and the door clicked open. I stepped inside. I expected a light to come on in the entrance way, but it didn't. I tensed. I stepped forward and realized my mistake. I was grabbed by my arms and shoved into the room. The lights came on. There were three men in my apartment. Two were holding me and the third had a gun pointed at my head. They shoved me into a chair. They did not say anything. I immediately gave them the names of the three stooges: Curly, Larry, and Moe. One had curly hair, one was big and round, and one had what appeared to be a bowl haircut. One of the men slapped me across the face. He hit me three times. I heard the man holding the gun shout, "Enough." My face was stinging, and I felt my cheek swell. I did not say a word. I figured that speaking would result in a few more hits to the head. I did not want to be hit again. "Secure him to the chair." The other two men used tie straps. I tried the ankle trick, but these thugs were wise to that. I felt my foot being pressed to the floor and the tie strap practically cutting off my circulation and it was pulled tight around the chair leg. They used zip-tie handcuffs to bind my wrists. We were sitting in my small kitchen at the table. On the table was a large tablet. The man with the gun, who I named Moe, turned the tablet and tapped the face. "We got him, boss."

I heard a muffled voice come from the tablet, and then it was held in front of my face. The face of Botox filled the screen. "What can I do for you Dr..." I paused. "Your real name cannot be Botox. What is it?" I paused again. "Never mind. It doesn't matter. So, what can I do for you, Dr. Botox? What do you need help with? Surgery? Butchery? Chemistry? I am not good at any of those. I don't know how to cook meth." The last bit was an effort on my part to let him know that I had a pretty good idea of how he made his money.

Botox chuckled. Then a nasty look slid onto his face. "Tell me where they are, and I will not turn you into a monster or make you into sausage." He grinned.

"Where what is?" I asked casually.

"Hit him." The man holding the tablet handed it to the man on his left and backhanded me across the face. He took the tablet back and put it in front of my face. "Now, let's understand each other. This is not a negotiation. I ask questions and you answer with what I want to hear. Understood?"

This was not going well. I tasted blood at the corner of my mouth. "I will tell you everything I know. I will not leave anything out, but it is doubtful you will believe me, especially with these medieval techniques your goons employ. Let's you and I sit down together and have a chat like civilized men. If then you feel I am not telling the truth, you can order these men to do their worst. If you want to use a polygraph, I will welcome it. What do you say?" I heard him laugh. "How about we meet at your warehouse?" I licked the blood leaking from the corner of my mouth and prayed Billie was still listening. "Assuming you still have it? It is only 20 minutes or so away, if I recall."

The man holding the tablet pulled it away from my face. I heard Botox say, "Bring him."

The two goons cut the straps holding my ankles and dragged me to my feet. I took the opportunity to look around my apartment. It had been trashed. All the cupboard doors were open and rifled through. I concluded that they had come through one of the walls from my outer office and searched my apartment. I was pretty sure they had not discovered the entrance to my lab. I was unceremoniously pushed into the back of another large Escalade-type vehicle. I tried to raise my zip-tied hands, but I was unsuccessful and ended up face down on the seat. My suitcase was tossed in and landed on my back. I scrambled to sit up, but before I could, one of the goons pushed my suitcase onto the floor, grabbed me by the scruff of the neck, and dragged me upright. The Escalade drove away.

"Search him," ordered the man in the front seat. He gestured with his gun. My guard quickly patted me down and found my phone. He held it up. "Get rid of it." He opened the window and tossed it out.

Twenty minutes later, we arrived. I was taken up to the private area of the warehouse. I recognized it as the same location as the last time I was here. They dragged me over to one of the cages pushed me inside and locked the door. I sat down on the floor and leaned against the back of the steel cage. I did not stay in that position for very long. The floor smelled bad. I did not want to imagine what had been captive before me. Standing allowed some distance and relief from the vile smell. I waited. A few minutes later, Botox arrived. One of the goons grabbed a chair and placed it in front of the cell. He sat in the chair. He turned to one of his men and said, "Search his bag." The suitcase was dumped onto the table. The man rummaged through the contents.

"Nothing here but clothes."

That seemed to satisfy Botox. He turned to me and stared. Finally, he spoke, "Convince me you have not found the diamonds."

I decided that my story must take some time. I needed to give Billie a chance to figure out where I was taken. I rambled on about how I found the pocket watch. I said nothing about the canvas. I mentioned the photo of Adare standing in the graveyard, which led me to the grave and the discovery of the watch. I spent much more time than necessary going through my thoughts on finding and understanding the microdot. I explained all about Brug 9 and the cellar. I enhanced the story occasionally to make me look like I was a brilliant detective. He stopped me once in a while to ask questions. I told him what I had found in the Brug 9 cellar.

He stopped me. "Yeah, I saw the picture of the grave."

I decided to act surprised even though I knew he had gotten it from the photographer. "How did you get that?"

He smiled as if I had complimented him. I kept the awed look on my face for more seconds than was necessary. "I have my ways," he said.

I decided to pop his bubble. "I bet you did not know what else I found." His smirk vanished.

"What?"

"Your men are not all that great at searching suitcases. Undo the zipper that runs down the center. There is a small pouch tucked in one corner. Open it." He turned and looked at the men behind him. He did not say anything. He didn't have to. One of the men checked the case where I had indicated. He came over with a small pouch and handed it to Botox. He dumped it out onto his hand. The two diamonds I had found in the cellar and the graveyard were shining in his palm. He looked up at me and I explained where I had found them. "That is it. You have in your hand the sum total of treasure I found. I have considered what might have happened to the rest of the treasure, if there really was any. I come up with two possibilities. One—Adare moved the treasure again and died before he could give any indication of where it went. Or two—he somehow sent it back to the States but died before he could tell his wife or give any clues as to where he put it. Either way, I do not have it, nor do I have any idea where it might be."

"These …" he flipped the two small diamonds onto the table, "are nowhere near the size of the two that Ms. Beal found in the flask. You could have picked them up in Amsterdam."

"As I said before, I did not find a cache of diamonds. Perhaps Adare returned them to the Dutch people. Maybe he gave them to some World War Two reparations group. I am not lying. I do not have the diamonds, and I have no idea where they are." I had plans to continue with a filibuster in the hope that I might be rescued by whomever Billie was going to send, but as it turned out, there was no need. I heard banging and voices down in the warehouse proper. All of Botox's men turned toward the door. Many footsteps were pounding on the metal staircase.

Several policemen burst into the room. A man in a suit, who I assumed was a detective, strode toward Botox, holding some papers in his hand. "Doctor Balzarini?" Botox stared at him. "Are you Lorenzo Balzarini?" Botox nodded his head. "This is a warrant to search your properties." The man looked over at me. I was still standing in the middle of the cage. I waved at him. He spoke my name. "Mr. Cervantes?" I nodded. He turned to one of the policemen. "Get him out of there." He turned back to Botox. "Dr. Balzarini, you are under arrest for kidnapping and unlawful confinement." At that moment, a policeman approached the detective and whispered something in his ear. The detective smiled and turned back to Botox. "It gives me great pleasure to add the production and trafficking of an illegal substance—meth amphetamine, to be precise." He turned back to the policeman. "Get this piece of shit out of here."

You could hear someone moaning and banging behind a door in the back of the room. Another officer started searching the room for the source of the noise. He jimmied a padlock from the door and went inside. He emerged with a woman in tow. She had a bag over her head. Her hands were tied behind her. You could still see the remnants of duct tape around her ankles. The bag was removed. I was staring at Beal. Her eyes were wide, and her mouth was covered with duct tape. She was trying to speak. The officer reached up and ripped the tape from her mouth. She yelled in pain. "Oh, thank God," she said as the officer removed the zip ties from her wrists. "Thank God, you found me. That freak was threatening to make me into sausage if I didn't tell him where the …" She suddenly stopped, realizing that information about the treasure was not something she wanted the officers to know. She continued, "…where you were. Are you alright Mr. Crervantes?"

"I'm fine, Sandra. How long have you been locked in that room?"

"Two days. They gave me water and let me use the facilities until I tried to escape. Then they never came back. I have to pee badly. There has to be a bathroom nearby." She spoke to the officer and he led her to a bathroom on the other side of the room.

The detective spoke. “I will need you to come to the station and give a statement.”

“No problem, but not tonight. I just got back to LA a few hours ago. I am exhausted. I am sure that Ms. Beal feels the same way. And please search Botox. He took a couple of small diamonds that I purchased. I would like them back.” With that, I repacked my case and headed out. I knew Billie was responsible for the police and she would have someone waiting for me. I was soon on my way back to my apartment. Once there, I saw that it had been systematically searched. I straightened my bed and fell into it.

THE ULTIMATE DISCOVERY

I thought that the morning would bring clarity. It did not. My night had been filled with circular dreams. That is a dream that never seems to end. The same events recur ad nauseum. It went something like *I found the treasure. No, I didn't.* Repeat. I got out of bed and went into the kitchen. Much of the cupboard's contents were strewn about. I looked at the chair they had bound me to. There were cut zip ties on the floor. I shivered. I had been fearful for my safety the previous evening but had to put on a brave face. The feeling would not dissipate quickly. I checked my hidden lab entrance. I breathed a sigh. They had not found it. It remained untouched. My stomach growled, and I decided to get out of the apartment, have something to eat, and call Billie. I needed to thank her for saving me the previous evening and get her to call a cleaning and repair service to go over to my apartment. As much as I wanted to hole up in my apartment and spend a week exploring the canvas, I would go to a hotel while the clean-up crew did their thing. Billie found a five-star property that would cater to my needs adequately. She also promised to run interference with the police to give me some time to recuperate. I must get my story straight, and that would require some solitary time.

The deli across the street called me for breakfast. I ate voraciously and then took a taxi and checked into the hotel. The room was unnecessarily opulent. It was an entire suite. I called the front desk and asked them not to disturb me. I dimmed the lights and lay on the bed. The canvas opened.

I was immediately disappointed. The canvas was no longer showing me lofty things of beauty but had grounded itself and grounded me—literally. I was once again a small insignificant rodent scurrying across a landscape littered with garbage. The fear was not as potent as my last experience, but it was still there. I hid under a rotting log and waited. My expectation of violence did not come to pass. The dark shadows slowly dissipated. A bright light seemed to fill all the nooks and crannies of the world around me. It ran across the ground until it hit the edge of the log under which I cowered. I was in the shadow of the log, but I feared going into the light that had overtaken everything. As I stared at a rusty jagged tin can just outside the protection of the log, I could see green begin to form under it. Grass was growing. I ventured a little distance out into the sunshine and then quickly scuttled back. The world of the canvas was changing. All that was ugly and rotten was being transformed into new life. Feeling brave, I stepped out once again. This time I felt a change in my body. I stepped out further, and the change increased the further I went until I realized that I was becoming the avatar I loved. I was becoming a kestrel again. I flapped my wings and lifted off with the ease of a wind-blown feather. As I flapped, I could see bright spots of light. Many tiny objects were falling all around me. They seemed to gather the sunlight and send it back out in a conflagration of rays. I swooped up above them just to watch them fall. They were never ending, for when one hit the ground, another appeared higher up to repeat the process. I rose even higher and as I did, I could see something forming on the land below. As each sparkling point of light hit the ground, it scarred the earth black. I flew higher still until I could see what was being drawn by the millions of points as they hit the ground. It was a letter. The lights were burning the capital letter 'A' into the ground.

I quickly sat up. The canvas was trying to tell me that the letter I had found in the graveyard was not just Adare telling me he had moved the diamonds. He was telling me how he moved them. I felt the urge to go back to my apartment to my lab, but I decided that I was just too tired to really think properly. The trip must wait until morning. I tried to sleep, but it was a waste of time. I got up and paced the room. My curiosity was getting the better of me. I knew I had to return to the lab. The restoration employees would still be working but I knew I could surreptitiously enter my lab and check something out.

Once in the alley, I stepped out of the taxi and into the alcove. I stuck out my tongue to be scanned, and the door lock clicked. I entered. I was surprised. The cleaning crew had not even arrived. I was glad I did not have to explain anything to the people Billie had hired. They would not like unexpected guests while they were cleaning. They did not know me and so they would go through the security protocol procedures. I would expect nothing less. The protocol demanded they follow stringent rules. It was lucky they had not arrived. I sent Billie a text telling her where I was and to inform the crew. She answered with an apology. The crew had been delayed and would not arrive for at least two hours. I went straight to my lab and slipped inside.

I sat on one of my lab stools. I took the 'A' out of my pocket and flipped it like it was a coin. I continued to flip in over and over. The act became hypnotic. I watched the golden metal letter rotate in the air. It seemed to slow down, giving me time to inspect each edge and indent. All of this was soon clouded over by an overwhelming 'why'. Why had Adare left this object along with a single diamond at the gravesite? Was this a final communication to his wife? If so, what was he trying to communicate? The first clue on the microdot led to the cellar beneath Brug 9. The second led to the graveyard. I assumed that the clue left in the graveyard would lead somewhere else. If that was its intent, then it was being very obtuse. I knew that the clue was not meant for someone like me. It was meant for his wife. Perhaps she had insight into the meaning of the letter besides the fact that it was Adare's initial. Samuel A. Adare. I had heard his name spoken by Beal. Samuel A. Adare. I had read his initials: SAA, but I had never seen his name actually written down. I got some paper and printed out his name. I suddenly had this feeling that I had seen it written down before. I had seen it, but what I had on the paper was different. I had seen the name Samual Adare without the middle initial. Seeing his full name would have left an impression on me. The pattern SAA was unusual, and it would always make me think of Adare and this case. I always looked for patterns. It was almost an unconscious act. Whenever I saw a full name, I would always think about the initials that the person would have to endure for their life. Some sets of initials were nasty. Why would someone give their child a name that resulted in the initials ASS for example? Albert Stephen Smith. Or Sean Howard Ian Teggarty that would result in SHIT for your initials. You would think that something like that would be very rare, but I assure you it is not. Even initials that were not complete words could result in something pretty hard to grow up with. Fredrick Urlic Kaufman. FUK. Alright in German, but not so good in English.

All this reflection on initials and Adare's full name twigged an image in my mind. I had seen his name somewhere without the middle initial. I glanced at the open footlocker. The letters and pictures on the inside of the lid stared back. They were telling me nothing. I flipped the lid closed in frustration and at that moment I knew where the diamonds were hidden for I was staring at some metal lettering on the front of the footlocker. The letters read SAMUEL ADARE. That was not unexpected. What caught my attention was the coloring of the wood between the names. It was lighter. I took out the letter 'A' and placed it between the two names. It fit perfectly over the lighter area with a small space on either side. The 'A' was originally part of the name on the footlocker and had been removed.

I started to think about Adare. He was a photographer. He loved puzzles. But mostly he was a spy. Spies had access to all sorts of equipment. I pulled the footlocker in front of me and flipped the lid closed. I made a solid thud. I opened it again and dropped it again. The sound was odd, as if the lid weighed more than it should. I inspected it closely. I saw that the external thickness of the lid was at least an inch and a half more than the internal depth. I shook the lid back and forth. The hinges creaked a little, and that was all. I looked very carefully at all the surfaces of the footlocker. Perhaps there was something inside that lid? I felt a rush. Adare needed a way to get the diamonds secretly back to the USA. He had the same problem I would have had if I had found the diamonds in Amsterdam. Getting them sent to his home by secreting them in his footlocker was a brilliant plan. As a spy, he might not make it home, but the treasure would, because the government would deliver his footlocker to his wife. The diamonds must be in a secret compartment in the footlocker.

I inspected every surface to see how the diamonds were to be retrieved. There must be a way to open up sections of the wooden footlocker. There did not appear to be any ingenious button or lever to push or pull to make the footlocker magically open and reveal the treasure. I took out a measuring tape and checked the height of the box with the depth of the box. Once again, there was a one-and-a-half-inch difference. The lid and the base were just too thick. That is why the locker was so heavy. Something was concealed inside. This footlocker had either been modified or specially built to conceal the treasure Adare had found.

I tapped and poked and prodded the edges and the corners and the surfaces, hoping to find a way inside. There was no obvious way to make the box magically reveal its contents. It occurred to me that there was no need to make some complex locking system. This was not an Indiana Jones movie where everything was absurdly complex. Once Adare had the footlocker safely in his possession, he could simply cut it open or, for that matter, smash it with a hammer or an axe. I scanned my lab, looking for a tool that I might use. I was sure I could open it without turning the box into kindling. I inspected the top again. The wood used was not the plywood commonly used to build these boxes. It appeared to be oak. It was painted a military grey. I took an Exacto knife and scraped away the paint from the corners of the top. It was then that I noticed a shift in the direction of the wood grain. With a little more scraping, I saw that a wooden plug had been placed in the top as if it was concealing something. The wooden plug was obviously hiding a nail, or more likely a screw. I continued scraping at the paint around the outside edge of the lid and found eight wooden plugs.

It took a while to drill out the plugs and remove the screws hidden beneath. I ran my knife around the seam and jimmied the top of the box loose enough to be lifted off. I breathed deeply in anticipation. I expected to see an entire tray of sparkling gems. Under the top was a series of packages two inches by one inch by a half-inch thick, neatly packed in a kind of cloth. There were dozens of them. I picked one up from the middle. My heart was pounding. I had found a lot of valuable things, but this topped them all. I picked open the package. One end opened easily, and I dumped a pile of gems onto the countertop. They were of various sizes, but I doubted any of the gems were less than two carets. This one little pile was worth a fortune.

I removed all the packages without opening them and turned the footlocker over. I found similar plugs in the bottom and proceeded to remove them and the screws they were concealing. The bottom held the same number of packages as the top. I found a cardboard box in my lab and removed the glassware from it. I put all the gem packages in the box and put it in my safe. I reassembled the footlocker as well as I could and set it on the counter. I was overwhelmed by the value of this treasure. There must be millions, if not billions, of dollars worth of gems in my safe. I knew they would present a new kind of problem. It was a problem for another day. I left the lab, secured the door, and headed back to my hotel. I fell into a deep, dreamless sleep for the first time in weeks.

TIDYING UP

THE morning slipped by, for I slept into the afternoon. I knew I would need to attend to the loose ends. My phone was shut off. I turned it on and regretted the action, for it seemed to buzz continuously seeking my attention. The buzzing was coming from text messages I was receiving. I was about to start reading them when the phone rang in my hand. I nearly dropped it. I answered the call. It was Beal.

"Tell me you found them. Tell me that what you said to Botox was a lie. You found them. Didn't you? You found them. Didn't you?" The last "didn't you" was much less sure and much more frantic.

"Perhaps we should have a chat. I think that would be a good idea. Don't you? After all, you went to the Dark Side. Did you think Botox would give you a better deal than me?"

"I was going to tell him everything I knew in exchange for at least 50% but I realized that I did not know very much about what you were doing in Europe, so I didn't."

"So how did you end up cozying up to that madman?"

"I left your apartment to get some wine when some of his goons grabbed me and shoved me in the back of an SUV. I ended up in one of his cages where you saw me. He questioned me with one of those sticks he uses to shock the animals he kills to make sausage. I have burn marks to prove it. He wanted to know a bunch of stuff I had no idea about. Once he found out what plane you were coming home on, he just ignored me."

"So, I delivered on the contract we made. I got you the pocket watch. You paid me. The contract was fulfilled. End of story. We discussed finding diamonds. I did not find them. We no longer have any business." I did not feel the slightest bit of guilt for lying to her. If I were to tell her all that I found in the footlocker, a whole other hornet's nest would open up. That was not going to happen. I had another plan that I hoped would satisfy her. "I did find quite a few gems that seemed to have been left in your grandfather's hiding spots. I am not sure of the reason. Perhaps they were left for whomever might follow his clues just to keep them interested. I do not know for sure. I will split them with you. Those and the two you got from the flask will set you up nicely." I waited for a response. All I heard was her expel her breath in resignation. "You can probably get your grandfather's watch back from Botox. When you chat with the police, you can ask them. I would, however, advise you not to mention anything about the treasure, especially if you want to keep the diamonds. Keep it simple. We thought there was a treasure in diamonds. Botox was told about the possible treasure by your friend Harry Kruger. Botox came after you and stole the watch. There is no need to tell anything about me except that I found the watch. Period." I waited again.

"Alright. How many diamonds did you find? I want to see them all and pick the ones I want."

"No. I do not wish to see you again. I will be fair. Trust me."

"When will I get them?"

"They will be delivered within the week."

"Alright. Goodbye, Cervantes."

"Goodbye, Ms. Beal."

I hung up. I needed to give some thought to the billion dollars in diamonds. Keeping them would be silly. Sooner or later the truth would come out and I did not want to be the target of that truth. I would keep enough to cover my time and costs, but that would be all. I knew there would be ways to ensure the treasure would be used to help the less fortunate. Perhaps an anonymous donation through a lawyer. I would come up with something.

I turned to the list of texts I had received. I scanned down and saw that one had come from Nora Braithwaite via Billie. I had forgotten about her. I smiled. I looked at the list and it appeared that Maggie had messaged me at least a dozen times. The last one made me laugh.

"Mathew, you bastard, where are you? Call me soon. A part of me needs you. I am sure a part of you needs me."

I would call Maggie very soon. I would let Billie deal with Nora. I did not need her to complicate my life. I needed some R&R. I looked at the last message. It came from Billie.

"A woman is trying to contact you. I intercepted the calls, but she continues to call. I don't know how she got your number. She is very insistent she talks to you. Something about her missing sister. She said you would know."

The woman with the ice-blue eyes I met at the airport in Amsterdam had called. I had no commitments. She was intriguing. I guessed I could find people as well as objects. Maybe I would take the case.

WAYS TO CONNECT

To learn more visit:
GMichaelSmith.com

Smith can also be found:

Tweeting @GMichaelSmithCA

on Facebook /people/Jerry-Smith

on Instagram @gmichaelsmithca

To leave a Goodreads review,
please visit Goodreads.com and search for
A Kestrel Circles by G Michael Smith.

ABOUT THE AUTHOR

G MICHAEL SMITH is a retired teacher of Computer Programming, Drama, Math, English, and Theatre. He's written and directed plays for both adults and children. He also writes poetry and novels.

Besides *A Kestrel Circles*, his body of work includes *The Prison of Power: A Man-Made Tale; The Forevers*, a YA SciFi series; *Hijacked,* a middle-grade mystery; an Early-reader Children's Books series including the titles *Lily Liar and the Eleventy Headed Monster*, *Tiny Tina and the Terrible Trouble*, and forthcoming *Ashley and the Hornets*, as well as a Children's Picture Book titled *The Accidental Adventures of Bernie the Banana Slug.*

Smith resides in Qualicum Beach, Vancouver Island, BC, Canada with his wife, Cheryl, and enjoys spending time with his three adult daughters and three grandchildren. He's also known to enjoy a rigorous game of pickleball, softball, squash, or badminton.